Christmas on

·CORONATION ST.·

Maggie Sullivan loves to travel, is an avid reader – never going without her Kindle – and her abiding love is watching football. She is also a freelance university lecturer and has a keen interest in drama and theatre.

Maggie was born and brought up in Manchester, where she acquired a lifelong passion for *Coronation Street* and its legendary matriarchs. After living abroad for several years, she settled in London where she still lives.

Also by Maggie Sullivan

Mother's Day on Coronation Street

Christmas on

·CORONATION ST.·

MAGGIE SULLIVAN

HarperCollins*Publishers*

HarperCollins*Publishers*
The News Building,
1 London Bridge Street,
London SE1 9GF

www.harpercollins.co.uk

This paperback edition 2018
7

First published in Great Britain in 2017 by HarperCollins*Publishers*

Coronation Street is an ITV Studios Production
Copyright © ITV Ventures Limited 2017

pg. 389 Archive photograph © ITV/REX/Shutterstock

Maggie Sullivan asserts the moral right to
be identified as the author of this work

A catalogue record for this book
is available from the British Library

ISBN: 978-0-00-825512-1

Set in Sabon LT Std by Palimpsest Book Production Limited,
Falkirk, Stirlingshire

Printed and bound in Great Britain by CPI Group (UK) Ltd,
Croydon CR0 4YY

MIX
Paper from
responsible sources
FSC® C007454

Thank you to Shirley Patton, Dominic Khouri, Helen Nugent and Kieran Roberts who gave invaluable advice and help on the Coronation Street details. I would also like to thank my wonderful agent Kate Nash and my amazing editor Kate Bradley without whom the book would not have existed. Special thanks also go to Ann Parker, Jannet Wright, Sue Moorcroft, Pia Fenton, Julie Leibrich, Brenda Squires and Mary Hughes for their unending belief, support and encouragement.

Mum, Dad and Bram, my everlasting inspiration.

December 1937

Chapter 1

Elsie Grimshaw stopped and stared at the newsagent's window, like she'd done every day since the small Christmas tree had appeared. The same as every year, it was draped in silvery tinsel and dotted with fluffy wads of cotton wool pretending to be snow. On the topmost branch was a fairy with a glittering wand. She shivered and wrapped her arms round her skinny body, trying to rub some feeling into them. It felt cold enough for real snow today though, and her arms were too puny and her coat too thin to offer any defence against the wind. Under the lower green branches of the tree, several gift-wrapped parcels were lying and she longed to pick them up. They were different shapes and sizes; all in fancy coloured paper, though much of it was faded. Some were strung with a ribbon that ended in a bow.

Must be some kind of chocolates, she had long ago decided as she gazed enviously at the packages. Seeing her own reflection in the newly cleaned glass, she was momentarily distracted and she stared at her outline. She pulled a funny face, laughed and then frowned, then stared straight ahead, a gradual smile coming to her lips. Her nose was all right, if a little pointed. She never had managed to scrub off the dusting of freckles. Her dark green eyes, which she knew were her best feature, looked huge against the paleness of her face. Lots of expression in those eyes, she was always being told. Nowt but bloody cheek and impudence, according to her dad. But it was her long eyelashes the girls at the factory envied. Much darker than the flame-red of her hair. She moved closer until they almost touched the glass. Everyone seemed to want long eyelashes. Not that she could see hers. Her fringe was too long. Long and lifeless, despite the curls, like the rest of the tangled mess that hung in different lengths around her shoulders. She'd tried to smooth it out but it wasn't easy. Maybe she could get her sister Fay to have a go at it if they could cadge some scissors off one of the neighbours. Of course, it would look quite different if it was washed and cut properly. She thought of the women she saw regularly coming out of the hairdressers in some of the nicer streets of Weatherfield. Then she could look like her favourite film star. Fiery hair, fiery temper her mother always said. But Elsie didn't mind, not if it made her like Maureen O'Hara. Maybe the hairdresser could make her look like that one day. Elsie peered again at her reflection and pulled another face, this time stretching her thin lips, then pouting. Nothing a spot of carmine couldn't improve.

She rubbed her fingers over her cheekbones, which Fay reckoned stuck out like film stars' bones. They stick out because I don't get enough to eat, Elsie had thought. Not the kind of problem Hollywood film stars have to worry about. She pictured herself stretched out on a sofa like she had seen in the films, munching through the contents of the chocolate boxes, deliciously soft and sweet. She imagined licking the melting chocolate from her fingers, though it wasn't chocolate that coated them now, stuck as they were with all the cotton fluff and grime from the machines at the factory. It never occurred to her the boxes might be dummies.

I'll be fifteen next birthday, she thought. In March. Not that anyone else would remember. Fifteen, and I've never had a present in me life. One of these days I'm going to have one and it will be all wrapped up just like those. She sighed before adding: And not only for me birthday, but for Christmas as well.

Suddenly, through the thin fabric of her shabby coat, she felt the touch of a hand in the small of her back and she spun round, feeling foolish and hoping she hadn't spoken her thoughts out loud.

'Bobby Mirren!' she squealed. 'What do you think you're doing?'

'Just being friendly.' He tilted his head to one side

and gave her a lopsided grin. 'Thought maybe you'd like Christmas to come early this year. If you know what I mean.' He winked. 'I'll make it worth your while.'

Elsie's hand closed on the wage packet that filled her coat pocket when he said that. Not for the first time she thanked no god in particular that she had a steady job at the textile factory. At least it meant the family could eat – most days. So long as her mam was smart enough to grab something back off her dad before he drank it all away.

She gazed at Bobby for a second or two then beckoned towards the end of the street with her head. There was still some daylight left in the early wintry afternoon. He crooked his elbow and she slid her arm through his as they sauntered off down the road together. She could feel the envelope in her pocket as she walked, but she was thinking that an extra ha'penny or two would never go amiss.

It was completely dark by the time she got home and as she opened the front door to number 18 Back Gas Street it wasn't much brighter inside. A dull glow was emitted by the small clump of coal that still smouldered in the hearth at the back of the room, but the single lightbulb that dangled from the low ceiling close to the room's solitary window was not lit. She flicked the switch on the wall but nothing happened. In the gloom, she stumbled over the pile of filthy clothes that still lay unwashed from last week. She sighed. Her mother had promised to do them today.

'Is that you, our Elsie?' There was no mistaking the bloated shape of Alice Grimshaw as she emerged in the gloaming from the scullery that was curtained off from the room, behind the stairs at the back. The telltale bump of her stomach looked about ready to drop, even though Elsie knew her mother had a few months to go before yet another wailing mouth to be fed appeared. In her arms, twelve-month-old Jack, favourite teddy in hand, struggled to get down, for once he'd heard the voice of his favourite big sister he was in no doubt about where he wanted to be. He grinned at her. A ghoulish grin, for his front teeth were already black and decayed from constantly sucking on the bottle he had inherited from his three-year-old sister Polly. It was kept almost permanently topped up with sugared water to keep him quiet.

'I managed to get us a yesterday's loaf,' Elsie said. 'I bloody hope there's some of that dripping left over what our Phyllis cadged off Mrs James next door.' Jack had crawled over the cold flagstones to where Elsie was standing and clasped her knees, his arms appealing to her to pick him up. It was hard to resist him with his blue eyes and blond curly hair, even if his head was scabby with lice. From a distance, he looked a bit like the little cherub in the soap advert they had in town, but close to it was hard not to see that his poor little face was too gaunt and his arms and legs too much like those of a matchstick man to really look like such a pin-up. His legs were too thin even to support the grey rag of towelling that served as a nappy. It had been pinned haphazardly around his waist and it slipped each time he moved. Now it looked as if it was about to descend below his knees. Not that Elsie cared. He would always be her favourite. The only boy at the end of a long line of girls. Normally she would have picked him up. But for now she was distracted. She could see that her mother had neglected her duties as usual, for the small inadequate sink was piled up with every dish they possessed. Not that there were many, and what they had was either cracked or chipped, even the tin plates they'd got from the rag-and-bone man, and all the cups had broken handles. No wonder everything gets damaged Elsie thought crossly. This lot's been lying here most of the week.

'There's a bit left for scraping,' her mother said, absent-mindedly bending down to pick up her son again. She groaned and quickly dumped him at the foot of the bed he shared with her and Arthur. Jack protested loudly, banging his teddy against the bedpost, appealing once more for Elsie's favours. But his sister still ignored him.

'Bloody good job,' Elsie said. 'Mr Whitehead at the grocer's up the passageway saved the bread for me special.' Elsie looked at her mother, wondering what she would say if she knew what the bread had actually cost her eldest daughter from the 'groping grocer' who worked in the shop at the end of the courtyard. Alice obviously had no idea, for she just smiled.

'Thanks, love. At least I've got summat for your dad's tea now. Can you give us a tanner for the meter an' all? Yer dad's still out and there's no one else to ask.' She made it sound like her husband Arthur was the usual provider of their basic necessities.

Elsie clenched her fists at the lie, though she knew she should have been used to it by now. It was one that tripped so easily off her mother's tongue, even though the old man hadn't done much in the way of providing since he'd been laid off at the mill five years before. 'Why does it always have to be me as feeds the lecky as well as feeding the whole bleeding lot of us?' Elsie's voice rose to a shout and she felt tears of anger scalding her lids. 'Why can't you get the little 'uns to run more errands for the neighbours so's we can have summat regular for the meter for once?'

Alice stared at her, but all she said was, 'You're a good 'un,' as the lightbulb sprang into life. Alice gave up then, abandoning the baby to the cold floor. She went back into the scullery, returning with a hastily washed plate with the last of the dripping and a knife for the bread. She banged it down on the table, which was surrounded by odd chairs in the middle of the room. 'Yer dad'll be back soon and you know how he likes summat to eat soon as he gets in.'

This time at the mention of her father Elsie quickly crossed the small dining-room-cum-kitchen that also served as a bedroom for her parents and Jack. She ignored Jack's outstretched arms as he tried to grab her and ran up the steep wooden stairs to the small first-floor bedroom she and her sister Fay shared with Polly, Ethel and Connie – some of their other siblings. She hoped that as usual they'd be running wild somewhere on the streets with no thought of coming home yet, giving her some precious moments of privacy, though that was a distant dream. Her other sisters, Phyllis, Iris, Freda and Nancy had the other bedroom upstairs while their parents slept below with baby Jack squeezing in where he could; Elsie thought the house generally felt like Piccadilly Circus but without the bright lights and excitement. Pushing her back against the door to bar entry, she took her wage envelope out of her coat pocket and scrutinized the contents. She skimmed off several of the loose coins and added them to the couple already in her pocket, stuffing a grey cotton square that served as a handkerchief in with them to prevent any jangling noises giving her away. Then she resealed the envelope and went back downstairs.

She was only just in time, for her father was already rolling through the door and as soon as he saw her he stretched out his hand.

'What you got for me, gal?' he asked.

'What makes you think I've got anything?'

'Because it's bloody payday, that's why, so don't get smart with me, lass.'

'Well, I ain't got nothing.'

Elsie stood arms akimbo and stared at him defiantly. For a moment he looked shocked but then before she had time to move he raised his arm and whacked her sharply on the side of her head.

'Don't you dare cheek me! How's a man supposed to get a drink round here? Gimme tha money.'

Elsie was aware of Jack screaming, though she wasn't sure where he was for the room was beginning to spin as she fell to one side. She didn't lose her footing, however, for her father grabbed hold of her before she hit the floor and with his huge hands triumphantly ripped the envelope out of her pocket. She tried to reach out for it but he snatched it away. Above the baby's shrieks she heard the loose change from her pocket spilling out on to the floorboards and knew she had lost everything.

'What the bloody hell is this?' Arthur shouted, stomping on two of the rolling pennies. 'You've opened it already! Trying to do me, are you? Well, I'll show you you can't swindle Arthur Grimshaw. Pick 'em up.' He pointed to the coins that had rolled under the chair.

Elsie glared at him for a moment then she spat on the money without moving.

'Pick 'em up yourself,' she snarled. But her defiance was short-lived. She was only to be rewarded by another clout, this time to the other side of her head. She heard as well as felt his knuckles make contact with her cheekbone and knew she would have a lump and a black eye by the morning.

'Don't you dare bloody cheek me!' he yelled. 'I'll make you pay for this.' Now her father grabbed hold of her shoulders and pulling her in front of him began to shake her violently. 'Pick 'em up, I said,' he shouted into her face. 'Now!' The cocktail of alcohol fumes, stale tobacco and the odours from his otherwise empty stomach, compounded with her spinning head, made her retch. Flinging her arms wide to fend him off, she raced out of the door and ran round the back of the house and across the tiny yard. She was heading for the midden they shared with four of their back-to-back neighbours, praying none of their snotty kids had noticed her plight and would deliberately block her way.

Chapter 2

Fay Grimshaw at the age of thirteen was still officially part of the Weatherfield school system, although not many of her teachers could attest to that fact for she played truant from her classes at every available opportunity. It wasn't that she didn't want to learn; she simply didn't believe the teachers in her school had anything left to teach her. They never seemed to talk about anything that related to her life, they weren't interested in understanding her problems and they certainly had no notion of her secret ambitions. If they had, they might have been impressed; for Fay wanted to better herself, to climb out of the Back Gas Street hellhole she and her eight siblings had been born into. But they never showed her any practical ways in which she could do this. They offered no help, gave her no guidance, so she saw no point in attending what she thought of as unnecessary and pointless lessons.

The fact that it was called a Church of England school and they regularly taught lots of religious studies was another mark against the teachers as far as Fay was concerned. No one in her family had anything to do with religion and she could only wonder that her parents had ever considered such a school appropriate. Elsie, her older sister whom she adored and looked up to, had certainly not been to any kind of religious school and she was now getting along very nicely in her working life without having owt to do with the church. Not that Fay had much to do with it herself. On the occasions when she and her classmates had been expected to go to a church service, she had managed to avoid it. And she would continue to avoid it. The only time she might consider entering a church was when she eventually got married. And then she would only agree to having a religious ceremony if her father promised not to attend and if she could guarantee her mother wouldn't turn up pregnant – again. Even as it crossed her mind now, her face flushed at the thought of her mother having yet another baby tugging hopelessly at her shapeless breasts like there had been for the last several years. It was bad enough to think that in a few months' time little Jack would no longer be the youngest member of the family. The thought of the same thing happening year after year put her off wanting babies of her own.

But the thought of her having a wedding at all made her smile. A big white wedding like she'd seen once or twice at St Mary's in Weatherfield. For it was something she and Elsie talked about a lot, her big sister being adamant she wouldn't set foot inside a church even for that. So maybe she should follow in Elsie's footsteps. It wouldn't be such a bad way to go, would it? Although, if she was honest, she would like to have a better job than her sister. It was true Elsie seemed happy enough in the textile factory, loading yarns on to the huge reels to be woven into different patterns of cotton fabric. But Fay had different ambitions. She was almost two years younger, she'd probably never be as big as Elsie, and she'd certainly never have Elsie's striking looks, but then she would be happy working somewhere quietly on her own. She wanted to do a college course and become a secretary.

When she was about eight years old Fay had seen a Charlie Chaplin film at the local picture house about a bank secretary, and she had fallen in love with the idea of working in an office. As usual, she and Elsie had sneaked into the cinema through the door people usually came out of, after one of their mates had left the emergency bar on the latch for them. Near the end of the first showing of the main feature they had slid in and gone to sit in the cheapest seats so they wouldn't be noticed while they waited until the film was shown again. She had eventually come out of the cinema, eyes blinking in the strong daylight, her mind full of the glamour of the important role the secretary had played within the bank and she had decided then that was what she wanted to do.

Fay liked the idea of working somewhere quiet and comfortably furnished, somewhere that was well organized and ordered. In the film and in offices she knew everything was neat and clean. The secretaries' desks always looked so tidy and there was even room for a potted plant or two. She admired the stylish way all the girls she knew who worked in an office dressed, and the way they came out of work looking relaxed and unflustered. Most had a smart coat and a pert little hat. So different from the way Elsie and her workmates came pouring out of the hot, noisy and horribly smelly factories where they worked. They were swathed in overalls and shawls and had untidy headscarves covering their curlers. No, the more she thought about it, the more she couldn't wait to leave school, though she had no idea how she would manage to pay the fees to enrol into a secretarial college.

'You don't want to be fretting about that,' Elsie had chided. 'I'll help you find a job so you can earn some money before you start.'

'Could you?' Fay was excited at the idea.

Elsie shrugged. Then she had suddenly looked serious. 'Of course the old man mustn't find out about it or you'll end up with nowt. And our mam must think you're still going to school, or she'll make you turn your wages over to our dad like I have to do.'

'Do you really think I could get away with it?'

'You, young lady can do anything you set your mind to do. You're pretty. You're not too skinny and you've got all the best features our mam must have had when she was a lass.'

'Do you really think so? Like what?' Fay was surprised to hear her sister talk like that.

'Well, for starters you've got our mam's lovely brown eyes, but yours always seem to be smiling. And look at the way they match the colour of your hair.' Elsie put a hand out to touch it. 'And the way your hair curls without ever having to put it up in rags. I'm dead jealous. You don't always have to drag it all back off your face, you know.' She gave her sister's ponytail a gentle tug.

'I know but it keeps it out of the way.'

'But there are lots of other things you could do to make yourself pretty. A bit of flesh on your bones, a spot of pink in your cheeks, rub some beetroot juice on to your lips and you'll have all the lads chasing you before long.'

'Nay, but I'm too small for anyone to want to bother.'

'Don't be so daft. You'll grow. And soon. Though you wouldn't really want to be as tall as me, now would you?'

'One thing, I'll never be as old as you,' Fay retorted and both girls fell about laughing.

'Seriously, Sis,' Elsie said, you're going to make something of yourself. I just know it.' She smiled as she looked away into the distance. 'The important thing is to hang on to the dream.'

Fay thought a lot about that dream and how she might be able to keep such a secret from her parents. She might even apply for the waitress job she had seen advertised in the café window in the centre of Weatherfield. As far as she knew, it wasn't a place either of her parents frequented so she wasn't likely to be found out. And though she had no idea what a waitress's weekly wage might be, she began to picture piles of threepenny bits, sixpences, even shillings and the odd half-crown being added to the few pennies she already had in the biscuit tin that was hidden under the bed. She might even have some money left over to buy presents for her siblings: a pair of silk stockings for Elsie, a new toy car for Jack. Soon she'd be able to leave home and find a room to rent, like she'd read about in a book once at school. It all sounded so romantic and so grown-up; she couldn't wait.

She was caught up in her dream while she was on her way to visit her best friend Valerie so she almost didn't notice Elsie staring intently into the newsagent's window on the other side of the road. But then she paused, wondering what her sister was doing. Fay was about to call out to Elsie to wait for her so they could walk home together, but before she could open her mouth she saw Bobby Mirren sidle up to her sister and cover Elsie's backside with his large hand. Elsie looked startled and Fay's instinct was to shout across to him to stop mithering and to leave her sister alone. But then she could see Elsie half turn and from the look on her face she seemed not to mind. Fay could only guess as to the exchange as she watched Elsie move Bobby's hand away, but to her surprise the next thing she saw was the two of them sauntering off arm in arm.

Fay held back a little way but kept pace with them on the other side of the road, curious about where they might be heading. She was surprised when they stepped off the pavement and disappeared into some bushes behind the bus stop. Fay took the opportunity to cross the road. She kept herself out of sight and found a spot half hidden by the shrubbery where she could see them without being seen. They seemed to be kissing, which Fay found strange for she knew for a fact that Elsie didn't particularly like Bobby. Hadn't she told her so only the other day? Not only that, but she had been adamant that she preferred Eric Ross and would welcome the chance to let him know that she fancied him. But now, as Fay watched, it was Bobby who had his arms around Elsie and they seemed to be almost devouring each other with ever widening mouths. Even more surprising, Fay thought she saw Bobby's hands slide inside Elsie's coat as the two became more entangled and Fay wondered what Elsie could be thinking. Of course Fay understood about kissing, she'd even tried it once with Brian Morgan. But it had made her feel dirty and messy and it wasn't something she was eager to try again. When she had told Elsie this, her big sister had laughed and told her not to worry about it for now. 'Mebbe you're a bit young yet. But you'll be at it again one day before long, I promise you – and you'll enjoy it too,' Elsie had assured her. 'But not before the time's right, and the lad's right too.'

Fay frowned. So did that mean Bobby Mirren was the right one for Elsie? Was she going to marry him? Suddenly Fay heard a shout, which she realized had come from her sister. She looked up to see Bobby pulling his hand out from under Elsie's skirt. Elsie's face was flushed as she patted down her clothing and rebuttoned her coat, but within a few moments they began kissing again, this time with even more energy. Feeling confused and not wanting to see any more, Fay crept away from her hiding place and started walking purposefully towards Valerie's house. Maybe her best friend would be able to shed some light on it all. But in any case, she would talk to Elsie tonight. She'd have to tell her what she saw and she'd ask Elsie what it all meant.

Chapter 3

Elsie lay in bed on her back, her face throbbing, her eye and nose already puffy and swollen. It was too painful to lie on her side as she usually preferred to do. Fay was asleep when Elsie had finally come back home and crept upstairs, and now she was gently snoring, snuffling each time she turned over and trying to snuggle up close. Elsie was also aware of Polly, Ethel and Connie, who slept top to toe with them in the same bed, and she tried to push aside their feet which seemed as if they hadn't seen soap or water for several weeks.

After being sick in the courtyard, Elsie hadn't made it to the midden, she had fled the house and gone to seek refuge, as she usually did, with her best friend Aggie. She had stayed there most of the evening. As she had hoped, by the time she returned home both her parents seemed to be fast asleep downstairs, their bed pulled out from behind the front door, closer to the hearth, to make the most of the remains of any heat from the coal dust in the fireplace. Her father was on his back snoring loudly, as a result no doubt from having retrieved the money that had scattered from her pocket, and having spent it, as usual, down at the Three Hammers. Her mother had turned her face to the wall as she always did, so it was impossible to be sure that she was asleep, but from the irregularity of her breathing and the stiffness of her pose, Elsie guessed she was not.

She had crept up the stairs, anxious not to disturb anyone. It was a bitterly cold night and she slipped gratefully into her only nightgown, a winceyette passion-killer her mother had found in a jumble sale. Then she wrapped herself in an old woollen cardigan and climbed into bed. There was a fireplace in the room but as far as she knew it had never seen a fire, so she tried to snuggle more closely to Fay. She was congratulating herself on having avoided her father during the time he was at his most dangerous when she was aware of a noise on the stairs.

Elsie knew she was most at risk of further punishment within the first twenty-four hours after a supposed offence, and her father was more than capable of humiliating her with more than just his fists. Sometimes, when he'd had a skinful and if he caught her unawares . . . She knew what he did was wrong, and hated him all the more for it. He certainly hadn't liked her behaviour tonight. She cursed under her breath. She had forgotten to wedge the old linen box against the door. She berated herself as she lay listening to the mounting footsteps. A hot wormy feeling crawled in the pit of her stomach as the sounds grew closer and she prayed that she would be able to hold down her meagre tea. She heard the final footfall stop outside the bedroom and then the groaning of the hinge on the rickety door. She closed her eyes, pretending that if she couldn't see anyone then no one was there. But she could still sense a body had entered the room. And she could hear the harsh whisper, 'Else.' Her eyes flew open. 'Else, are you all right?' She couldn't see her face but she could make out the silhouette in the moonless night against the sheet that acted as a makeshift curtain: it was Phyllis with her fists clenched.

Phyllis was shivering as she stepped inside the room and brought her face close to Elsie's. 'Are you all right?' she asked again. 'Only I heard you'd got batttered by the old man.'

'Is that you, Phyllis?' Elsie asked, relieved. 'You frightened the life out of me. What the 'ell are you doing up at this hour?'

'Sorry, but I couldn't sleep. I was worried that he might come for you again.' Phyllis paused, her pale and pinched features barely visible in the darkness of the shabby room. 'I know what he's like.' Phyllis's hand touched her swollen face and Elsie pulled back; the bruise was still tender.

'Sorry I wasn't here to help you,' she said. ''Cos I would 'ave, you know.'

Elsie tried to smile, though it felt forced. Phyllis was one of the toughest kids in the family, maybe even as tough as Elsie herself, though she was barely into her teens.

'Don't worry, lass, I can look after meself. I'm all right and you'd best be getting back to bed before you catch your death.'

Phyllis lingered, and Elsie felt her sister's cool hand clutch her own. 'It's not right, Elsie, what he does to us.'

'No, it's not, pet, but we look out for each other, don't we?'

'Aye,' said Phyllis. 'But I can't take much more of it. I tell you, the first chance I get, I'm off.'

Elsie was shocked, 'You're talking daft. Where would you go at your age?'

Phyllis sounded defiant. 'There's plenty of places, places where Dad would never find us 'n' all.'

'Don't do anything silly, Phyllis, promise me.' Elsie squeezed Phyllis's hand.

'It won't be silly – anything's better than this miserable life. Anyway, so long as you're OK, Else. G'night then. I'll see you in the morning.'

'Night, Phyllis. Sleep tight and don't let the bed bugs bite.' As Phyllis crept across the bedroom and quietly clicked the door shut behind her, Elsie lay wide awake, mulling over what her sister had said.

Chapter 4

It took longer than usual for the swelling to go down, by which time Elsie had made up her mind. She needed money. A second job. One that offered more than a quick grope and a few pleasures behind the shrubberies. But it also had to be one where the old man couldn't get his hands on a penny of what she earned. What was the use in finding extra work if the money was only going to be poured down his disgusting throat? She couldn't go on like this, starving for lack of a regular daily meal, watching the kids being whittled down to scarecrows. But she had no idea what she could do, for she had no particular skills. It was a pity she couldn't get an office job like Fay had set her heart on, but she needed to work different hours. She couldn't work during the day while she hung on to her job at the factory. She needed extra hours. Some kind of evening shift work like in a hospital or a factory that never closed down. She would have to think of something.

The next day was bright but cold and by the time she came out of work and the sun had gone down, a frost had already begun to form. Elsie was still smarting from the run-in with her father and didn't feel like going straight home. So she did what she often did when she felt one of her moods coming on and wanted to be left to herself; she went to the Field. It was a strip of waste ground that had not a blade of grass on it, a few minutes' walk away from the factory; she always went there whenever she wanted to think. She would sit, head in hands, on the remains of an upturned barrel that lay among the debris in the far corner of the stony ground, and mull over whatever problems were uppermost in her mind. Sometimes her thoughts would be interrupted by someone walking by. If it was someone she knew, she'd often play a game. First, she would catch their eye, for the gas lamp on the corner where the Field met the main street usually gave her a clear view of their face. Then she would shout something saucy or rude in the hope of making them respond, and finally she would award herself a score according to the level of their response. She'd give herself five if she raised a little smile, seven for a laugh, ten if she could get them to halt their journey and engage in a few moments' banter. She was good at that. People hardly ever failed to respond in some way, even if it was only to shout rude words and obscenities at her. She would set herself a target for a total evening's score and she rarely missed her mark.

But tonight she'd seen no one and she was wondering how much longer she could remain before she became frozen to the spot. She was about to give up and move off when a young man walked past. She smiled at him and he tipped his cap to her – that was seven points for a start. But she was prepared to give him a few extra points because he had such a pleasant face. He wasn't very tall but he seemed surprisingly muscular and his gait was forceful and determined. She thought he might be a few years older than she was, maybe seventeen or even eighteen, though a cowlick of hair darker than the rest flopped forward, giving him a sort of boyish charm.

'Hello again,' she called, realizing that although she didn't know him, she had actually engaged in her game with him before. The thing she had liked most about him then was his broad, cheeky smile. As he drew level with her, she saw a flash of it again.

'Sorry, can't stop today – I'm already late,' he called, and as he increased his pace she could see his face break into a broad grin. 'And if I don't get to the pub on time tonight the bloody landlord will have me guts for garters, 'cos they'll be all out of clean glasses.'

'Which pub is that then?' Elsie shouted, though she was unsure if he was still within hearing distance. Not that it mattered. She'd already awarded herself a full ten points.

'The Butcher's Arms.' She heard his reply only faintly and it set her a fair puzzle, for she had no idea where that was. She stared at his back as he slipped out of range of the lamplight and disappeared from view. There was one way to find out. She would follow him. Sliding from her perch she set off after the young man, running the first few steps till she got him back into view then slowing to walking pace, for she didn't want to get too close else he might realize he was being followed.

They seemed to have walked quite a long way through parts of Weatherfield Elsie had never seen before and if she hadn't come to a crossroads with a sign that pointed to Westerley Cross in one direction and Town Centre in another, she wouldn't have known where she was. She might even have thought she was in a different town completely. The young man had disappeared by now, but she spotted a pub on the corner and to her relief found it was called the Butcher's Arms. It was not a pub she knew, but the good news was that she had never heard her father speak of it either, so she wasn't likely to bump into the old man. She stood for a few moments wondering, having come so far, what she should do now. If anyone had asked her, she couldn't have explained what had made her come all this way.

As she stood dithering in the chilly night the bar door was suddenly flung open and two raucous men rolled out, laughing drunkenly. The door swung back, lighting up the pavement for a few seconds. As it closed, she saw a notice was pinned lopsidedly to the diamond-shaped stained-glass panel cut into the wood. She tilted her head following the direction of the piece of paper, which seemed to be hanging by a thread and read: *Experienced barmaid wanted for late shift. Must be 18 or over*. Elsie hesitated but only for the minute it took to pat down her hair, pinch her cheeks and bite some colour back into her chapped lips. Then she pulled open the swing doors and was sucked inside by the warmth of the bar.

It was brightly lit and noisy but her appearance caused a stir from the moment she entered. Most of the younger lads wolf-whistled while some of the older ones were positively leering, reaching over to touch her as she stepped in among them. Her response to this instant reaction was to exaggerate the sashaying move-ment of her hips, a movement she'd been practising a lot recently. She even winked and raised her eyebrows at those close by, like she'd seen the film stars do in the pictures. She pinned an immediate smile on to her face and she could almost feel the twinkle in her eyes as she glanced flirtatiously round the dimly lit room. There were several men who obviously hadn't seen her, for they were standing by the bar rail shouting their orders and a few obscenities to the young redheaded man who was running backwards and forwards behind the bar. He seemed to be trying to serve at least six people at once but couldn't make up his mind who he should serve first.

A quick glance confirmed to Elsie that she was the only woman in the crowded room and she couldn't deny she was enjoying the attention. If it was anything like the pubs she'd been in with her father, there would be other female patrons tucked away in the ladies' snug, which would be approached by its own separate entrance, but she wasn't in a hurry to join them. As she moved closer to the bar, she caught a glimpse of the young man she'd trailed all the way from the Field. She was right: he was worth following. Not only was his face pleasant but he was kind-looking too. And she liked the way he stopped now and then to flip the lock of hair out of his eyes. He was gathering empty glasses, gripping them tightly between stubby fingers. He carried them behind the bar and placed them in a large sink. There a boy was washing them in what seemed from the blueness of his hands to be cold water. A large man with heavy jowls and a ruddy scowling face, doubtless the landlord, was ringing up a variety of prices into the cash register as the redheaded barman called out the amounts of money he had taken. The landlord handed back the change and the barman's cash was emptied into the till. When Elsie appeared, the redhead stared at her for a moment then he nudged the older man, who peered at her over his glasses and frowned.

'This bar's not for the likes of you, even if you were old enough,' he said, his voice surly. 'So go on, 'oppit.

Unaccompanied women, entrance round the corner.'
He indicated with his thumb.

'I'm here about the job.' Elsie jutted her chin out and
spoke with as much confidence as she could muster,
hoping she sounded stronger than she felt. 'The one on
the door.' She indicated the glass panel where she had
seen the advert. 'Who do I need to see?'

The man took off his glasses and peered down at
her. 'You don't look half old enough,' he said.

'Oh, but I am. It's me birthday very soon. I'll be
eighteen,' she put in for good measure, remembering
what she had read on the poster. Thankfully, she had
always been tall for her age – she would look even
taller if only she had the money for a proper pair of
shoes. But she was glad at least she had put her hair
up that morning with some pins she'd found in the
toilets at work. She only wished she had a bit of carmine
to dab on her cheeks as she bit her lips again to redden
them up. Unfortunately, the landlord was not impressed.

'Oh yes,' he said, 'pull the other one, it's got bells
on.'

'It's true.' The young man from the street stepped
forward, his fingers gripping a couple of dirty drinking
glasses. He had stopped by Elsie and moved closer to
her as he spoke.

'Oh yes, and how do you know that?' the landlord
asked.

"Cos I knows her. We're mates. Ain't that so, Else?'

Elsie tried not to show her astonishment, not only

31

that he knew her name when she hadn't a clue about his, but that he dared to shorten it in such a familiar way. But she wasn't about to contradict him. 'Yes, that's right, mister.' She looked back at the heavy-set older man and fluttered her eyelids like she had seen Mae West do in the cinema. When the landlord began to smile, she hoped she hadn't overdone it.

But he did seem to be taking her more seriously now. 'Have you worked in a bar before?' he asked.

Elsie thought back to the time a few years ago when her father had taken her with him into the Three Hammers at the top end of Back Gas Street. She was so young the innkeeper had declared her, 'The youngest child that ever set foot in my pub!' Since there were no customers about at the time, he had lifted her on to his knee and let her pull a pint. She recalled the way he'd instructed her to tilt the glass so that there was just enough of a head on it rather than a glassful of frothy foam. After giving her a sip, he'd downed it himself in a few long gulps.

'Yes, I know how to pull a pint,' Elsie said, crossing her fingers behind her back in the hope that she wouldn't be caught out in the lie. 'Any road up,' she thought she'd better add, 'I'm a fast learner.' She winked at him. 'If you know what I mean.'

Elsie caught his astonished gaze and was aware of his sudden scrutiny. She willed herself not to look away, knowing that if she wanted to get anywhere she was going to have to brazen it out. Just then there was an icy blast as both the double doors were pulled open sharply from the outside and a crowd of men rushed in. They were a mixed bunch. Some were young, some middle-aged, one or two were positively old, but they were all jostling for the honour of being first through the door like it was the most important thing in the world.

'Now then, gents. Easy does it. Slow down a bit, will you,' the man at the till called out, his attention diverted from Elsie. 'We've room for you all, so what the hell's the rush?'

There were several shouts of, 'We're thirsty,' which for some reason made everyone laugh.

Then someone called from within the crowd, 'Aye, aye, landlord,' and he raised his arm in an exaggerated mock salute.

'He thinks he's in the bloody army already,' his mate shouted, elbowing his friend in the ribs, to much general laughter.

'I'm as good as,' the first man said.

'That's right. Going to be shipped off to Spain to fight in the bleeding Civil War,' one of the old men explained proudly.

'I suppose they can do with all the help they can get out there,' another agreed.

'They must be bloody desperate to want him, is all I can say,' a young lad muttered.

'Can anyone sign up?' Her new 'friend' the bar helper was trying to pass through the mob with more dirty glasses between his fingers. The crowd fell silent for a moment when he spoke; Elsie was taken aback by how serious he looked.

'Of course. It's a bloody fiasco out there.' It was the newly enlisted man who replied.

'They say Madrid's under siege and things are going to get worse,' the old man who could have been his father went on.

'Well, I've signed up,' the soldier said, trying to lighten the mood, 'and I'm off in the morning. So this will be my last drink on English soil for quite some time. Let's make the most of it, eh lads?' He turned to look at them all. 'Are you ready, fellas?'

The helper put his head down now and scurried back to drop off the glasses to be washed. Elsie stood uncertainly in the centre of the sawdust-covered floor. She was completely surrounded by the excited group of men until one of them moved away to go and stand at the end of the bar. He banged his fist on the countertop that was already swilling in ale and shouted, 'Landlord, let's be having some pints over here,' and a loud cheer erupted from the crowd.

Elsie still didn't move. She was mesmerized by the scene that had so suddenly changed with the arrival of the newcomers. War, war, war seemed to be all men wanted to talk about these days. Even her father had been moaning about Hitler invading half of Europe. Only this morning he'd told her mother, 'It won't be long before we're dragged into a bleeding dogfight.'

Elsie had tried to shut her ears. She avoided looking at headlines about a possible war although there were often newspapers lying around at the factory. She didn't want to talk about it, even though some of the older girls could talk of nothing else. What if Britain did get involved in a major war in Europe? What if their sweethearts were called up for active duty? They seemed to be proud and excited, but afraid at the same time. Elsie couldn't make sense of it. Weren't we already supposed to have had the war to end all wars? She was thankful her only brother was far too young to be called up into any army; as she had no proper sweetheart yet she refused to think about what war would mean for her. Not that she could avoid it completely. Even their Phyllis at almost thirteen years old was earning a few coppers shouting out the headlines about the latest German invasions from the *Weatherfield Gazette* stand. Let's face it, she thought. No one could be sure what was going to happen.

Elsie was far more interested in the Royal fairy tale that continued to fill the newspapers than the chances of Britain getting embroiled in another war. To her the story of the abdicated King and his stylish American wife was worth talking about any day of the week. During the summer months, she had eagerly looked for discarded newspapers with that story in the headlines. She had been captivated the day the front page of the *Weatherfield Gazette* had been devoted to their magical wedding in France; she had even cut a picture of the happy couple from a copy of the paper she had found several weeks after the event.

Now she took in the room full of chattering men and smiled. None of them were talking about love stories with fairy-tale endings. Men never seemed interested in things like that. They were so engrossed in their talk of war that they seemed to have forgotten all about her.

Unsure what she should do, Elsie hesistated. The last thing she wanted was to make a scene, so perhaps she might as well go home. The landlord was rushed off his feet, helping the redheaded barman to serve the new customers who were now standing two and three deep at the bar, waving their money and shouting their orders. The young man she had followed had disappeared completely, probably taking another batch of glasses to be washed in the sink.

The whole group had moved away from the entrance and Elsie noticed that the advert that had first drawn her in had fallen to the floor and been trampled underfoot. As she reached the door, she bent to pick it up. Suddenly the landlord called out, 'Hey, you – Else or whatever your name is. Get your coat off and give Stan a hand collecting them glasses or we'll never get this lot served tonight.'

Elsie turned in surprise. 'You mean me?'

'Well, I don't see anyone else, you daft ha'porth.'

She turned and walked back.

'I reckon the customers will welcome a fresh face, so

long as I don't hear you squawking if someone takes a fancy to pinching your bum now and then.'

A huge cheer went up among the crowd as he said that and as she made her way over to the bar she had to dodge the hands that were eagerly trying to take him at his word. But she didn't have to be asked twice.

'How much?' she said as she ducked under the counter to join him behind the bar.

'How much what?'

'Me wages,' she said, trying to look him straight in the eye.

'I can't afford to pay you no set wages,' he said, averting his gaze. 'But you can keep all your tips. Be nice to the customers, keep them well-oiled and don't keep them waiting, and you can do well here, particularly on payday. I'll give you a bonus if the takings are good. And if someone buys you a drink, you put the money in the till and save it till home time which is nine thirty most nights and later on Fridays and Saturdays. I don't want to see you drinking on the job.'

Elsie was disappointed. She had hoped to get some kind of regular wage. She had no idea what tips might amount to at the end of the day, or how she would know whether or not the takings had been good, but she couldn't afford to turn it down. Beggars can't be choosers, as her mam was fond of saying, and she wasn't about to pass up this opportunity. 'OK,' she said, and was about to add something but he gave her no chance.

'Right, come and help me deal with this lot,' he said, tossing her coat like a bundle of rags over a stool behind the bar. 'And when things quieten down you can give a hand to young Ray there, washing the glasses.' He went away to serve a customer leaving her wondering what she should do. But very soon she was pulling pints like she had been born to it and passing the money along for Mr Tony Harehill – he pronounced it like Arial – to put in the till, which he made very clear she was not allowed to touch.

'Me and Phil there,' he indicated the redhead, 'are the only ones to handle the cash,' the landlord explained when she had taken her first order. You don't go near that thing – get it?' He nodded towards the cash register.

'Got it,' Elsie agreed.

She was nearly on her knees when 'time' was finally called, though the satisfying clink of all the pennies, threepenny bits and even sixpences in her pocket more than made up for her aching legs. What she hadn't decided was where to stash her new earnings so that they would be safely hidden from any prying eyes. Whatever I do, she thought, I must be careful not to let on at home that I have even one extra penny.

She wouldn't even tell Fay, she decided; it wasn't fair to burden her young sister with her secrets. At least, not yet. She would give no sign to anyone about her new job. Elsie wondered how she would explain her absence every evening. Thinking on it, she thought she could get away with saying that she was working nights at the factory. The place often operated around the clock at busy times of the year and the factory had been much busier than usual of late. Word had it that it was in case there was a war. Anyway, Elsie knew her lackadaisical parents were unlikely to check. The others would just have to do more of the housework now – as the eldest, she'd more than done her bit.

'It's gonna get busier than this before Christmas is over,' Mr Harehill told her as he prepared to lock up for the night. 'And I'll expect you to work a full shift over the holidays.'

She readily agreed. The young man she had followed, who had spoken up for her at just the right moment, the one that the landlord had called Stan, seemed to have disappeared by the time she was ready to go home. She felt strangely disappointed that she hadn't been able to thank him for the part he'd played in securing her the job, though she was sure she would be seeing a lot more of him now they were both working at the Butcher's Arms.

Chapter 5

Stan had intended to see Elsie safely home after her first successful night in the pub. Apart from anything, he fancied her and thought he might be in with a chance, as he'd been so helpful and actually found her the job. But instead, when the noisy crowd of young lads and men who had invaded the pub were preparing to leave, he grabbed his jacket and slipped out with them. He was keen to latch on to the newly enlisted soldier. The lad said he'd come to say goodbye to his family as he was off to war the next day and Stan, who'd been thinking of joining up himself, desperately wanted to grab the opportunity to find out more.

'Which way are you walking?' he asked. When the lad told him, Stan suggested they walk together since he was going that way too. In truth, his home was in the opposite direction, but he had endless questions to ask and the lad seemed only too eager to answer them. They walked for quite some time, but Stan was too busy chatting to pay any attention to where they were going. So engrossed was he in the stories the young soldier had to tell about his recent experiences, they'd reached the lad's house without Stan realizing how far out of his way he had gone. He didn't want to admit how long it would take him to walk home, so he waved goodbye and waited for the lad to let himself into the house before turning around and walking home. But he didn't mind the walk, even though it turned out to be several miles. It enabled him to clear his head, mull things over and consider again the decision he had made almost as soon as he had first met the young soldier.

By the time he was back in Weatherfield, Stan was certain he knew exactly what he was going to do. He too was going to volunteer to fight in the Spanish Civil War. This wasn't the first time he had heard about it, but it was the first time he had met someone who had actually enlisted. The previous year a mate had persuaded him to go to a summer camp run by the Labour League of Youth. He knew it was something his dad would have approved of if he'd still been alive as he'd been a keen supporter of the Labour Party. So, Stan hadn't taken much persuading. And he'd been pleased with his decision. All the lads he met there were working class like him and they turned out to be a great bunch. Mostly, it had been a good laugh, but things had turned serious when they got to talking about the latest war in Europe. It seemed that in Spain the democratically elected Republicans were being threatened by Francisco Franco and his gang of fascists. With Adolf Hitler supporting Franco, the Republicans needed as much help as they could get to stop the fascists taking over. The International Brigade was recruiting soldiers from all over the world and although the English government was against young Brits signing up, many of the lads at the camp were determined to go. The stories Stan had heard there were enough to convince him it was the right thing to do. Besides, it sounded exciting, a chance to make his mark on the world. What's more, he reckoned he could make far more money fighting for a good cause than he could ever earn collecting dead glasses in a crummy bar in Weatherfield.

Stan had always considered himself a bit of a warrior and a chancer, though in fact his biggest adventure to date had been a day trip to Glossop. But fighting in a foreign country, even for a cause he didn't fully understand, sounded thrilling. From the first moment, he was enchanted by the notion of going to Spain. He was already imagining the stories he would be able to tell when he eventually came home a hero, and the thought of impressing Elsie wasn't far from his mind either. It didn't trouble him in the slightest that he wasn't sure how to get down to London, where the soldier had said he would find the recruiting office for volunteers.

Elsie saw Stan again sooner than she'd expected. Early the next morning as she came out of the front door ready to go to work, she was surprised to find him leaning against the wall, one foot flat against the brick-work. The window beside him was so grimy it was impossible to see in or out. Casting an anxious glance over her shoulder, Elsie was relieved to see that she was the first one up and out of the house as usual. If for once her father had been up and about, he would have had a mouthful to say about a lad sniffing around at that hour of the morning.

'What are you doing here so early?' she said. 'Couldn't you sleep?' She treated him to one of her teasing smiles. 'Nice of you to want to walk me to work, but it's only just down the road, you know. By the time you've said, "How do you do?" we'll be there.'

Stan grinned. 'I know.' He lifted his cap to flick the straying lock of hair underneath it, then jammed it back down again. 'I wanted to see you.'

'You'll be seeing me soon enough at the pub tonight. Can't it wait?'

'No, it can't. But don't fret. It won't take a minute. Shall we just nip down the side so no one can see us?'

At this Elsie giggled. 'Why? What are you planning on doing? Isn't it a bit early in the morning for that?' She was surprised to see him blush.

'It's nothing like that. I want to tell you summat, and it's a secret.'

'Well, that's all very flattering. Thank you very much. But I daren't be late for clocking on or they'll be docking me wages. They use any excuse they can get, you must know that.'

'Aye, I do. They're all the piggin' same, the bosses.'

They scurried to the end of the James's house next door at number 20, and Elsie leaned up against the wall in what she thought was a provocative pose. But he didn't seem to notice.

'Well?' she said. 'I'm waiting.' She was aware of the minutes ticking by. 'Spit it out.'

'Can you keep a secret?' Stan looked suddenly agitated and Elsie felt a tingle down her spine. What was this about?

'Of course I can,' she said. 'What kind of secret is it anyway?'

He hesitated before blurting out, 'I'm going off to war.'

Elsie was puzzled. 'But there is no war. Not yet, at any road. And there may not—'

'Not that war,' he cut in. 'The civil war in Spain.'

'Oh.' Not wanting to admit she wasn't sure of the difference, she nodded as if she knew all about it and then said, 'Why?'

'Because we have to stop the bloody fascists from taking over the country.'

'I see,' she said, though she wasn't sure she did. 'But

why do you have to go? Spain's a heck of a long way. Haven't they got enough men in their own army?'

'No. Not now that people like Hitler have muscled in. They need help or the next thing we know those fascist buggers will be running all over the shop here, too.'

'It doesn't sound right that you have to go all that way to fight someone else's war.'

'Actually, there's men going to fight from all over the world.'

Elsie was flummoxed. She was only just getting to know Stan Walsh as she'd heard one of the regulars call him. So far she liked what she saw. She certainly didn't like the idea of him buggering off to Spain to fight in some war. Who knew what might happen. He might never come back. 'So what does your mam have to say about all this?' she said.

'I haven't said owt to her. I told you: it's a secret.'

Elsie frowned. 'Don't you think we've got enough problems here in Weatherfield, without the likes of you waltzing off to Spain.'

'But it's important that Franco is stopped.' Stan was adamant.

'Well, that's all very well. But why do you need to get involved? And what if Hitler takes a fancy to coming on to us? Don't you think you'll be needed here?'

Stan looked thoughtful. 'I can see what you mean, but . . . ' He looked uncertain.

Elsie moved away from the wall, preparing to leave.

'Look, I haven't got time to stand here arguing the toss. I've got to get to work.'

'I know, I'm sorry.' Stan took off his cap and raked his fingers through his hair. 'I just wanted you to know what I was thinking, that's all.' Stan lowered his eyes. 'I shan't be telling anyone else.'

'I see.' Elsie didn't know what to say. 'Well, thanks for telling me.'

'So, I'll see you at the pub tonight?' His voice was eager.

Elsie liked that. She nodded. 'Right.'

'And you won't tell anyone what we talked about?'

'No, of course not.'

'Only I don't want Mr Harehill to know what I'm planning.'

'You've no need to worry. He won't hear it from me,' she said. She started to walk away but Stan caught hold of her by the shoulders. He leaned forward with pouted lips, but Elsie had turned her head so he ended up pecking her on the cheek.

'Thanks, Else. I'll see you tonight then.' He turned to go. 'And don't forget: mum's the word.' He put his finger to his lips and disappeared while Elsie had to run all the way down the road to reach the factory gates on time.

Chapter 6

It was exhausting being rushed off her feet at the Butcher's Arms, particularly after a long shift at the factory, but Elsie enjoyed working alongside Stan. As Mr Harehill had predicted, Christmas was a particularly busy time, but it was also a time when customers were more generous than usual with their tips. In the privacy of the bedroom, when she was sure none of the other occupants were around, Elsie was gratified to see her small stash of money was steadily mounting as she carefully checked it on a Saturday night. She shared knowledge of the contents of the old biscuit tin with nobody. Not even Fay. And she made certain never to touch it if any of her sisters were around. She was looking forward to the day when she would have enough to buy her first present for herself. It would have to be something new. That would make it very special and it would be her very own. She dreamed of having her first proper lipstick.

Although she saw Stan every day, they never had time for more than a bit of playful banter as they were flying about clearing and refilling the glasses. Mr Harehill didn't encourage what he called 'chattering' among the staff, and most nights she left before Stan did, so he couldn't even walk her home. But there was something comforting about him just being there that gave her a warm glowing feeling inside. She was considering hanging around after her shift now and again so they could have the chance for a chat, but before she had a chance to act on it, she was surprised one night, a few days before her birthday, to find Stan had come in search of her.

Elsie and the other workers at the factory came out of work late that day as they'd been asked to put in an extra shift. Things were changing in the factory and rumour had it they would all be expected to do different kinds of work soon, though nobody knew quite what that meant. It was as if, despite all the optimism that was in the air, the country was still preparing for war.

As always, Elsie came out arm and arm with her friend Aggie and they said goodbye at the gate. Then as she turned to head for home, she felt someone tug at her sleeve.

'Stop messing about, will you – let go of me,' she

snapped, thinking it was one of the ragamuffins who hung around the factory gates. They loved to plague the life out of the young workers, waiting with their hands out and pleading for spare change in their pitiful, whining voices. She turned round testily, ready to give the little so-and-so a telling off, for she was tired and ready to go home. But to her surprise, she came face to face with Stan.

'Hello,' he said, touching his cap as she'd seen him do before.

'What the hell are you doing here?' she asked.

'Waiting for you,' he said. 'I assumed you still worked here. I thought I'd come and look for you.'

'Well, you didn't have to look far.' Elsie grinned. She was pleased to see him, but then began to worry that something might be wrong. 'Is anything up?' she said.

He shrugged. 'Nowt much.' He paused. 'I wanted to tell you I got a promotion.'

'What, at the Butcher's?'

He nodded.

Elsie's jaw dropped. 'When was that then?'

'This dinner time.'

'How did you manage to get that stingy bugger to agree?'

'Fancy a bit of a walk? Come with me and I'll tell you.'

Twilight had given way to darkness as they'd been standing and everyone else had suddenly disappeared. Only the nightwatchman was left, and he was busy fixing a sturdy padlock on to the factory's wrought-iron gates.

'Which way?' Elsie asked.

'How about we go to the Field?'

'All right.' Elsie was sure Fay would cover for her at teatime. She felt him fumble in the darkness for her hand. He put it with his into his coat pocket. It gave her quite a thrill and made her think twice about commenting on the hole she could feel in the pocket lining.

'What's your promotion then?' Elsie asked.

'I'll be taking over Phil's job.'

'Wow! How did that happen?'

'Till was a bob short. Old Hairy accused him of pinching. There was the heck of a row, then he told him to go. Straight up. No explanations. No second chance.'

'Had he really nicked owt?' Elsie wanted to know. 'I didn't think Phil was like that.'

'No, I don't think he is. Kept swearing he hadn't touched anything, but Hairy didn't give him a chance. You know what he's like about that cash register.'

'He'd take it to bed with him if he could.' Elsie giggled. 'Don't tell me the mean bugger's going to trust you to use the till.'

'Not yet. He said I'd have to prove myself first. But that's OK. I don't want ever to be accused of anything. He can have it all to himself, for all I care. Less work for me. But he has agreed to upping me wages.'

'Well done. That's great. Did you have to beg?'

'No more than usual.'

'Then he must like you, is all I can say,' she teased.

They had come to the flickering gas light at the end of the row of the houses. Beyond was the wasteland they knew as the Field. Elsie's favourite upturned bucket seemed to have disappeared and there was nowhere for either of them to sit. Stan propped himself up against the end wall of the terrace and pulled Elsie towards him.

'I first met you here, didn't I?' he said.

She nodded. 'And then you saw me here the second time, the night I followed you to the pub.'

'I remember,' he said. 'You shouted something to me, but I was in such a hurry I didn't even realize you were following me.'

'It was thanks to you I got that job. He never would have believed I was eighteen if it hadn't been for you. But I've always wondered: how did you know my name?'

Stan's lips twisted into a smile and he tapped the side of his nose with his finger.

'Ah, that's not fair,' she complained. 'Go on, tell me, I really want to know.'

'No big mystery. After seeing you the first time, I asked one of your mates from the factory who you were. They told me your name.'

Elsie laughed. 'Simple as that!' But she did feel flattered. Her instincts about this lad were serving her well. She didn't have long to dwell on the thought, though, because Stan put his hand up behind her head and pulled her face towards his. Then he kissed her full on the lips. At first, Elsie was surprised. Then she relaxed as she felt his mouth, fleshy and warm against hers. She responded to the stiffness of his tongue as he explored her mouth. This felt different from most of the boys she had kissed before. This felt really grown-up. They stood for a few minutes, holding each other, gently kissing. Then the light drizzle that had begun as soon as they started walking turned into a heavy downpour. Elsie pulled her thin coat tightly around her, but her hair began to drip into her eyes and she couldn't stop shivering.

'Bugger!' Stan said. 'What a bloody nuisance. I suppose we can't just stand here and get wet.'

'Too late,' Elsie said, putting her hand to her already bedraggled hair. 'I reckon I'd best get on home.'

'I'll walk you back,' Stan offered. 'Maybe it'll stop.'

'Yes, and pigs might fly!' Elsie laughed, as they set off at a brisk pace.

Stan reached for her hand and held it in his, although this time he didn't try to put it into his pocket. 'Do you fancy going out on Sunday?' he asked.

'Out? What, like together?'

'Yes, of course together.'

'Where to?'

'I dunno. I could meet you by the factory gate after dinner. We can go for a walk. I'll think of somewhere to go by then.'

Elsie hesitated, then she said quietly, 'It's me birthday on Sunday. I've never been out on me birthday before.' She wasn't sure why she had told him that.

'Well, in that case you can't say no.'

Overcome by a sudden shyness, Elsie smiled.

'Tell you what – can you ride a bike?' Stan asked.

'A bike? I don't know as I've ever tried. But I've not got one anyway, so it makes no difference.'

'No, but I've got one and I can lend you me brother Charlie's. I bet I could soon teach you to ride.'

Elsie frowned, not sure if he was being serious. Riding a bike wasn't something she'd ever thought of doing. Not recently, at any rate; she had longed to have a go when she was a kid. Fay had once found a tricycle on the tip. It didn't have a seat and the handlebars were a bit wonky, but they had taken turns to ride it standing up while desperately trying to steer. She had ended up with the bike on top of her when it had tipped over as she tried to turn a corner, and that was the end of it. Since then, she had never attempted to ride again. She certainly had never tried on a real bike that only had two wheels.

'We could go out on to the moors,' Stan said.

Elsie hesitated, considering his suggestion, but he was persistent. 'Tell you what, if you want to meet me tomorrow I could teach you to ride in no time. I'll keep hold of the seat till you get the hang of it. It won't take long, I'm sure.'

Elsie wasn't at all sure, but she was willing to give

it a go. It would be exciting to do something special for her birthday.

'Do you know Coronation Street?' Stan asked.

Elsie did know it. Coronation Street wasn't that far from Back Gas Street, but they might as well have been on opposite poles they were so different. Coronation Street was a tidy row of neat terraces that had been built to house the workers from the old Hardcastle mill, which had long since shut and was now the raincoat factory. The residents who lived there now were ordinary working folk, just like she was, but Coronation Street had a proud air about it, everyone seeming to sense they were lucky to live there. It was very different from the squalid slums that were all she knew.

'Of course, why?'

'Because it's got a good stretch of fairly flat cobbles. And that lot are so houseproud they always clear up the horse dung after the milkman's been, so it's never too slippery. You'll be able to learn right quick there. And there's a good straight run from one end of the street to the other.'

'I don't know—' Elsie began, but Stan wasn't listening.

'There's a slight slope that you'll have to pedal up, but on the way down all you have to do is steer. Tell you what – why don't I meet you at the factory gates, like I said, and I'll bring the bike. We can walk to Coronation Street from there.'

Elsie wasn't at all convinced she would be able to do it. To her, it sounded a crazy idea, but Stan was so enthusiastic she didn't want to be a spoilsport and say no.

'If I learn how to do it, can we really go out for my birthday?' she asked, spurred on by the thought of such a treat.

'Like I said, it could be fun. And me brother need never know I've borrowed his bike.'

Elsie for once was speechless. No one had ever done anything special for her birthday before. So that made her more determined than ever that by Sunday she would learn how to ride a bike.

Chapter 7

By Sunday morning the rain had stopped. Elsie couldn't see out clearly through the grime on their bedroom window, but when she made her way downstairs she couldn't hear any rain pattering against the glass pane. She was up even earlier than usual, wanting to make the day stretch out as long as possible even though nobody else in the house would be stirring for another couple of hours. She was determined to enjoy every minute of her birthday. Others down at the factory were forever talking about the things they had done to celebrate their birthdays; now, for the first time in her life, she wanted to be able to experience what it was to feel pampered and special. She wanted to go back to work on Monday morning and talk about what she had done and how much she had enjoyed herself on her big day. And Stan Walsh was going to make sure she did.

As she cautiously descended the stairs, however, she felt as if the day was already less than perfect. It might be her birthday, but she still had to do her early morning chores. Collect the water from the pump in the court-yard. Set up the cauldron. Rake out the ashes and get a new fire going in the grate. She needed to get through as much as she could and be gone from the house before anyone else was awake.

As she got dressed, she wished she could have worn something different. But that of course was impossible. She was by far the tallest in the family so she couldn't even pinch anything from one of her siblings. At least today she didn't have to cover up her dress with her work overalls or wear a wretched headscarf. The flow-ered print of her cotton dress had once been quite pretty, she thought as she smoothed her hands over the tight-fitting bodice and gathered skirt, but that was before all the flowers had faded. The only thing she could find to wear that made her feel different was a pair of fine lawn knickers that she pinched from her mother's drawer. Alice had shown them to her once and said she'd only worn them on very special occa-sions. What kind of occasions her mother would have needed such pretty delicate underwear for, Elsie really couldn't imagine. Not that Alice could fit into them at the moment, so Elsie was sure her mother wouldn't miss them. They felt really light and special as she ran her hands over the fine gauze material. The knickers were still pretty even though they were no longer white. Just the thing to comfort her aching sit-upon.

The chill of the early morning was likely to remain throughout the day, so Elsie would need to wrap up warm. But when she had worn her coat last night for the trial run on the bike, it had flapped annoyingly around the chain, getting in the way, so today she put her cardigan on instead. She fastened all the buttons against the wind, but even so she found herself wishing she had darned some of the larger holes.

Elsie was still excited by the fact that she had learned to ride a bike last night. It hadn't been easy, but she had conquered her fear and maintained her balance and by the time Stan had said they should call it a day, she'd been riding up and down the street in triumph. She'd never have believed it could be so exhilarating, riding the length and breadth of Coronation Street without anyone holding on to the saddle, and when she wobbled off a couple of times it had cost her nothing more than her dignity. But now she realized she was paying the full price for Stan's tuition, for this morning her legs ached when she tried to walk, and sitting down was so painful she didn't know how she was going to get back on to the bike.

They had taken a chance and hidden Charlie's bike overnight under some old rags in the courtyard, and when she went out to use the privy she was relieved to find the bike was still there. She wheeled it to the factory gates where she was to meet Stan, hoping that by walking slowly alongside it she would be conserving her energy for today's ride. She had no idea how far they would be going, Stan was keeping that a secret, but it was bound to be a fair way.

He was already at the factory and was leaning on his bike as it stood propped up against the iron gates. He was wearing his cap as usual, but today he had tied the bottom of each of his wide trouser legs with a band of string. Elsie thought he looked very dapper and dashing, smoking a cigarette while leaning casually on the gates, and she had to pinch herself it was so hard to believe that a man was taking her out specially for her birthday.

As always, Stan doffed his cap when he caught sight of her. 'At your service, madam,' he said as she drew near, giving a slight bow and making Elsie giggle. 'And some little bird has told me it's your birthday today,' he said. From behind his back he whipped out a small package covered in pretty paper.

Elsie turned away to brush her eyes with the back of her hand. 'No one's ever given me a present on me birthday before. Is this really for me?' she asked, overwhelmed at the gesture.

'Really.' He laughed as she began feeling the package, trying to guess what might be inside. 'You'd better open it or you won't be able to see what it is.'

It was just like one of the packages under the newsagent's Christmas tree. She unwrapped the paper carefully, so as not to tear it. Inside, as she had suspected, was a bar of dark brown Bournville chocolate. A lump rose in her throat. 'Thank you – thank you very much, Stan. I shall treasure it.' She wanted to hang on to her precious present but realized she had no pockets to put it into.

At that Stan laughed again. 'I was rather hoping you'd eat it. And you can give me a bit an' all. But for now you can put it in me saddlebag.' He indicated the small leather pouch on the back of his bike. She handed the chocolate over reluctantly. It did make more sense to put it away for the time being. And afterwards she would keep the paper he had wrapped it in. This was her first-ever present, and that was something she would never forget.

'We can have it when we gets to the moors,' he said.

'The moors?'

'Aye, I thought it would be nice to get out into the country. It's not far, not now that you can ride.'

She nodded. She couldn't tell him she was too sore to get on a bike today. Not when he'd gone to so much trouble. And after all the effort he'd put into teaching her to ride last night. She remembered how pleased he had been and knew she really couldn't let him down.

'Look, I brought this too.' He brandished another package, this time in a brown paper bag. 'It's a sandwich, in case we get hungry at dinner time.' He leaned towards her and kissed her lightly but tenderly on the lips.

A bar of chocolate and a sandwich! Elsie's stomach fizzed with excitement; she felt really special now.

'So, let's go,' Stan said, turning his bike. 'You can follow me, I know the way. I've been up on to the moors loads of times.'

Elsie was afraid that he would see how difficult it was for her to lift her leg over the crossbar of Charlie's bike, but as it turned out it she didn't need to worry. He wasn't watching; in fact, he was already halfway down the street. She wobbled along behind him for a short way then gripped the handlebars tightly while she tried to shut her mind to the pain.

'I'm going to have a lovely time,' she repeated over and over, trying madly to convince herself. 'I'm not in pain and I'm going to have a very nice day.' She lifted her head and felt the breeze in her hair. She thought of the sandwich and the chocolate bar in Stan's saddlebag and like a miracle the pain seemed to drift away.

They were well out into the country and seemed to have been pedalling for ages when Stan signalled for her to stop. Elsie was some way behind him and it took a few minutes for her to catch up. But as there was no one else on the narrow ribbon of road, apart from the occasional car, she had never actually lost sight of him. When they stopped, the view was amazing. The choking fog and grime of the city were still within sight, yet she had never been here before. High up here on the moors she had a bird's-eye view of Weatherfield;

the rows and rows of brick terraces looked like one of those paintings you could see in the library and it seemed hardly possible that the houses were teeming with noisy and chaotic life, so peaceful and calm did it seem from this distance. And up here, amongst the soft, springy turf and the heather, was another world. There was so much space, almost no people, with only the occasional sheep. Stan had laid his bike down in the short stubby grass and was crouching beside it when Elsie eventually came to a halt. At that moment she wished she had been riding a girl's bike. But somehow she managed to swing her leg back over the crossbar. She flopped on to the grass next to him and lay for a moment, spread-eagled, enjoying the silence, mesmerized by the hugeness of the sky. It was mostly grey with clouds that looked low enough to touch and only occasional pockets of blue. She'd never really looked at the sky before. At home it was difficult to see any of it between the buildings.

'Not sure you should do that. It'll be wet down there.' Stan was watching her. 'You'll get yourself all muddy, if you're not careful. People come up here with their dogs.'

Elsie sat up. Her dress was already mucky so it didn't matter much. But she didn't want to be the one to say that. Thankfully, she had just avoided a puddle.

'You're doing well for a beginner,' he said, and smiled. 'You OK?'

Elsie nodded but didn't say anything.

'I thought we'd go on just a bit further.' He pointed ahead. 'Over that next hill there's a terrific view of the Pennines.'

She wasn't sure how much further she could go, even if the view was better from the other side. It was all uphill from here, as far as she could see. In the far distance there was snow on the higher peaks. She trusted they weren't headed there. The only thought she could console herself with was that there must be some bit where it was all downhill.

When they set off again, she slowed down considerably and at times lost sight of Stan altogether. But she kept doggedly at it and gritted her teeth until eventually she rounded a rocky outcrop and found him lying on an old newspaper in a grassy hollow. He was smoking, looking very relaxed.

'What kept you?' he said, his face creased into a grin. He patted a big sheet of newspaper that he'd placed beside him. Elsie was panting from the spurt she'd had to put in for the final hill and didn't answer right away. But then she dismounted and sat down beside him to catch her breath. She nudged her elbow into his ribs.

'You're a cheeky sod. Do you know that?' she said. 'Pretending you're so much better than me. Here, give us a puff of that.' She grabbed the cigarette from between his fingers and took a long drag. But she dropped it as quickly as she had picked it up when she began to cough and choke. Stan rescued the remains of his home-rolled fag from the heathery stubble. 'What did you do that for, you daft cow. Trying to be clever? I bet you've never smoked before, have you?'

Elsie shook her head, unable to speak. She got up and ran away as quickly as she could from where they were sitting. She needed to throw up.

Stan tutted. 'I can see I'll have to teach you a lot more than just how to ride a bike,' he said.

The coughing fit slowly subsided and Elsie came and sat down beside him.

''Ere, let me make it better,' he said, pulling her towards him. He put his arm round her and she let herself be comforted as he stroked her back.

Now that her breathing was almost back to normal, she could feel the cold striking up from the sodden grass.

'Damn!' she said. The back of her dress was wet. The wind had also picked up and it didn't take long before she was chilled to the bone. But it felt so nice being there, just the two of them, that she didn't want to spoil the moment.

It was Stan who jumped up, realizing he too had been getting his backside wet. 'Fancy a sarnie?' he said.

'Oo, that sounds good.'

'You've got a choice. Jam or jam?' he laughed as he proffered the bag. Elsie stood up too. She realized when she peered into the packet that she was hungry and didn't wait before she sank her teeth into two of the thickest chunks of bread she'd ever seen. There was a thin smear of red jam in between and it tasted good.

Stan demolished his half of the sandwich equally quickly.

'What's for afters?' he said.

Elsie raised her eyebrows.

'As if I didn't know,' Stan said. He pulled out her present, still in its gift wrap, and handed it to her. Elsie broke it up into squares. She took a large one before passing the rest to Stan. She put the whole piece into her mouth and sucked on it. It tasted delicious. It didn't take long before they'd finished the entire bar. She had eaten so quickly that for a moment she thought she might be sick again, but she was determined not to let her birthday present go to waste. She took a deep breath and neatly folded the coloured paper. I'm going to keep this, she thought, and tucked it into her cardigan sleeve.

'We can go for a walk,' Stan suggested. 'Might help to warm us up a bit.'

'Good idea,' Elsie said. She was trying not to think of the long journey home, however much of it would be downhill. 'I wonder who lives over there?' she said, pointing to what looked more like an unlived-in old cottage than somebody's current home.

'Let's go see,' Stan said. 'I'm sure our bikes will be all right here for a bit.' And he reached out to take her hand.

As they had thought, the cottage was abandoned. Inside, the roof sagged ominously, but they crept through the door into the shelter of the ruin. As soon as they were hidden from view, Stan pulled Elsie towards him and kissed her. His breath was warm and sweet, and as his tongue probed her own gently, she felt a ripple of desire shoot through her. She responded eagerly, but at the sound of masonry dislodging itself above them, they pulled apart. It looked as if the roof might collapse at any moment.

'We'd best get out of here before there's an accident,' Stan said, taking her hand as they picked their way out of the ramshackle building and down the path into what might have once been the garden. In the centre there were the remains of some small trees, and where flowers may once have grown there were now tall upright stones and boulders. At the end of the garden was a signpost but the names on the two arms had long since worn away.

'Here.' Stan's voice was thick as he pointed to a clump of several rocks. They formed a dry platform with a back wall that would shelter them from the wind.

Elsie followed him out and they sat down together against the largest of the rocks. It was warm and dry, and as she made herself comfortable Elsie was aware of him looking at her with raw desire. Next thing she knew, they were wrapped around each other in a passionate clinch. This was even better than the last time. There's something different about Stan, she thought as his hand worked its way up the back of her dress to unclasp her bra. There was something that set him apart from the boys who hung around the courtyard. Clearly he was older than she was. Not so much a boy, more of a young man. She could feel her nipples standing erect as his assured touch lingered over them and she knew that this time it really was special, for her body clearly wanted more. Shocked at her own reaction, she made no attempt to stop his hand when it slid effort-lessly under her skirt. His fingers dipped inside her soft cotton knickers and she was glad that she had put them on. She almost wished she could display them. Suddenly it was as if Stan had read her thoughts, for he pulled them off – tearing them in the process.

'Hey! What do you think you're doing?' she gasped. She was about to add that he should take care as they weren't hers, but fortunately she stopped herself in time, realizing how stupid it would sound.

'Well, we've got them out of the way,' he said, his voice husky. 'Now it's back to the serious business.' His beaming smile made him look anything but serious. But when she felt his hand between her legs again she realized what he had meant. Elsie had let some of the local boys have a grope and feel before, but for the first time in her life she was transported, carried on a rush of longing that flooded her whole body. Elsie wasn't sure what to expect but when Stan pulled down his own trousers and she felt him enter her, she gasped in surprise as the pain and the pleasure entwined deli-ciously around each other inside her body.

Afterwards he took off his jacket and wrapped it round her as they sat together on the boulder. But then she remembered something.

'Where's me drawers?' They looked around them, and saw that the wind had caught the flimsy strips of cotton and carried them as far as the nearest small tree, where they'd caught on one of the branches and now hung flapping precariously. Elsie could only laugh. And she could see that Stan was laughing too.

Once her knickers were reinstated, Stan offered her a cigarette. When she hesitated, he showed her how to hold it between her fingers and to breathe in gently. She remembered how Deanna Durbin had done it on the screen and did the same. She felt very grown-up and sophisticated. And so she should. For hadn't she now got her first boyfriend. A special someone who bought her presents and made her feel like a real woman and not just young Elsie Grimshaw from Back Gas Street.

Chapter 8

Elsie spent the next few days almost dancing, feeling as if her feet were not touching the ground. I have a proper boyfriend, she kept saying to herself over and over, and no one can take him away. She was fifteen years old and she had at last found the kind of boyfriend who bought her presents. The kind who would stick around for a very long time. Stan had proved that, hadn't he, when he'd asked her to go out with him again the following week. And hadn't they been seeing each other whenever they could ever since. He must like her. And she certainly liked him.

After that first time they went back to the moors on Sunday afternoons whenever the weather held. Sometimes they rode together over to the other side of Weatherfield, up and down some of the hillier streets, to help her improve her skills. Elsie was quite proud of herself. Not only was she able to ride more smoothly as time wore on, but it wasn't long before she was able to negotiate the narrow, unevenly cobbled streets and alleyways on the outskirts of the town without falling off. And she was no longer feeling sore whenever she mounted the saddle. She loved the freedom of getting out into the country, the feel of the wind in her hair, and she was happy to take any opportunity to get away from the foul air and grimy streets of her home town. Stan taught her how to control the bike properly and how to use the brakes to stop instead of dragging her feet along the ground.

'Keep doing that and you'll soon have no shoes left at all,' he warned. Elsie tucked her feet away behind the pedals when he said that, not wanting to draw attention to the fact that there wasn't much left of her shoes as it was, without them having to act as bicycle brakes.

She was so grateful for all his teaching, she thought she should offer him something in return. So she showed him how she and her sister often sneaked into the cinema for free of an evening.

'I'm surprised you and your mates don't know about it already. It's somewhere to go when the weather's bad.'

'I've never been mithered to go to the cinema,' he said. 'Me mam took me a few times when I was little. But she only wanted to see soppy love stories. You know the sort. Lots of mushy kissing.'

Elsie stared at him, her mouth open. He looked a little sheepish as he grinned. 'It's one thing doing it, quite another having to watch others at it. So I stopped going.'

But once Elsie had introduced him to the likes of Billy the Kid and Roy Rogers, he changed his mind. Randolph Scott became his particular hero and after that he was happy to go with her to see pretty much any action film.

Whilst it wasn't easy for them to find time to go out together, they did see each other every night at the Butcher's Arms. Whenever she could, Elsie waited for him so they could stroll home together. If it wasn't too cold, they would sit out on the Field for a while, smoking one of Stan's roll-ups between them. One evening they came to the waste ground to find it looking quite different. Two or three small mounds had appeared that definitely hadn't been there before.

'What the hell's this?' Elsie asked, poking at one of them. Although it was sticking up quite a way out of the ground, when they peered inside it was possible to see from the light of the nearby gas lamp that it had been dug out of the mud so that part of it sloped down underground. It was dark inside and smelt of freshly dug earth.

'It looks like it could be used as some sort of shelter in case there is actually going to be a war. They say the Germans have bombs that they would drop on us, if they can. I've read about it in the papers,' Stan said.

Elsie was sceptical. 'You bloody men, that's all you ever think about. Why can't you get it into your thick heads that there's not going to be a war?'

Stan shrugged. 'I dunno. We can't be sure, Else. There still might be one. Then we'd all need one of these.'

'If there was a war, I can tell you I wouldn't fancy being holed up in one of them for very long,' Elsie said. 'You can't fit many people in there, for a start. You'd need one for each of us or a bloody great big one for everybody in the street.'

'I suppose each family could have their own.'

'Oh yes, and where the hell would they put it?'

'In the back garden.'

'And who the hell's got one of them?' Elsie wanted to know. She was thinking of Back Gas Street and wondering where all the residents would go. In the midden off the courtyard?

'That's true,' Stan said. 'Not many folk in these parts have got that much room.'

'Never mind that. The blooming thing itself is scary. It would make me feel like one of those animals that you see in books. Don't they live in little tunnels like this? What do you call them? Is it badgers or something?'

'It wouldn't matter what it made you feel like, let me tell you if the bloody Germans did start dropping bombs on us we'd be glad of having one, even if we had to crawl into it.'

'Frankly, I wouldn't mind if someone bombed our house,' Elsie said. 'It's about the best thing that could happen to it. It's no better than a mudhole right now.'

'Yeah,' Stan said with a rueful snigger, 'I know what you mean. It's true of a lot of places round here.'

Elsie smiled. 'Can you imagine – the kids would be like pigs in clover if these things started popping up all over the show! They'd want to be playing hide and seek in them all the time.'

'True, and you couldn't blame them.' Stan went to investigate the little tunnel more closely. He ducked into the entrance. 'You can just about stand up in it.' He chuckled. 'I can think of better uses than kids' games.' He stepped further inside, but not before he had grabbed hold of Elsie's hand to take her with him. Then he pulled the tin door over the entrance.

Elsie was stunned into silence for a moment as they were plunged into pitch darkness. Before she could say anything, Stan covered her mouth with his own. She giggled as she sensed his hand groping under her skirt. Feeling him hard against her, she immediately began fumbling with his buttons.

It was over very quickly. Elsie hardly had time to catch her breath. It felt so amazingly daring; although the door was closed and no one could see them, they were practically standing in the street. Elsie started to laugh but it turned into a coughing fit and she lunged for the entrance and fresh air, with Stan hurriedly trying to straighten her clothing as she emerged into the yellowy gas light. She was still choking but Stan was right behind her, slapping her on the back. Then he fastened his own buttons before putting his arms round her.

'Our secret,' he whispered into her ear. 'This is only between you and me.'

The idea of having such a secret with someone as special as Stan thrilled Elsie. Which was why she was so upset to discover that it didn't remain a secret very long.

One night after work a few days later she went home with her friend Aggie. It was something they liked to do when Aggie's family were all out and they had the place to themselves. They would sit together on the couch in the front room swapping stories and feeling proper grown-up. Elsie had told her friend lots about her new boyfriend and Aggie had been thrilled to share in Elsie's excitement about her birthday present and the trip to the moors. But tonight when they sat down in front of the fire, Aggie wasn't her usual smiling self. In fact she had a frighteningly serious look on her face.

'Is summat up, Aggs?' Elsie asked. 'You know you can tell me, whatever it is. By the look on your face, anyone'd think the dog ate your dinner.' Elsie nudged her friend, trying to chivvy her into a smile.

But Aggie didn't smile. Her forehead puckered into a frown. She didn't answer immediately and when she did, she refused to look directly at Elsie. 'There's something I've got to tell you,' she began, as if Elsie hadn't spoken. 'It's about Stan, and I think you should know.'

'Why, what's up wi' 'im?' Elsie was beginning to feel anxious now.

'I mean, I know you two have been doing a spot of courting,' Aggie said hesitantly.

'I don't know as I would say we were *courting*.' Elsie relaxed a little and grinned. 'Not yet awhile.'

'No, well, you know what I mean. You have been sort of "stepping out".'

'Good God, Aggie, that makes it sound dead posh. It's just me and him . . . like. Well, we work together at night in the pub. He walks me home afterwards. You know . . . '

'No, that's just it. That's the point. I don't know.'

'You don't know what? Now you're talking in bloody riddles.'

Aggie hesitated, then said, 'I suppose what I'm really asking is, do you know him well enough to trust him?'

'Course I do. I don't know about courting, but he is me boyfriend, isn't he? He bought me a birthday present an' all.' Elsie jutted her chin out defiantly.

'I know about that and you've said nice things about him.'

'Well, I like him, why shouldn't I? It's only natural.'

'It's just, what I'm trying to say is . . . ' She hesitated again, then blurted, 'He's not saying such nice things about you.' She stopped when she had said that and looked anxiously at Elsie.

Elsie frowned. 'How do you mean? What kind of things is he saying?'

The colour had risen in Aggie's face and there were two rosy spots on her cheeks. 'I don't know if I should. I—'

'Course you should. You're my mate, aren't you?'

Aggie remained silent, avoiding her gaze. Instead she looked down at her hands, which she was clasping and unclasping in her lap.

Elsie didn't know what to think. 'C'mon, spit it out,' she said. 'I want to know what he's been saying.'

Aggie took a deep breath. 'He's saying . . . ' She had been unwilling to tell her friend the awful stories Stan was spreading about her, but now it felt as though she had opened the floodgates. Aggie sat forward and Elsie looked at her in anticipation, but her friend only sagged back into the chair. The rosy spots had disappeared and her face now looked drained.

'For crying out loud!' Elsie was torn between irritation and alarm. 'You can't stop in the middle like that.'

Aggie spoke again and this time the words came out in a rush, although her voice was barely above a whisper.

'It's about that day on the moors. Your birthday. And you finding that old house and . . . '

Elsie felt the blood drain from her face. Knowing what must be coming, she wasn't sure now that she wanted to hear it, but Aggie was still speaking softly. 'You kissed him? Right?'

'Yeah, I bloody kissed him. Isn't that what people do when they have a boyfriend? Don't you and Danny . . .?'

'I'm not talking about me.' Aggie dismissed the question sharply. 'Did you . . . ? You know . . . did you go any further?'

Elsie felt the blood rush to her face. The girls at the factory giggled about what they got up to with their boyfriends, but it was all very 'nudge nudge, wink wink' and no one talked in any real detail about what went on between a man and a woman – not to girls of her age, at any rate. Elsie knew that she wasn't like most of the other girls and she was starting to realize that doing things your own way could attract the wrong sort of attention.

'He's my boyfriend, I told you,' Elsie said, as convincingly as she could. But then she stopped. No longer so sure of anything. A cold shiver ran down her spine. 'What's he been saying?' Elsie demanded. 'I've got a right to know.'

'Stan's been boasting. About what you two got up to – not just on the moors, but on the Field as well.'

Elsie felt the gorge rise in her throat. She was so angry, she couldn't speak. The toad. For that's all he was. A snitching toad. And all the while she'd thought they'd had something special.

'I hope I did the right thing, telling you.' Aggie's voice was tentative. 'Only, I was mithered about what other people might be saying. Some of the girls at the factory . . . well, they've not been saying kind things about you. Calling you a slut and rotten stuff like that.'

Elsie gave her friend a doleful smile. 'Ah well, you should know me well enough by now to know I don't give a bugger what other people might say. What I do or don't do isn't any of their bloody business.' She sighed. 'Isn't life hard enough as it is, without having to fight for me sodding reputation.'

'Oh, Elsie, are you a slut?' Aggie had such a worried look that Elsie couldn't take it seriously. To her friend's astonishment, she burst out laughing.

'I don't know whether I am or not. What's more, I don't care. All I know is the way Stan makes me feel – or he did, at any rate. Stop looking so worried, Aggs.'

'But aren't you worried about getting . . . you know . . . in the family way?'

Elsie cocked her head to one side. 'Stan said he was careful, whatever that means.'

Aggie threw her arms round her. 'Elsie Grimshaw, you're a one and no mistake. What am I going to do with you?'

'Still be my friend, I should hope.'

Aggie nodded. 'Of course, I'll always be that.'

'It's that bloody Stan,' said Elsie, still fuming. 'He's the one needs pulling down a peg or two. He swore on his life not to tell another living soul. Wait till I get my hands on him!'

Chapter 9

Elsie left Aggie's house in such a fury it was all she could do to contain herself. Somehow she was going to have to keep a lid on her emotions until closing time at the Butcher's. With old Hairy watching like a hawk, she would have to be civil to Stan during the course of the evening shift; she daren't let her anger spill over and risk upsetting her boss. In the event, all she could manage was short, curt responses whenever he spoke to her. The first time she did it, he looked at her surprised for he had no inkling of what was going on. She quite relished the fact that he would have to remain puzzled, for there was no opportunity to talk once they had set to work.

Fortunately, she had no time to think about it after pulling the first pint, for it was the stag night of one of their regulars who was getting married the next day. As she watched the men in the party became more and more drunk, Elsie thought with pity about the poor bride-to-be. The young groom must have spent the whole of his wage packet standing drinks for everyone at the bar, even sending some through for the ladies in the snug. Elsie was pleased with her own pickings, for she did well in tips by the end of the evening. And she could have been flat-out drunk too, if she had taken up all the free drinks every time they were offered. She did sneak a couple of shorts at the end of the evening when she knew everyone had been served. Not that she needed Dutch courage, but when she saw Stan slip himself a Scotch or two she thought it wouldn't do any harm to be well fortified for what she knew was to come.

When she and Stan finally quit the pub, the rowdy mob from the pre-wedding party had left before them, nursing their already sore heads. Stan was in a mellow mood. Before they'd gone as far as the top of the lane that led to the main road, he was feeling for her hand. Elsie snatched it away and folded her arms firmly across her chest. Stan stopped walking. He was laughing as he stood in front of her, imitating her posture.

'Blimey, Else, you look fierce tonight,' he said. 'If I didn't know you better, I'd say you were mad at me for summat. You've been snippy all evening.'

'You do know me well enough, Stan Walsh,' she said, moving her hands to her hips and planting her feet firmly apart. 'The way I hear it, you've been telling the world just how well you know me.'

At that Stan laughed and looked relieved. 'Oh, is that what this is all about? Me showing you off as my girlfriend? If a bloke can't boast around the place about his woman, then the world is a sorry place.'

'Is that what it was, boasting? Boasting about your easy conquest, more like.' Elsie felt as if every nerve ending was fired and ready to explode. No doubt this was how her father felt when he came home sozzled and let fly at her or one of the kids. The booze definitely gave her that extra edge. But she didn't need any more alcohol to finish this fight, thank you very much. Her anger was already well fuelled.

'Of course. I wanted to share my good fortune. Tell everyone I'm the happiest man there is.'

'What about it being "our secret"? "Just between the two of us", like you said.'

'Yes, well, doesn't everybody say that? But it doesn't mean you have to stick to it totally.'

Elsie opened her mouth to contradict but was so flabbergasted she couldn't find the words. She didn't have to worry though, because now that he had started, Stan kept going. 'Anyway,' he said, 'I should have thought you'd be pleased. I want everyone to know I've got the best girl in the world. C'mon, Elsie, don't be cross. You know I think you're a smasher. I'd never say nowt bad about you. It's those jealous old bags at the factory that have twisted it.'

It was the whisky talking. Elsie knew that. But Stan's words seemed to be having the desired effect and she could feel her temper starting to lessen, 'Do you mean it?' No one had ever said such a nice thing to her before.

He nodded.

She was horrified when she felt the prickle of tears and she brushed them away hastily with the palms of her hands before they could plop on her cheeks and embarrass her. 'Gerroff with you!' was all she managed to say.

'Surely you didn't think I meant to hurt you, did you?' Stan stepped closer and wrapped her in his arms. 'I wanted to shout it from the rooftops!' At that he ran off to the nearest lamppost chanting, 'I've got the best girl, Elsie Grimshaw!' as he swung himself round. When he ran to the next lamppost, still singing out of tune, Elsie yelled, 'Shut up, you daft sod! You'll wake the neighbours.'

'Good. That's the idea.'

His grin was so cheeky, Elsie found herself grinning too. It was impossible to stay mad at him.

He came back to stand in front of her again and put his hands on her shoulders. 'Do you forgive me?' he said, and this time he looked so apologetic she had to laugh. He might have given the spiteful gossips at the factory more grist to the mill, but could she really withhold her forgiveness?

At that moment a thought crossed her mind and she

stared up at him, determined to meet his gaze. As she locked eyes with him, she thought: Bloody hell, I love him! And I think he loves me. I've seen enough films to know.

'Yes, I forgive you,' she said, and she put her hands up to his face. He kissed her eagerly and she felt herself melting as if he were Errol Flynn. It was worthwhile getting angry once in a while if the making up was always as rewarding as this.

'What did you think to the stag do tonight?' Stan's voice brought her back to the street and the fine drizzle that was hanging in the chilly night air. They were strolling hand in hand now and it was as if the previous few minutes had never happened.

'I've not been rushed off me feet like that since Christmas,' Elsie replied.

'They enjoyed themselves.' Stan seemed deep in thought for a moment but his voice was casual when he said, 'Shame I won't be able to have my do there. But I'm sure you wouldn't want to spend the night watching me and my mates getting pie-eyed.'

'Your do?' Elsie queried. She was not sure she had heard right, though she could feel her heart beginning to pound. 'Have I missed something?'

'You don't have to worry. I'm not about to tie the knot yet. But you know we will one of these days, don't you? I reckon we shouldn't leave it too long to get wed.'

Elsie was choked. 'The two of us, getting wed?'

He nodded. 'Why not? I've told me mam about you and she thinks it's a good idea. She'd like to meet you. I reckon we should think about it as soon as I get back.'

'Back from where?'

'Spain.'

Elsie felt a boulder hit the pit of her stomach. She didn't know whether to laugh at the casualness of what she assumed was a proposal or to cry at his mention yet again of going off to fight in a foreign war.

'What are you talking about? You said you weren't going to go.' Her voice betrayed her exasperation. She didn't know what to make of him and his sudden changes of mind.

'No, and I didn't go then, but I didn't say I would never go at all. It seems things are getting worse. They need foreign help more than ever now.'

'But it doesn't have to be you as goes, does it?'

'Like I've said before, I don't have to go, but I want to volunteer.'

'What about if we have a war here?' Elsie knew Stan had wanted to go for ages but things were different now, surely?

'All the more reason to go to Spain now. Maybe we can stop fascism spreading across Europe. If we can beat Hitler there, he won't be able to come over here.'

Elsie was trying her best to follow his logic, but it was difficult for her to understand.

She shook her head. 'I don't know, one minute you're

talking about marriage then you want to flit the country and leave me behind. What's a girl supposed to make of it, I ask you?'

'I have to leave you, and the country, because I love you and I want to make the world a safer place for us and our kids.'

Elsie snorted. 'How are kids ever going to happen if you're not here? I do know the facts of life,' she mocked.

He tried to put his arm round her, but she shied away. 'Oh, Elsie, my love. Don't make a fuss. I'll be back before you know it. Just promise me you'll wait for me, that's all.'

'Seems to me you're not very good at promises, so why should I bother making any?' Elsie said, all the thrill of the last few moments gone.

'Yes, well, I've explained all that. Besides, this one is different. It's a real promise. An important one. We'll get married as soon as I come home from Spain.'

'Oh, a *real* promise,' she sneered. 'Why should I believe you this time? You've not only been bragging about what we've been up to but now you're buggering off and leaving me to face all those guttersnipes back at the factory. You'll only let me down again. I can't trust you.'

'Are you saying you won't wait for me?'

'What I'm saying is, I'm not prepared to make any promises in case I can't keep them either.'

Stan looked staggered at her words. 'Well, if that's your attitude, I may as well go and fight.'

'I agree. Go to Spain and don't worry about ever coming back,' she added spitefully. His eyes were filled with such sadness at her harsh words that she regretted saying them the moment they left her mouth. But it was too late. She couldn't take them back. All she could do was let the darkness swallow her up. Without another word, and with such a look of hurt and pain across his face, Stan let go of her hand. He didn't move and made no attempt to follow her as she ran off into the night, her mind fizzing with anger and betrayal.

Chapter 10

Stan didn't say a word about his intentions to his mother or his brother Charlie, with whom he shared a home. The following morning he packed his few belongings in a bag and set off into the centre of Manchester. He thought he would catch a train from there to London, but when he found out how much a ticket cost he realized he could only afford to go as far as Crewe. From there, in order to preserve his meagre funds, he thought he would try to hitch-hike. When the train finally arrived at Crewe he came out of the station unsure of which direction he wanted to go. He set off walking on what he took to be the road south and stuck out his thumb hopefully. Eventually someone did pick him up and drove him a significant number of miles, but mostly in the wrong direction. It took several more days and a lot more walking than he had anticipated to reach his final destination.

When Elsie turned up for work the following night she was not surprised to find Stan was missing. She had hardly slept for worrying about the angry note on which they had parted and she regretted the words with which she had let him go off to war. She wished she could find a way to tell him that she would surely wait for him and to let him know that she was missing him already. She didn't tell the landlord what she knew about Stan's whereabouts and she wondered vainly if there might still be a chance he would change his mind and not go.

'Well, where is he?' Mr Harehill greeted her when she arrived at the Butcher's.

'Who?' Elsie pretended not to know what he was talking about.

'Stan, your pal, that's who. What have you done with him? Never bloody turned up this lunchtime, did he!' Mr Harehill was furious and she couldn't blame him, but she wasn't going to let him know that. 'I can't believe the cheek of the lad. He never even let me know.'

Elsie had no idea what to say, especially when the landlord poked at her shoulder and said, 'You know him. So where's he disappeared to then?' He stared at her as if he trying to read her mind, then poked at her again, 'Where is he, eh?'

'I don't know. He didn't say anything to me,' Elsie said, remembering a long-ago promise not to talk about the possibility of Stan volunteering to go to Spain.

'Well, where does he live? I could send one of the lads to give him a kick up the backside and tell him to get himself here at the double.' He clenched his fists. 'I promise you, I'll give him a piece of my mind when he does turn up. Bloody cheek, leaving me in the lurch like that.'

'I've honestly no idea where he lives, I'm afraid,' Elsie said, relieved that on that score she could at least tell the truth. And I'm never likely to now, she added silently, thinking of the terrible things she'd said to Stan last night.

Mr Harehill shook his head. 'I don't know. Kids these days. He knows how busy we are. How am I going to replace him at such short notice?' He looked at Elsie. 'You'll have to do his work, that's all there is to it,' he said and he turned and walked away.

'For his wages?' Elsie called after him without thinking. The landlord stopped.

He twisted his head to look at her. 'What was that?'

'I said, I'll do his work for his wages.' She could feel the colour rising to her cheeks but she was determined to stand her ground now that she had said it. 'Only seems fair. If I'm to do his work, I should get his money for doing it.' Mr Harehill opened his mouth to speak but she wouldn't let him get a word in. 'Otherwise I'll be doing two jobs for no wages,' she added quickly.

'And them as collects glasses are hardly going to get any tips, are they?'

Mr Harehill thought for a moment. Then scratched his head. 'I'll admit you got me there. I tell you what. You can have half his wages, 'cos after all you're only a woman. I think that's very fair.'

Elsie didn't think that was fair at all and was about to protest but then she thought better of it and nodded her agreement. If she tried to insist on being paid more, it might enrage the landlord so much she could end up with nothing.

'I'll pay you half what he got till Wakes Week – and no fingers in the till, mind,' he said. Then we can look at things again. We'll see how you do.' He winked at her. 'If you're any good, I might have no need to replace him. Know what I mean?'

Elsie was sure that she knew what he meant, but she had no time to say more than, 'OK. Thanks,' for the doors began to swing as customers started to arrive and she was kept busy serving, clearing and even helping Ray to wash glasses for the rest of the evening.

She thought about Stan again as she set off on the long walk home. It was the first time in ages that she had to walk back alone. Not that she'd call it walking. More like hobbling. She'd managed to find some shoes at the Sally Army charity shop, but they were too small and having worn them all day her feet were killing her. It always helped having someone to talk to on the journey, to take her mind off the pinching of her toes.

For that reason – though it was not the only reason – she found herself wishing Stan was walking along beside her. She even imagined their conversation and how it might go, for the memory of their joyful making up was still vivid in her mind. She was sorry that they'd parted in the way that they had and she blamed herself and her quick temper for the guilt she was feeling now. But she had had her first proposal, and that she could never forget. Nor would she forget the man who had made it, for he was also the man who had given her her first-ever birthday present.

If she was honest, Stan Walsh was a really nice bloke and she had been a fool to let him go. He was a hell of a lot nicer than most of the lads that usually chased her. The ones who only wanted her attention. He was much nicer than those who expected her to give in to their advances without any thought of offering her anything in return. She should have told him that she would wait for him, instead of almost willing him to go.

By the time Stan finally arrived in London he was exhausted, hungry and wondering whether he was doing the right thing after all. It took him another whole day and much of his precious funds to get himself cleaned up and to find the recruiting office. He wandered the streets fruitlessly for most of the day and it wasn't until the late afternoon that he came upon it. He had thought then that the actual process of signing up would be easy, but he was wrong. The building seemed smaller and less significant than he had imagined. There was a wrought-iron handrail and stone balustrade running alongside some steps that led up to a wooden door. The steps were not steep and should have been easy to negotiate. But the approach to the front door was blocked by a small crowd of people. Several men on crutches, some with bandaged heads and limbs, and one with an alarming empty jacket sleeve were standing or sitting on the steps and doing their best to bar entry to anyone who tried.

'You don't want to be going in there, mate,' they said each time he tried to walk purposefully up the steps.

'Whyever not? I've come to join up,' Stan said, in what he thought sounded a reasonable tone.

But the men took no notice. Some even shouted at him to 'clear off'. They kept milling about in such a way that no one could get past them. They bumped and jostled; not roughly, but sufficient to deny people access. Stan hovered uncertainly, wondering what to do. He was tempted to turn and walk away, to forget the whole thing. No one knew he was here, so no one would be any the wiser if he didn't complete his mission and no one could call him names for running away. No one but Elsie Grimshaw, that is. And she wouldn't care either way.

At the thought of Elsie, Stan shook his head. He really thought he loved her, but now he knew he had to forget her as quickly as possible. She was nobbut trouble. He looked up at the wooden door. He had come such a long way, spending considerable time and money in the process, and he was reluctant that all that effort should go to waste. He tried once more to climb the stairs and this time one of the men on crutches hopped directly in front of him and made no attempt to move out of the way. Stan found himself staring into the young man's pale blue eyes that were watering even as he looked. The man swiped the back of his knuckles over his face and his look hardened. He lifted one crutch and waved it in the air.

'Is this what you want to sign up for?' he said. From his accent, Stan reckoned he too had travelled a fair distance to be there, and he wondered what story the young lad had to tell. 'Is this really what you want?' The lad nodded towards the door. 'I'm eighteen and I'm on the scrapheap because I've lost one of my bloody legs.' He prodded one of Stan's feet with his crutch.

'I . . . I'm sorry about that,' Stan mumbled. 'I never really thought about people getting injured.'

'Well, think about it now, before it's too late. Before your life is ruined like mine was.'

Stan gulped, not sure what he should say. But the lad hadn't finished.

'Another few days and this could be you,' he said, engaging Stan's gaze, refusing to let him move or even look away. 'I was full of idealism. I thought I was going to change the bleedin' world. Well, I found out the hard way that I couldn't do that, but the world sure as hell changed me.'

Stan was dumbfounded. He had to admit he had his own ideological beliefs. He was there because he believed he could be a hero by saving Spain, and possibly the whole of Europe too, from the right-wing upsurge. Because clearing dirty glasses was the best he had been able to manage so far and fighting in a war, even someone else's war, seemed like a much better thing to do.

'Go home before it's too late,' the lad said. 'Let me and all my mates here be a lesson to you.' He waved his crutch in the direction of the other wounded men. 'Do you really want to end up like one of us?'

Stan backed away. Hell, no. He didn't. 'I'm not sure that I do,' he voiced the words. Then he shivered. It felt as if someone had chucked a bucket of cold water over him.

'I bet you've given up a good job to come here,' the young soldier went on. 'Like I did an' all.'

Stan nodded.

'But take our word for it' – the lad indicated his companion with the bandaged head who had come to stand next to them – 'and go home now while you've got the chance.'

At that moment a huge man in a dark suit, like the pictures he'd seen of the men who sat in parliament, bounded up the concrete stairs two at a time, pushing the wounded and anyone they had accosted to one side. Then he turned to face the small crowd that had now gathered on the steps.

'All right, everyone, may I have your attention please. Would all those wounded in the battle for the noble cause please stand aside and make room for those who still feel they have a duty to perform. Make way, everyone, please. You lot' – he indicated the ex-soldiers 'come on now, off with you or I'll have the police on to you for causing an affray.'

The man with the crutch laughed. 'You wouldn't want to be doing that now, would you? The police are the last people you want here right now. What you're doing ain't right.' But no one took any notice, least of all the man in the suit. The crowd parted and without looking right or left he strode through. One or two new arrivals started up the steps after him and Stan took the opportunity to do so too. He could hear the man with the crutch calling out to him to think again and come back, but he followed the dark-suited man through the wooden door and into the forbidding-looking building. Stan told himself there was no going back now. He had come here to fight for what he believed was right and had even sacrificed the love of Elsie Grimshaw to do so. He was going to Spain to fight the fascists, and no one – man or woman – could stop him.

Chapter 11

Fay found it hard now that Elsie was out of the house so much, for all the skivvying work fell to her. In the past she had never minded mucking in with the household chores, or looking after the younger kids whenever Elsie asked her to help out, because it was always fun being with her older sister and she was happy to share the work. Elsie had an endless stock of stories, real and made up, that made Fay laugh and she was always getting into scrapes with her silly pranks. Elsie didn't like the harshness of their life any more than Fay did, but somehow she never let it grind her down. The face she showed the world nearly always had bright eyes and a ready smile. Fay didn't know how she managed it or where she got all her energy from. Fay always felt tired and the days when the younger children were her sole responsibility were often more than she could cope with. Yet her mother seemed to think that Fay should take on all the duties whenever Elsie wasn't around and used her pregnancy as an excuse for not doing them herself.

'You know how difficult it is for me to be getting around, love,' was her favourite plea for not doing what Fay would have considered her fair share.

Maybe Elsie was right with what she said about their mother. It would have helped Alice to build up her strength if she had done some work around the house instead of sitting in the threadbare armchair most of the day gazing out through the mud-speckled window into the street. Alice spent hours watching the neighbours going by, occasionally chiding the younger children who tried to scramble over her as she sat listlessly picking at dust on her shabby housecoat. Meanwhile Fay was expected to cook as best she could in the blackened pot that hung permanently over the fire, to clean as much as the house ever got cleaned, do the washing, and to keep an eye on the little 'uns just as Elsie did whenever she was available.

The house was permanently dirty and keeping the children clean was impossible. There was mess everywhere and Fay dreaded laundry day on a Monday when she'd spend all day slaving over the tiny copper in the outhouse at the back. Scrubbing and washing for the whole family was backbreaking work – the clothes never seemed to get any cleaner and were often sodden and damp-smelling for days afterwards in the colder months. Fay was sorry now she had left school. She thought she was being helpful to Elsie, doing her bit for the family. But all she had done was to scupper her own life. Her chances of fulfilling her ambition and getting to a college to learn how to be a secretary got slimmer every day.

One of the problems for Fay about working so hard was that she was permanently exhausted. She was so tired that most evenings she could hardly stop herself falling asleep as soon as she sat down. She almost had no energy left to drag herself up the stairs to bed. What she missed most, now that Elsie was not around so much, was the long chats together they'd both enjoyed. Of course she understood that of late Elsie's time had been taken up with Stan. Fay liked him and she could see that Elsie was really sweet on him too, but something had gone seriously wrong recently. She hadn't yet seen Elsie to find out what it was. And then there was the second job Elsie had, working in the pub – the job that she had somehow managed all these months to keep from her father; the job Fay had only recently found out about.

Often of an evening if there was no mending or darning to be done Fay would go next door where she wouldn't have to worry if she nodded off. Megan James's children were grown up and had fled the nest and the older woman was lonely. She invited Fay to join her to keep her company whenever she wanted and didn't seem to mind if the young girl fell asleep. She seemed to value Fay's company any time she felt like coming to sit in the warm, which Fay loved to do, particularly of a winter's evening when the embers would still be glowing in the grate. She didn't know how Mrs James managed to keep them going all day. And Fay would sit in the alcove and enjoy the cosy warmth. It always amazed Fay to think that the layout of the next door house was identical to her own, because from the inside they looked in no way the same. For one thing, Mrs James's oven door was still in one piece and with no family left to cook for she had the luxury of using the oven to keep warm.

'We don't use either of the upstairs' fireplaces,' Fay said chattily one late afternoon when she was at her neighbour's. She had watched as Mrs James put another small scrap of coal in among the twigs and had a sudden picture of having to heave a coal bucket up the narrow stairs. 'At least it's one less chore for me to do.' She sighed. 'You don't light a fire up there, do you?'

'Nay,' said Megan James. 'Too much like hard work – and for what? Between you and me, I never wanted to encourage any of the buggers to stop in bed.' She chuckled.

'I'd rather have a cold bedroom than have to drag coal all the way up there an' all to light a fire,' Fay agreed. 'You can always keep warm if you gets dressed fast enough. And it's first up best dressed in ours anyway. If there's only one clean dress to be had of a morning, I like it to be for me.' She stretched and yawned. 'I wonder if the rain has stopped yet.' She got up and peered out of the window. Night was drawing in. 'I'd best get home and see what scraps I can find to make for tea. My dad's bound to be yelling for summat as soon as he gets home from the pub.'

There was a smell of grass and fresh mud in the air as she walked over the wet cobbles, stepping gingerly for they felt as slippery underfoot as they looked in the yellow gaslight. As she crossed to the passage beside the houses, she heard a commotion from number 18 and hurried along to see what the matter was.

The front door was ajar and she pushed it open carefully. Her father was standing in the middle of the room and he was slowly and menacingly taking off his belt. Two of her sisters, Phyllis and Nancy, were standing in front of him, their faces set. Fay was surprised to see they had their fists raised. A stranger to the scene would have been forgiven for thinking the two young girls were seriously thinking of squaring up to their father. But anyone who lived in the neighbourhood would have known that, for all the bravery of their stance, in a matter of minutes both girls would be left with black eyes and raised welts across their backs. Phyllis, the older girl, already had a black eye swelling up where she had obviously been punched.

Fay rolled her eyes. None of them could ever escape the old man. Except her mother, it seemed. For today at least she was nowhere to be seen, probably hiding in one of the neighbours' houses while they were left to his wrath.

The scene was not unusual in the Grimshaw house and as Fay came into the room and took it all in, her first instinct was to ignore it and duck right out again. She could go back next door till it was all over. But when she caught sight of a stranger standing near the table, she stopped and looked again, not sure what was going on. He was standing with his cap and a small bag in his right hand, his left hand supported by a grubby-looking sling. He was staring down at the sawdusted floorboards as though trying to pretend he had no part in it all, but when she entered he looked up and for a moment she met his steady gaze. She had never seen such pale blue eyes before. And he seemed equally taken with hers, which she knew were by contrast the darkest of brown. His face had a boyish look though his skin was tough and weathered; she put him at about nineteen. There was a keenness and earnestness to his expression that set him apart from the usual reprobates and chancers that her father hung around with. He gave her a smile of crooked chipped teeth, but before she could smile back she was distracted by a sudden movement. She turned to see that her father now had his belt off and was binding his fist with it, leaving the buckle dangling like the sizable weapon it was. Usually whenever he took his belt to any of the older girls there wouldn't be a peep from them, except maybe some swearing under their breath. But tonight the younger one, Nancy, was crying.

'I don't want to share our bed with him,' Nancy wailed. 'He smells.' Her voice was surprisingly strong and she jerked her thumb in the direction of the stranger. 'There's hardly enough room for the four of us as it is. If he comes, it'll be a right squash – and him with a bad arm an' all.'

'Where's your sense, lass?' her father snapped. 'You'll not be sharing with him. You'll be moving downstairs to muck in with your sisters.'

At this, both girls looked astonished. 'What, all nine of us? We can't all be sharing one bed.'

'You'll share with who I says you'll share with, my lass, and there's an end on it.' Her father took a step towards her and Nancy backed away.

Phyllis scowled and rubbed her distending eye with her grubby fingers, which only made the swelling worse, but she said nothing.

Arthur Grimshaw glanced at the stranger, then turned to Fay. 'See this young man here . . . ' he began to say. He didn't get any further. Fay doubted he would for she could already hear the slur in his words. 'See this young man . . . he's our new lodger.' He tried again and this time he turned to face the stranger. 'What did you say your name was?'

''arry. 'arry Wilton,' the young man said modestly as he fidgeted with his cap.

'Yes, well,' Arthur said, looking back at Fay. 'It seems

young 'arry Wilton has fallen on hard times and is in urgent need of some decent lodgings. I seed him down at the Three Hammers. And do you know what I thought? I thought, it's the least we can do, to offer him somewhere to sleep for a while.'

Fay stared first at her father then again at Harry. It seemed unbelievable, but she knew she had better believe it. For a lodger, in her father's book, meant money. And Arthur Grimshaw was never far away when there was a bit of cash up for grabs. She would have liked to know how much this poor man was being stung for, for the privilege of sleeping in a damp bed on the second floor in a filthy bedroom. She couldn't help wondering whether he knew just how many of them there'd be in the bed downstairs so that he could be accommodated.

'My lass here, Fay, will be pleased to give you a bite of bread and cheese, I've no doubt.' Arthur seemed to have got the hang of talking again even if he didn't always manage to keep control of his tongue. 'Though that will be extra, of course.' He gave a toothless grin. The belt had slipped off his hand and he seemed to have forgotten it for a moment when he put his arm round Fay's thin shoulders. Instinctively she shook him off and without looking at Harry again she went straight into the back scullery, thinking she couldn't remember the last time they'd had any cheese in the house and hoping to salvage some scraps.

* * *

'What the hell's going on 'ere, then?' Elsie wanted to know when she finally climbed into bed alongside Fay later that night. There were more little girls than usual and they were all asleep, if the level of snoring was anything to go by. She and Fay could barely make themselves heard as they were whispering, snuggled up close. 'Ain't we got enough mouths to feed? What's the old bugger thinking of, taking in someone from the streets?' Elsie wanted to know.

'A couple of extra bob to chuck down his throat, that's what he's thinking of,' Fay said. 'Must have seen a row of pint pots in his dreams.'

'But who is this . . . what can I call him?'

'I believe the fancy word is lodger, but scruffy tramp is more like.'

'You're not far wrong there. Where on earth did Dad pick him up?' Elsie demanded.

'In the pub of course. Apparently, he's not long back from Spain. Got shot there in the war – or so he says.'

'Not sure I'd believe a word he says. He's got those shifty-looking eyes.'

'Oh, I don't think they're shifty – he looks interested, that's all,' Fay said coyly, then she grinned. 'Though they were following me all round the room.'

Elsie laughed when Fay said this. 'Oh aye. Or so you'd like to think. Is that what you mean by "interested"?'

'Why not?' Fay sighed. 'Thinking costs nowt.'

'It's the only bleeding thing that doesn't.' Elsie shifted

position though it was almost impossible to get comfortable. 'Do you think he might have seen Stan in Spain?' Elsie said, for she had already confided in Fay about Stan's disappearance and whereabouts.

'I suppose it's possible. But Spain's a big place, isn't it?'

'Bigger than England?

'It certainly looked that way on the globe we used to have at school.'

'So why didn't this Harry bloke go home once he got back to England?' Elsie changed the subject. 'He's not from these parts, is he?'

'Stockport way, so he says. According to him, when he got back he found he had no home to go to. Someone else was living in his house and both his parents had been sent to one of those Public Assistance Institution places while he was away.'

'What's one of them when it's at home?'

'You know, they're like the old workhouse. Same thing really; it's for folks on their uppers with no one to look after them – mostly old codgers and vagrants. Unless he wanted to go in there too, seems he had nowhere to go.'

'That is, until he met Mr Muggins in the pub who saw pounds, shillings and pence signs flash in front of his eyes.' Elsie sounded sceptical.

'Summat like that. He's supposed to be looking for work in one or other of the factories, so maybe he'll be able to earn a bob or two soon enough.'

'And till then? All I can say is, I wish him luck. Not

much in this neighbourhood for a one-armed pirate.' That made Fay laugh. 'Seems we're stuck with him for the time being.'

'I can tell you, the little 'uns aren't happy about it,' Fay said.

'Me neither,' Elsie agreed, aware of little Freda's elbow digging into her back. 'But they'll have to put up or shut up, like the rest of us.'

Chapter 12

Alice Grimshaw went into labour at ten o'clock on a Friday night at the beginning of April. Elsie had just returned home from a long shift at the pub which followed on from a full day's work at the textile factory. All she wanted to do at the end of the day was crawl into bed. But as soon as she entered the house and saw her mother doubled up on the bed behind the door she knew she was in for a long night. Her father wasn't home yet and she had no idea what time he might arrive, if at all as he'd probably got a lock-in at one of the local pubs. So the first thing she was obliged to do was to wake Nancy and Phyllis and send them to forage for bits of wood and coal scraps, and to bring in a fresh bucket of water from the pump in the court-yard so that she could put the pot on to heat on what was left of the embers in the hearth. Phyllis prided herself on being more responsible than all her siblings and Elsie knew she could trust her to come back with enough fuel to keep the fire going for most of the night and into the next day.

'You'd best get the little 'uns to alert the neighbours now. I think it's me time. They're old enough to know what's what.' Alice gasped her instructions in between the waves of pain that were wracking her body. Elsie sighed. She hated seeing her mother like this year after year, but there was nothing she could do about it except to do as she was asked. Although they were only five and six years of age, Ethel and Freda had indeed been through this before so Elsie packed them off to fetch Vera Clegg from next door and was dismayed when they returned on their own a few minutes later to announce that Vera had gone down with 'flu only that morning and was in no fit state to come and oversee a birthing. Alice looked panic-stricken when they made their announcement and she turned her face to the wall, her body shaking with sobs.

'Don't fret, Mam, I'll find someone to help us.' Elsie tried her best to comfort her mother, afraid that if there was no one else available the task would inevitably fall to her. So she set about touring the neighbourhood, trying to find someone who would be able to come immediately to act as midwife. Eventually, to Elsie's great relief, Doris Wiggins from down the street agreed she would come. She was very experienced, having over the course of the years delivered more than half the babies in their street alone and Elsie knew that if Doris was involved everything would be all right.

'I won't leave you to struggle on your own, lass,' she assured Elsie as she gathered up the essentials in her little bag. 'And we can stop off on the way and ask young Molly Fletcher from across the yard if she could come an' all.'

Elsie was impressed how quickly the neighbours gathered to help the family out and readily agreed to Molly's suggestion that some of the young Grimshaw girls should go to her house for the night to mind her youngest babe, as her husband was working nights. Elsie agreed that it was a good idea, so long as they could take young Jack with them as well and Phyllis and Nancy jumped at the chance. They skipped off eagerly to Molly's with Jack and his beloved teddy in tow. They knew from previous visits that there would be bits of food lying around that they could pinch, not to mention the warm blankets they could all wrap up in on the couch in the living room, which was just the thing on a chilly night such as this.

Elsie had known for a long time how babies arrived into the world, having some memories of her horror and fascination from as far back as when some of her sisters were born after her mother had spent the night screaming with pain. She remembered she had been shocked at seeing so much blood. Then she remembered her mother squeezing her hand painfully during a short labour when Freda – now a gangling six-year-old – had made a rather sudden appearance. And then there was Jack. She was especially proud of the more important role she had played, actually helping Vera Clegg clean up the baby when he was born. A son, finally, after the long line of girls. Her mother had been really poorly on that occasion and Elsie had been the first to hold him. It was teatime and she had shooed out all the younger children while the ladies from the neighbourhood had gathered solemnly at the foot of Alice's bed. They had all looked so grave and one had even told Elsie her mother's life was in danger, she had lost so much blood. Then they had finally agreed to call out the doctor, who had sent Alice into the hospital. Elsie never understood where the money had come from to pay for the few days Alice spent there, but she was mightily relieved when her mother finally came back home, the baby glued to her breast. Not that she had enough milk to give him. Jack had spent the first few months of his life wailing with hunger. But Martha Jones, who lived across the street, had had a baby the same day as Jack was born and she came by each morning with her baby suckling on one breast, letting the youngest Grimshaw suckle on the other until eventually he had begun to settle.

Elsie bustled round the living room now, following Doris's instructions, confident she had a clear notion of what was to come. It was only when dawn arrived and she found herself drowsing on a hard stool by the bed, her mother grey and exhausted and no sign of the new child, that she understood what she had been told on several occasions: every birth was different and you never really knew what to expect.

Fay spent the night sleeping on the stairs, unsure whether she really wanted to be part of this process. She didn't wake until a brood of her sisters clattered downstairs when it was time for school.

'Hush, your mam's exhausted,' Doris Wiggins warned.

'Where's the new babby, then?' four-year-old Connie wanted to know.

'Not ready to come out just yet,' Doris answered, trying not to show her concern. She wiped Alice's brow with a strip of old sheeting and then wiped her own as well. 'Now you'd all better be getting off to school. The baby will no doubt be here by the time you get home tonight.'

'I don't go to school any more.' Fay was now fully awake. 'So I'm here to help me mam.'

'And what about Elsie?' Doris asked.

'She needs to be getting off to work,' Fay said, and she roused her sister, who had fallen asleep on the stool.

Elsie stretched herself awake from the uncomfortable crouched position. She shook her head, trying to clear it, and ran her fingers through the curly mess of her hair. 'What's happened?' she said, trying hard to focus her eyes.

'Nothing yet,' Fay said. 'But don't worry. You can get off to work. I'll help Mrs Wiggins when the baby actually comes.' She announced the words now with a feeling of pride that she would be the responsible one at home today. Once Elsie had reluctantly gone off to the factory, Fay looked around to check what she might do.

Doris Wiggins and Molly Fletcher had been whispering together at the foot of the bed but Fay was aware of a sudden silence. She looked at her mother, her eyes had sunk into her grey face. Then she looked from Doris to Molly and back to her mother, who seemed to have exhausted her strength. Both of the other women had a defeated look too.

'Remember last time,' Doris said with a sigh.

'Aye, lass, I do,' Molly agreed and they both turned to look at Fay.

'I think you need to run and fetch the doctor,' the older woman said.

By the time Elsie got home from the factory, everything had been cleared away and there was no evidence a child had ever been expected. Elsie quickly took in the unexpected scene. It was Jack, arms wrapped about his teddy, who was stretched out next to his mother and both were thankfully asleep. But there was no sign of a new baby. Alice looked gaunt and ill and for a moment Elsie was afraid to ask what had happened. She put her hand out to touch Jack, and when he stirred but continued sleeping she smiled down at him. At least he seemed to be all right.

Fay was sitting by the bed while her mother slept

and she stood up as soon as she saw Elsie. She flung her arms round her sister and burst into tears.

'The doctor had to come. He said . . . he said . . . the baby was . . . the baby was already dead inside her,' she sobbed.

Elsie felt the sharpness of her sister's shoulder bones through the flimsy shawl she wore. She held her while they both wept.

'Where's Dad? Does he know?' Elsie said eventually.

Fay shrugged. 'He didn't come home last night and he's not shown his face here all day.'

Elsie's jaw clamped tight shut for a moment. 'Do you know what the hardest bloody thing is?' she said at last.

Fay shook her head.

'When he does eventually turn up, he won't sodding care either way. It'll be same as it bloody always is. Like it's nothing to do with him.' Elsie was breathing hard, her mouth twisted, her fists clenched. 'One of these days, I swear I'll bloody swing for that man.'

Fay was staring at her, her eyes wide with fear. 'Oh, Else, don't say that.'

Elsie hugged her and tried to smile. 'Don't worry, lass. I wouldn't give him the satisfaction.' She gave a grim smile. 'I suppose we should try to look on the bright side of all this.'

Fay looked up eagerly. 'And what's that?'

'At least we won't have another mouth to feed.'

At this Fay burst into a fresh bout of tears. 'Oh, Elsie,

I hope it's not wicked to think that, I were thinking the same thing,' she said.

'How can it be wicked to spare a kid the misery of coming to live in a dump like this?' Elsie looked about the wretched room and it was as if she was seeing it for the first time, even though she had lived there her whole life.

The house was supposed to have been part of the slum clearance after the Great War, she knew that, but somehow they had stopped the demolition work when they got to Gas Street and Back Gas Street. Suddenly, it seemed, such houses were desperately needed for large families to live in who couldn't afford to be housed elsewhere. So they were patched up, made barely habitable and people like her gran who had twelve children and nowhere to live, had gladly moved in. It was that or going to one of those institutions that had replaced the old workhouses – and she knew which one she preferred.

But not all of the houses were in fact habitable, even then. Especially theirs. Most of the other houses in their block at least had an inside tap with cold running water in the downstairs room. The Grimshaws had not been so lucky. So not only did they have to go out through the front door and walk all the way to the back in order to get water from the pump in the courtyard, but they still had the lead sewer pipe leading directly on to the street, making the sanitation of the whole block questionable. Inside the house, they had a fireplace but the door was hanging off the oven and there was no storage tank or boiler for cold or hot water. They could only cook on old grindstones in front of the fire or boil water in an old black cauldron that hung over the grate.

Elsie remembered her gran well. A strong, spirited woman, she had not let the awfulness of the house get her down. She had papered the walls in the downstairs room herself. She'd got some gaudy-coloured rolls of paper off the rag-and-bone man and tried to cheer the place up. She'd done a good job at the time. The torn remains of it still clung to the damp walls in some places. After Elsie's gran had died, all her children moved away except for Arthur, who seemed happy to live there with his wife and two young children. And when the family had grown, the house had become more and more neglected. The only wonder was that all of the children, apart from a few miscarriages, survived. And now they shared it with the rats and mice that ran freely across the courtyard and used it as their second home.

Elsie sighed. She had lived her entire life in such squalor and she honestly believed she had become immune to the diseases that had carried so many young children off. The mildewed damp that had long been running down the walls – removing much of the plaster and wallpaper in the process – didn't help her perpetual cough, but she had learned to live with it and tried not to let it get her down. But she was never happy at the thought of bringing a new baby into such a filthy existence, and that was why she had such mixed feelings now.

Fay pulled away from her sister's embrace. 'Well, we won't have to worry about that ever again, according to the doctor. He said there'll be no more like this one. No more miscarriages. No more babbies. She's all buggered up inside now.'

Elsie was shocked and stared at Fay. 'He said that to you?'

Fay shook her head. 'Not to me directly. But I heard him telling Mam and Mrs Wiggins.'

'Well, all I can say is, I'm glad for her sake and Dad won't care so long as he can have his way.' She looked across at her mother, her brow creased.

'Yes, me too. But I bet our mam won't be so quick to tell him that.' Fay wiped her nose with her shawl. 'It was sad though. He was a tiny scrap. I held him in my arms for a few minutes, you know.'

'It was another boy?'

'Yes. You could see his little willie. There were nowt wrong wi' 'im. He looked just like he were asleep. Only the doctor said he was never going to wake up.' She began to sob, loudly this time, her entire body shaking. 'I held him in my arms, but the poor little mite was cold. And he was quite blue. He was already gone, Mrs Wiggins said. I couldn't save him.'

'Of course you couldn't. You're not a doctor. Even the doctor couldn't save him.'

'It all seems so unfair.'

'Unfair? Maybe. But then again, maybe it's for the best. I'm sure he wouldn't have wanted to come and live in a midden like this, and I can't say as I blame him.'

Elsie felt tears flowing, only hers were silent. She could almost feel the baby in her own arms and she shivered. Then she reached out and touched Jack's face once more, relieved to find it was still warm. He opened his eyes and began to whimper and she gathered him into her arms, rocking him to and fro. It was the closest she had come to understanding her mother's pain. It was for a moment as though she was holding her own child in her arms. And Jack would probably be the last baby of the family, thank goodness. Until she started having babies of her own.

Her father didn't come home until the following day, and when he did, late in the evening, he acted as though nothing had happened. He didn't lift a finger to help when Alice dragged herself from her bed to tend the meagre fire, and he said nothing other than to complain when she produced only bread and dripping. It was as if she had never been pregnant. As if she had never suffered the agonies of a stillborn child. And when Elsie had climbed the stairs and fallen into bed exhausted from her full day of work, she felt a surge of roiling anger at her mother when she heard the familiar rhythmic creaking of her parent's bed downstairs.

Chapter 13

Apart from the discomfort of having to share her bed with all her sisters, Fay was surprised to find she quite liked having their new lodger Harry around the house. He helped her with her chores, even though he only had the full use of one arm. He carried buckets of water and found much larger chunks of coal than she was usually able to unearth. He rinsed off the dishes and one morning after he had cleared up the sink she found him washing his sheets. Later that day, she noticed he'd somehow managed to make up his bed. He washed himself daily at the pump in the courtyard and took a razor to his face. He no longer smelled like he had on that first day. In fact, when he was freshly scrubbed, he looked quite handsome with his slicked-back blond hair and his piercing blue eyes. She caught herself whistling softly as she went about her chores and realized it was something Harry did all the time. He didn't talk much about his experiences in Spain, except when she asked him a specific question.

When Elsie was around, Fay avoided the subject of Harry completely. Her big sister seemed suspicious of his motives: 'First bloke I've seen rolling his sleeves up to help with the 'ousework.'

'I think it's nice of him. He's grateful that he's not out on the streets and just wants to show his thanks.'

Elsie gave her sister an old-fashioned look. 'Just be careful he's not looking for you to show your thanks in return, if you know what I mean.'

Fay frowned. 'You're just miffed that you're not the centre of attention for once.'

'What, you think I'd want ogling by that scruffy layabout? No fear!' Elise scoffed.

Harry did so much to help Fay that when he asked her shyly if she could possibly change the dressing on his wound, she didn't feel she could refuse.

She had never fancied the idea of being a nurse because she was squeamish, so she wasn't sure how she was going to react at the sight of blood. Harry took off his sling and Fay stared down at the old dressing, not sure where to begin. There was some dried blood showing on the outside of the bandage and she didn't know what she would find as she unwrapped it hesitantly. The old gauze dressing was stuck to the wound but Harry bravely ripped it off himself. He gave a shout and visibly winced but it was over quickly. To Fay's relief, what looked as though it had been a nasty injury was obviously now healing well.

'It's wonderful to be able to move my arm freely,' Harry said, swinging his arm in circles.

'So long as you keep it well wrapped up,' Fay agreed, 'and don't knock it, then it should be fine in a few weeks.' She discarded the sling and found some clean rags to wrap it up again.

'I can see I shall have to call you Fay Nightingale,' Harry quipped. Fay blushed. 'Is that what you want to be when you grow up?'

'I'll have you know I am grown up,' Fay responded, more tartly than she'd intended. She stood up quickly.

Harry laughed. 'You may not have the red hair in the family, but you've got the temper that goes with it.'

At this Fay laughed too.

'Thank you for your help. I can see that I'll be fully healed very soon.'

'And for your information, I've no intention of ever being a nurse.' And she told him of her dream of becoming a secretary.

'That sounds like a noble ambition,' he said.

'Now you're making fun of me,' Fay said, her face serious.

'Not at all. I mean it. And I hope you get what you want.'

'I will if I can work out how to pay for the lessons.'

'What about your sister? She's got a job. Can't she help you?'

'Elsie has to give everything she gets to me dad. He'd flay her alive if she didn't.'

'I saw her down at the Butcher's Arms, working behind the bar.'

Fay was stunned, but she reasoned that someone was bound to see Elsie there at some point. 'Me dad doesn't know about that. She only gets tips, not a proper wage. Promise you won't tell him.'

'I suppose she must do quite well down there for her tips, good-looking lass like her.'

'I don't really know. She has to be careful – if he found out, he'd not only take them off her, but he'd give her a good thrashing too for being deceitful.'

Harry flashed her a reassuring look. 'Don't worry Fay, her secret is safe with me.'

'Thanks, Harry.' Fay smiled gratefully.

'Now, about those lessons,' he said. 'That's easily sorted. You go to the college and ask them for a job.'

'But I won't be qualified.'

'I meant a job as a cleaner. You could clean their offices before anyone else gets there in the morning and then instead of wages they could let you stay on for free lessons.'

Fay clapped her hands with delight. 'What a great solution! I think I'll try that. I may as well get some benefit from all the cleaning I do. It's not like anyone here is ever going to pay me.' And she grinned.

Harry waved his arm in the air. 'And I'll also be able to look for a job soon.'

'It must be frustrating, having been handicapped for so long,' Fay agreed. It was on the tip of her tongue to ask him how he was managing to pay the rent without a job but she decided that seemed too rude.

Not everyone in the family liked Harry's presence. He had been in the house for a week when Fay realized Phyllis had not come home for three nights in a row. Always the wild one with the same wild flame hair as Elsie, she had taken to staying away overnight sometimes. Elsie had told Fay what Phyllis had told her about being determined to get away from their father, and they had both noticed that her absences had increased of late. When Elsie had mentioned it to Phyllis, she had been mysterious, just saying that she had made new friends and was perfectly entitled to do whatever she pleased. But when Fay realized Phyllis had hardly been home much at all that week she thought it best to alert Elsie when she came in for her tea. Her mother had popped out to have a natter with a neighbour in the backyard and they had the downstairs room to themselves for once while the other children were out at school.

'Do you think we should tell our mam?' Fay was anxious to share her concerns.

But Elsie wasn't so sure. 'What will she do, apart from tell Dad?'

'Are you suggesting that we should tell him, then?' Now Fay felt positively afraid.

'I'm not suggesting anything,' Elsie said. 'Perhaps we don't need to tell anyone yet. After all, no one in this madhouse would have noticed, 'cept us. And probably nobody will.'

'She didn't take kindly to Harry coming to lodge with us. She was the one who most hated us all having to share the same bed,' said Fay, remembering the day Harry had first appeared with her father.

'True enough, but is that any excuse to run away? We're all in the same boat, after all.'

'Where does she go when she goes missing for the odd night or two?' Fay asked, knowing that Elsie was closer to her lookalike than she was.

Elsie shrugged. 'I don't think anyone knows.' Phyllis had always been a tomboy and could give as good as she got with any of the local bully boys. She was tough as old boots, but she was still barely into her teens. Anything could happen to her.

Suddenly Elsie jumped out of her chair and went to pick Jack up from where he was playing with his teddy on the floor. She gave him a fierce hug and rocked him back and forth.

'At least we know where you are, don't we? All the time, thank goodness. But then you would never do anything like Phyllis, would you? You'd stick with your Elsie and always tell her where you were going, 'cos you know I'd worry otherwise.'

Jack responded with a loud 'yes' and then 'no', but not in the appropriate place. Elsie didn't care, she rejoiced in the warmth of his little body as she held him close, and the love she felt when she hugged him tightly and he hugged her back. Maybe no one had done that with Phyllis – or with any of them, come to that. Maybe Phyllis was craving love too and had decided to flee the nest in search of it, earlier than any of them. Who could blame her? Elsie certainly intended to get out as soon as she could.

If Phyllis's absence was not noticed by her parents, it was certainly noticed by the teachers at school. A week after her disappearance, a letter came through from the headmaster of the school. Unfortunately, it was addressed to her father and as Phyllis herself was not there for a beating he took it out on all the sisters instead.

'Are you trying to tell me no one in this family knows where she is?' He swiped out with his arm, each girl jumping back in turn as he looked for the next one to hit. Their mother fretted about where Phyllis might be, but only in her usual half-hearted fashion. Neither of them remained interested for long and within a few days it was as though Phyllis had never existed. Only Elsie and Fay worried about her. They had looked everywhere they could think of, asked the other children in the courtyard and in the surrounding streets. Elsie even went down to her school. But she seemed to have disappeared leaving no trace.

Fay found Harry's presence comforting and they took

to having a walk most afternoons. She really enjoyed talking to him. He was full of big ideas and encouraged her to talk about her plans and her dreams. He oozed a certain strength. Despite his weakened arm, she felt she could lean on him and he wouldn't break. She told him about Phyllis, not mentioning that she feared he might have been the cause of her disappearance. But he had no idea where she might be. Fay feared she was getting quite fond of him and didn't know what to do. She had never had feelings like this before and wasn't sure how to behave. Was this the way Elsie had felt about Stan, she wondered. She resolved to ask her big sister about it when they were in bed later that night. When Harry had finally admitted that his dream was to join the navy so that he could travel the world, she was really disappointed.

'I've had a taste of living overseas, even if it wasn't in ideal circumstances. It made me realize I wanted more.'

'So you won't look for a local job?' She felt sad.

'No, not now. I worried at first my arm might become infected, but now I know it's healing well I can think about getting a job aboard ship.'

She believed he would do it, though she knew how much she would hate to see him go. She could sense he was getting impatient for his arm to heal and then for her it would all be over.

Chapter 14

Elsie was missing Stan more than she would have thought possible. She had hoped that maybe he might write to her, but her hopes were in vain. She even thought of writing to him but she didn't have an address. There wasn't a day went by that she didn't think about him and wish she could have taken back her harsh words. She only hoped he would come home alive and then she could tell him herself.

Even with Stan gone, she was still enjoying her job in the pub and the freedom it gave her compared with the repetitive and boring work she did at the factory. At the Butcher's Arms she got to meet and talk to different people, and for once she found that how she looked really seemed to matter to the customers she engaged with. At the factory it was important to cover her hair to keep it out of the way of the dangerous machinery. She was also required to cover up her clothes. Even when she was wearing her oldest of rags she needed to prevent them being completely ruined by contamination from the cotton waste and fibres that came flying off the looms.

At the pub she was encouraged to take pride in her appearance and she soon found she wanted to look her best to impress the customers – and her boss. She tried to keep her hair clean so that her bright red curls always looked their best. She went down to the charity shop where the Sally Army lady she knew picked out a pretty green dress that suited her well. She slept with it as a pillow so that her sisters all knew it was hers and she would run the flat iron over it before she put it on each day. And eventually she got some shoes that nearly fitted from the rag-and-bone man.

All she needed now was something she couldn't yet afford. Make-up. It would help to make her look a little older than she was so that no one would think to complain that she was too young to be working behind the bar, or that the landlord might be exploiting child labour.

She loved the idea of wearing make-up just like the film stars and she studied how they applied it in the film magazines she found lying around at the cinema. She would spend ages looking longingly at the cosmetics and make-up counters in the shops. If only she were able to buy a little rouge, a touch of flesh-coloured face powder or maybe some trial-sized lipstick, she was sure they would help bring her face alive. She wanted to replace what she thought of as her current death-like colouring with something more pink and rosy that would be altogether more healthy looking. Make-up, she was sure, would help her soften what she knew to be her sharp, rather angular features. But she could only do this if she could afford to buy some of the things she had seen. She was fed up always having to rely on the scraps and dregs she found in the waste baskets in the ladies' toilets. She thought about this every time she walked up and down the aisles in F.W. Woolworth. And she sighed each time she passed by the items she knew would be ideal.

The first time she didn't pass them by she stopped to look at the prices, wondering if the collection of coins so long hidden under her bed would be enough to buy any of the make-up she craved. Perhaps a lipstick. She knew she nearly had enough money, for the last time she had counted her stash she was surprised how much she had accumulated. She hoped that with some of the extra tips she had earned this week she might at last be able to splash out.

On Saturday night when she was sure she was alone, she crawled under the bed as she usually did to retrieve her precious tin. She reached out to where she normally was able to touch it with her hand. But all she came back with was a handful of fluff. She swept her arm in an arc but still she couldn't feel the tin. Damn! One of the kids must have knocked it far under the bed without knowing what it was. The dust flew in all directions as her search became more frantic and she emerged from underneath the iron bedstead coughing hard. She dived back under and this time to her relief she felt the cold metal square which had somehow been pushed up against the wall. As soon as her fingers touched it, she knew something was wrong and when she brought it out her worst fears were confirmed. The lid was missing and the box was empty.

The first thing she did was so unlike her that she was shocked at her own reaction. She burst into tears. The tears were of rage and frustration that someone had dared to touch her hard-earned cash. But she felt humiliated all the same. Not caring that she would now have to reveal her secret to all her sisters – it was too late anyhow – she called downstairs to Fay. Her sister came running, looking puzzled and then alarmed as Elsie explained what she had found.

'I didn't know it was there, honestly,' Fay said, her cheeks flaming.

'I'm not accusing you, you daft thing.' Elsie gave her a hug. 'I just needed to tell someone else and maybe we can think together about what might have happened.'

'Could it be one of the little 'uns?' Fay suggested.

'I don't know.' Elsie's voice was grim. 'But I mean to find out.'

The girls were all in the house, avoiding the sudden downpour that was crashing down outside. Except, of course, for Phyllis, who hadn't been seen by anyone and who still hadn't come home. Elsie called for them to come upstairs at once. Mystified, they all sat down on the bed.

'OK. Who's had it?' Elsie shot out the question.

They each turned to the other. 'Who's had what?'

'Whatever was in my box,' Elsie said.

'What box?'

'What was in the box?'

'Where was the box?' came the questions.

'Never you mind,' Elsie said, still sounding stern. 'You'd know if you'd taken it, wouldn't you?'

The little ones began to cry. The older ones shook their heads. And Elsie knew they'd had no part in it. Whoever had taken it, she would never find the money. It was well spent by now. Five-year-old Ethel seemed to be crying the hardest and she continued crying long after the others stopped.

'Stop snivelling, Ethel, for goodness' sake,' Elsie snapped at last. 'I know it wasn't you, so what are you crying for?'

'Harry. He told me not to tell or he'd cut all my hair off.'

'What?' Several of the sisters gasped at once.

'I saw Harry. He was in here. I saw Harry in here when he didn't oughta.'

'When was that?'

'Yesterday night. When I was going to bed.'

'Why didn't you say so before?'

'He told me I mustn't tell anyone that I'd seen him. It was our secret.'

Elsie didn't wait to hear more. She rushed up the second flight of stairs to what was now the lodger's bedroom. She didn't knock but flung open the door. The first thing she realized was that his cap wasn't there but, more telling, his small bag had gone.

Elsie was devastated. Her stomach churned. Not only had she lost all her hard-earned savings but she would have to tell her father Harry was gone. And she would have to be quick. Before the old man drank more rent than would be coming into the house.

Elsie couldn't tell her father that she suspected Harry had taken all her money for he didn't know anything about her separate earnings. And she had sworn all her sisters to secrecy about that too. But she still got a beating for needlessly reducing the family's earnings. He blamed her for chasing away the most profitable source of income they had ever had as it required no work at all on his part.

Chapter 15

Elsie couldn't stop herself looking in F. W. Woolworths, even though the lipstick was no longer within her reach. The only thing she had been saving up for and now she couldn't even afford that. But she stopped to admire the rest of the items on the counter more closely and to make a note of all the different names and shades of the powders and creams. She tried to decide which colours would be most suitable for her and even picked one or two up, turning them over to see the price. That made her laugh out loud. Whoever can afford all these things, she wanted to cry out. Would anyone seriously pay such a price for some colours to brighten up their face? There was a display picture of a beautiful, long-haired, blonde model her face painted with a set of sample colours. She was smiling, lips slightly apart, showing a hint of her pearly white teeth. That's who can afford them, she thought. People like her who have ladylike jobs and who weren't brought up in a slum. She touched the picture of the woman whose skin looked like spun silk, but of course all she could feel was the cold gloss of the printed cardboard.

She picked up the metal case of the sample lipstick she so admired and spun it open. She dabbed a little on the back of her hand like she had seen some of the ladies do before grudgingly putting it back. But then as she was about to leave the counter something happened inside her head. The resentment against the thief, the frustration of being so nearly able to afford her first special lipstick and now not being able to afford it at all built up until there was an explosion in her brain. Without thinking about what she was doing, she watched like a helpless onlooker as her hand shot out and her fingers coiled round the lipstick, this time covering it entirely from view. In a split second she had whipped it into her pocket, where she continued to keep it covered with her hand.

Before she walked away she scanned the shop anxiously to make sure she hadn't been seen. Unlikely, as there were so few people about. The assistant was at the other end of the counter, trying to help someone who was asking about something called sanitary towels. Otherwise the only person she could see close by was a man in a grubby beige raincoat and he was taking no notice of anyone as his head was buried in a newspaper. He did look up for a moment, although not in her direction, but she caught a quick glimpse of his face. For a second she thought he had a familiar look about him, but then there were a lot of men in mucky raincoats, especially at the cinema, and she always took pains to avoid them.

She was about to move away when the assistant left her customer and came to hover nearby, which made Elsie realize how close she had been standing to the till. 'Can I help you, miss?' The assistant spoke stiffly with a strained smile.

Elsie tried to look casual and unruffled, as villains always did in films. 'No thanks. Yer all right,' she said, and not wishing to engage further headed straight for the door. She had just stepped outside and was about to join Fay, who had been to the hardware store and was waiting for her, when she felt a hand grasp hold of her arm by the elbow and pull her sharply around. It was the man in the raincoat.

'Just a minute, young lady,' a gruff voice thick with a local accent said. 'I think you might have something there that doesn't belong to you.'

Elsie tried to pull back her elbow, hoping to catch him unawares with the intention of running away. But the heel of one of the shoes she had found abandoned on the tip that morning gave way and she twisted her ankle painfully.

Fay hovered for a moment, but when Elsie made a

shooing gesture with her hand she ran away quickly down the street and turned the corner out of sight.

'Who's that?' the man said. 'Have you got an accomplice?'

Elsie didn't want to show him she didn't know what that meant. 'Of course I have,' she said brazenly. 'I'm not like you. I'd never be bloody daft enough to be without one.' She was surprised and puzzled when he laughed.

The man didn't remove his arm but instead used his grip on her elbow to steer her back inside.

'This way,' he said dourly. 'We're going to pay a little visit to the manager's office.' And he didn't let go of her arm until they were inside and the door was closed.

The man behind the metal table that served as a desk may have been the manager of this particular store but no money had ever been spent on furnishing his office to make him look as if he really belonged in that important post. For apart from the table and a metal filing cabinet, there were just two simple wooden chairs, a wastepaper basket, and a framed advertisement for Colman's mustard on the wall behind him. However, that didn't stop him from doing his best to look intimidating.

He stood up when she entered. 'Empty your pockets,' he ordered, trying to sound menacing. He indicated the space he had cleared on the table.

Elsie kept hold of the lipstick tightly in her hand and managed at the same time to pull out her pocket linings to show they were empty. But the man in the raincoat, who she now realized must be the shop's detective, prised open her fingers to reveal the rogue lipstick.

'Hey, what do you think you're doing? That's mine!' Elsie tried to brazen it out.

'Oh yes, and I'm a Dutchman.' Both men laughed. They clearly didn't believe her.

The manager put out his hand and she had no option but to pass the lipstick to him. He looked at the price ticket, which was still attached, and then at her.

'How old are you?' he asked.

'Eighteen,' she said. She struck a pose like she had seen in the cinema, raising her eyebrows and turning her eyes away in disdain. She was miffed when he laughed again but was determined not to show it.

'Let's try one more time,' he said. 'How about something closer to fourteen?'

Now she tried laughing and was furious when he didn't look impressed. 'That is not true,' she emphasized each word and tried to stare him out.

'Well, what then? You tell me. And mind you tell me the truth this time.' He wagged his finger at her.

Elsie folded her arms but she couldn't look at him as she finally said, 'Sixteen next brithday,' delivering the words like they were poison in her mouth.

'That's more like it.' He gave a self-satisfied smile. 'So, do you have the money to pay for this item? Maybe it was just an oversight? You forgot you hadn't yet paid for it?' There was a sarcastic ring to his tone.

Elsie shook her head. Her cheeks were burning and she blinked back the tears that maddeningly threatened to rain down her cheeks.

'Have your parents got the money if we escort you home and explain the situation to them?' he continued.

She shook her head. She tried to look as if she didn't care, but she knew she couldn't hide the alarm from her eyes.

'No, I didn't think so,' he said. 'So, how are we going to solve this difficult situation?'

Elsie hesitated then she cleared her throat and said, 'I've got a job. Evenings. I can pay for it tomorrow. Tonight's payday.'

As she said this, the detective stepped forward. 'Wait a minute,' he said, 'I thought I knew you from somewhere. You work at the Butcher's Arms at Westerley Cross.'

Elsie stared at him and then realized why he had seemed so familiar when she had first set eyes on him in the store. He was one of the regulars at the pub. One of those who had first come in with that crowd the night she got the job. Damn it, why hadn't she recognized him when he was peeping out from behind that newspaper? Her original fear was that her father would find out what had happened and give her a beating. Now she was much more upset that her job would be in jeopardy if Tony Harehill got to know.

She was aware the manager was scrutinizing her face and she stared back with feigned indifference. But it worked. After a few moments of consideration, he said. 'So, you think you can pay the money back by tomorrow?'

'Yes. Definitely, sir.' Elsie did her best to sound contrite and sincere.

'Well, there's absolutely no reason for me to do this,' but let's say I'm feeling tolerant today. I'd like to give you a chance as this is your first time.'

First time I've been caught here, at least, Elsie thought. She couldn't believe her good luck. She'd never been treated so leniently before.

'I'll expect to see you here tomorrow with the money. On my desk at nine o'clock prompt. Understood?'

Elsie nodded. 'Understood, sir, and thank you kindly,' she said, though she didn't like to ask if that meant that she could keep the lipstick after all. Because if not, then she wasn't sure what all the fuss was about. 'And we won't prosecute if you promise never to do anything like that again.' He sounded more like a favourite uncle now rather than an angry store manager and she wanted to laugh. But she lowered her eyes reverently and said, 'No, never,' while thinking: Never again to be caught, that's for bloody sure.

'And you must promise never to come to this store again.' The manager made a sign to the detective and the man in the raincoat who had ushered her in, now steered her out, his hand still painfully controlling her elbow. He didn't speak until they set foot outside in the street, then he turned her so she was facing him.

There was an unpleasant leer on his face and she noticed for the first time the ruddiness of his nose and the web of fine red threads on his cheeks. He seemed to be breathing hard as he bent down and spoke into her ear. 'Of course there is another way of solving this rather "difficult" situation,' he said. 'A way that means no one else ever has to know.' His grip tightened. 'I could, let's say, "lend" you the money, or even, if the mood took me, "give" it to you. Right now, if you'd like. Well, not perhaps right now you understand,' he emphasized the word 'right'. 'But shortly after . . . ' He looked down at his crotch, where she noticed a huge bulge had appeared almost popping the buttons of his fly. 'Shortly after . . . I'm sure you catch my drift.'

Elsie stared at him, appalled at his lewd suggestion. He was an old man. Almost as old as her father. How could he even suggest? How dare he even think? The thought of it made her want to vomit.

'Otherwise,' he went on in his coarse voice, 'I shall be forced to tell your boss – Mr Harehill, is it? I shall be forced to tell him all about your little escapade here. And of course I shall just have to tell him how old you really are.'

She suddenly found the strength to yank her arm out of his grasp. 'No thanks. You'll probably snitch on me anyway.' She spat out the words then ran as fast as her cracked-apart shoes and painful leg would allow.

* * *

146

That evening when she turned up for work at the Butcher's Arms, Elsie was surprised to find everything seemed to be as normal. Mr Harehill greeted her cheerfully, she pulled pints as usual and the customers came and went in an unremarkable way. She breathed a huge sigh of relief and let down her guard a little when she didn't see the store detective in any of the bar rooms. But her relief was short-lived, for halfway through the evening the detective arrived while she was buzzing about collecting dirty glasses. He brushed by her shoulder, though he pretended not to see her, and made straight for her boss who was at that moment feeding customers' coppers into the till. At first she was filled with dread when she saw him whispering out of the side of his mouth to Mr Harehill, but when the two men disappeared into the office on the other side of the bar all she could do was resign herself to her fate.

Should I just get my coat and go home, she wondered. Or should I wait for the inevitable and try to cadge a few more tips in the meantime? She knew there wasn't much she could say in her defence. Her only error was in getting caught. But before she had decided what to do, the two men emerged laughing together and the detective was handed a pint, obviously 'on the house'. This time he smiled at her as he projected the pint-pot towards her in a mocking gesture and mouthed the word 'Cheers'. She knew then that she would find out her fate tonight.

She didn't have to wait long. In fact, she hardly had

time to blink before she was summoned into Mr Harehill's office. He was standing behind the small desk, his arms folded, a grim look on his face.

'Shut the door,' he snapped when she appeared. 'You know what this is about, I'm sure.'

Elsie nodded. 'I suppose I best get me coat.' She tried to use her normal voice, but only a whisper came out.

'Not before you give me back your tips from tonight.' He put out his hand.

Elsie looked at him, astonished. She had hoped at least he would pay her for the work she had already done this week, but it seemed as if he was in no mind to be generous.

'Tips? But what about what you owe me in wages?' she dared to ask.

'I owe you nothing,' he snarled. 'It's you who owes me, more like.'

'How do you work that out?' She was so shocked she felt bolder now, ready to shout for what she felt must be her rights.

'What you've no doubt been stealing from me all this while. I told you expressly never to go near the till.' He put his hands on his hips and stared fiercely at her.

'And I never have been.'

'What about the other night?'

Elsie's jaw dropped and she found it difficult to find the words. 'But you asked me specially to put that half-crown in the till. You even watched me do it. I've never ever been near that till otherwise, before or since,' Elsie protested.

'Aye, that's what you say, but it's not difficult to cheat on a publican. How do I know what you've been up to, eh?'

Elsie felt dismayed to be so falsely accused, but she couldn't provide any evidence to support something she hadn't done. In the meantime, Mr Harehill was ranting on and there was nothing she could say in her defence.

'I can't measure what's gone from each barrel and compare it with the takings, now can I?' he was saying.

'No, of course you can't, but—' she began to argue, stung by the injustice.

'But nothing. How can I trust you about anything, when all you've done is lie to me?'

Elsie looked at him quizzically.

'Don't you give me those Miss Innocent eyes,' he shouted. 'Turns out I don't even know how old you are.'

At this Elsie stopped, for she had no answer.

'You led me to believe you were old enough to work in a pub, but I now understand that's not true.'

Elsie hung her head and stared down at her clasped hands.

'How old are you, eh? Just as a matter of interest. I hardly know what to believe any more.'

She didn't reply. What was the use when he obviously knew already from Mr Woolworth's store detective?

'And who did I trust to back up your story? Stan Bloody Walsh, that's who. Someone else who let me down in the worst possible way.' He gave a false laugh. 'For all I know, the two of you could be in cahoots. So you can't blame me if I think it only fair that you at least turn over your tips. Tonight's tips and we'll call it quits. I think that's a pretty generous deal. You should consider yourself lucky.'

Then how come I don't feel lucky? Elsie had the words on the tip of her tongue but she managed to hold them back. She was about to leave, there was no point in trying to put her case when she really had no case. 'I'll get me coat,' she said and she turned to go.

Mr Harehill held out his hand to bar her way. 'Tips,' he said again.

She dipped her hand into her pocket and reluctantly handed over the coppers that she had scrimped from this evening's customers. She was tempted to hold a couple back but then decided it wasn't worth it. The way things were going, the detective might try to hang her upside down on her way out to make sure she wasn't stealing anything else precious from the bar. The thought suddenly made her want to laugh as she pictured it and despite her misery it was all she could do to stop herself smiling.

When she came out of the office it was the detective's face that was split into a wide grin. He raised his glass to her once more and walked beside her to the door.

'Sorry you didn't want to do it my way,' he whispered. 'You know we'd both have been far better off.'

She could feel the spittle gathering in her mouth and it was all she could do not to gob it out into his face.

'Thanks for nothing,' was all she said as she pushed past him and left the bar for the final time.

'Of course there's still the little matter of the price of that lipstick, which I presume you won't now be producing at nine o'clock tomorrow morning.'

Elsie stared at him. She'd had more than enough for one day and she certainly owed him nothing. 'No thanks to you,' she spat out.

'Sorry to have put a spanner in your works, Miss High and Mighty. Perhaps you should have taken me up on my offer.'

'I'd rather be dead in a ditch than be pawed by you, you dirty old bugger.' That wiped the smile off his face, Elsie was pleased to note, as she flounced past him with as much dignity as she could muster.

Chapter 16

Stan stared across the road and read the sign King's Cross Station which stood out in bold letters across the roof of the large building opposite. It felt strange, seeing a sign in English. That proved he was still alive. And he was back in London. He could hardly believe his luck. The joy he felt at being back home in England was having a positive impact on his wellbeing and he didn't feel quite so ill today. There was even a spark of hope that maybe the army doctors had got it all wrong. What did they know? After all, they hardly spoke any English and he'd had to rely on one of his Spanish comrades to translate for him. All the same, he knew deep down he was clutching at straws.

He had no idea what day it was or what month. The weather gave him no clue as to what time of year it was either. It was cold and damp, like it usually was for most of the year in England, and he felt chilled to the bone. He only knew that it was seven o'clock at night because the clock hanging from the station roof told him so.

It felt like years since he had last been in London, jostling through the crowds, desperate to join the International Brigade. Though he knew it was probably only a few months since he had sailed from Dover with all the other English lads, full of dreams and hopes. But none of that mattered really. So much had happened since then. He didn't think he'd ever forget some of the terrible things he'd seen. Pitched battles in the streets, comrades killed as they fought alongside him; the hunger, disease and insanitary conditions. He couldn't be sure where he'd caught the tuberculosis that was now killing him; they had all been through so much . . . . Now all he wanted to do was go home – and he knew in his heart he was going home to die.

In the meantime, he was going to have to work out how to get back to Weatherfield, for his memory wasn't everything it should be. He wasn't even sure if this was the right station. But at least he'd be able to buy a ticket, for with his discharge papers had come some money. Not as much as was owed to him. Not as much as he reckoned a proper private's salary should have been for the months he was out there fighting for the future of Spain. But it should be enough to see him safely home, back with his mother. At the thought of her surprise and delight when he walked through the door, he felt a tightness in his stomach, knowing that his return would be tainted by his illness. It was a far cry from his dream of coming home the all-conquering hero.

Right now he was exhausted and wasn't sure how much longer he could go on. So the first thing he needed was a cup of hot sugared tea and something to eat. He'd not tasted anything sweet since he'd left home and as he hadn't eaten since the measly breakfast he'd had at the camp, his head was now throbbing and he was having difficulty organizing his thoughts. He crossed to the other side of the street, nearly getting knocked down in the process by a taxi cab which seemed to be driving on the wrong side of the road. He reeled on to the pavement, grabbing hold of his trousers which felt as though they were slipping down. He pulled his belt in a few notches at the waist. Before he'd left the hospital in Spain they had given him back the civvy clothes he'd arrived in and it was only then he realized how much weight he'd lost. Even his shoes felt too big.

He went into the station where he was certain there would be a café. He ordered a cup of tea at the counter and slid his hand inside the pocket of his thin coat for his wallet. But his stomach did a somersault and he immediately began to panic when he discovered it wasn't there. Without waiting to pick up his order, he hurried away, ignoring the shouts of the man behind the counter. He walked out of the station in a daze. His thoughts were spinning and he went down the first street he came to without thinking about where he might be going. He plodded on till he came to the river. He hadn't been walking quickly but he was badly out of breath and he bent over, trying to draw as much air as possible into his lungs with each gulp.

When he could breathe again without pain he stood for a few moments looking out over the water and considered the gravity of his situation. Some light-fingered young whippersnapper must have taken advantage of the free-for-all when he got off the train from Dover. They'd picked his pocket clean without him feeling a thing. So, right now he had neither the means of getting a ticket to Weatherfield, nor anywhere or anyone to go to in London. He was hungry and tired. He couldn't walk around all night, and it was too wet to sleep on a bench in a park. Even the homeless tramps he noticed had built themselves a small fire under the arches along the embankment. When he caught sight of its flickering light, he found himself drifting in their direction.

'Down on your luck, mate?' the old man who was stoking the fire called to him.

It was confirmation that, with his oversized clothes that had been rolled up in storage for months and his flopping shoes, Stan looked no better than they did.

'Need a warm? Come and share the fire. No extra charge.' The man gave a rumbly cough that was probably intended as a laugh. The other men eyed Stan suspiciously, but the first man, whose face was framed by matted hair and a matching beard, encouraged him to come closer. 'There's not many as dare to come down here, but as you have, you may as well get warm.'

Stan cautiously approached the tiny bonfire and held out his hands towards the glowing embers. He would have liked to sit down, but there was nowhere to sit.

'You look like you lost a pound and found a penny,' the tramp said.

'That about sums it up,' Stan replied. He was trying hard to concentrate but the tramp was drifting in and out of focus, and he was having difficulty hanging on to his thoughts. He needed to eat something and to lie down somewhere warm. Most of all he craved sleep.

'By the looks of you, what you need right now is the Sally Army,' the tramp said. 'There's a hostel not far from here.' He jerked his thumb down the road. 'They'll give you a bed and some grub too, if you're lucky.'

Stan thanked him and wandered off in the direction the man had pointed.

The man behind the desk asked no questions but gave him a bed number and a blanket. 'First floor, turn left,' was all he said. 'Breakfast at seven, you need to be gone before eight.'

Stan wondered if he should tell him he hadn't eaten all day, but in the end he went straight to the bed, though he tossed and turned restlessly for most of the night with his stomach growling.

He woke up coughing, not feeling at all well. He was sure he had a temperature.

'You're a bloody screamer, aren't you just?' the man in the next bed grumbled. 'You needn't bother coming back tonight if all you can do is rattle on all night. You'll not be welcome.'

Stan apologized. There wasn't much he could do about that. He wondered if he'd been delirious as his comrades had complained of in Spain. He pulled his coat round him and went downstairs. It was a new day but he still didn't know how he was going to get himself home.

He exchanged his blanket for a bowl of thin broth and sat down at the refectory table, trying not to drink it too fast as he pondered on the seriousness of his situation. Nobody knew where he was. Only Elsie. And they hadn't exactly parted on the best of terms. He'd lost count of the nights he'd lain awake thinking about her, wishing he could change things. She was a corker she really was. But unless he could get hold of some money and get back to Weatherfield soon, he feared he might never see her again.

His thoughts were interrupted a cultured voice saying, 'Good morning, sir, and how are we today?' as an older man sat down beside him. He wore a Salvation Army uniform and his deep voice with its well-rounded vowels was unlike anything Stan had heard outside of BBC broadcasts.

'I've been better,' Stan said. With his head still banging

from the night before, he wasn't in the mood for chatter but he didn't want to be churlish.

'Just back from Spain?'

'How did you know that?'

'The eyes are a dead giveaway,' the man said. 'You can always tell.'

Stan blinked his eyes shut, suddenly overcome with a deep wracking cough. It took him a few moments before he was able to breathe normally.

'You don't seem well. We have a doctor who visits the hostel once a week and gives his time free of charge to needy people like you. He is coming later this week – perhaps you would like to see him?' the man said.

'I need to get back to my home town more than anything.' There was a kindness and concern in the man's eyes that Stan hadn't seen for some time and he was touched.

'We have a prayer meeting today, won't you join us? We think of ourselves as God's Army, you know. We have much to offer young men like you. God is here for you if you would only open your arms to him.'

'I'm not sure God has much to offer me now, thank you,' Stan said, wishing he could get away from the man's piercing gaze. He knew he meant well, but he found it unnerving.

'I bet you've seen some sights,' the man said.

'I . . . I'd rather not talk about it, if you don't mind.'

The man looked at him kindly. 'It's entirely up to you. Only, we get many young men like you through

159

our doors and, in my experience, unburdening your thoughts can help open you up to God's grace.'

Stan hesitated but kept his mouth shut. It would have been a relief to talk but he couldn't afford to open some of the floodgates he'd tried so hard to slam shut. He closed his eyes but now he couldn't keep out the images the man's seemingly harmless words had conjured up. For he saw clearly all the filth and squalor they had lived in on the battlefields, the dead bodies and wounded comrades, the hundreds of refugees being mown down as they fled. Even in the hospital, foot soldiers like him were being left to die. He had been one of the lucky ones, being thrown out of the hospital.

Stan felt tears sting his eyes. He had never really thought about the realities of war before he went out, which was why he had been so shocked when confronted with it all face to face. He had learned the hard way what war was all about.

'I . . . I can see that you've got good intentions . . . but I just need to get back to my home town, that's all.'

The man looked as if he were about to say something else but changed his mind. He stood up and put his hand on Stan's shoulder. 'Make sure that you get that cough seen to, won't you,' was all he said before he walked away.

Stan sat for some time after the man had gone, struggling to get his thoughts straight. Try as he might, he couldn't figure out a way to get some money. And all the while, his mind kept wandering, going to places he didn't want to go. He tried to think only pleasant thoughts: Elsie, her soft fleshy lips, her flaming red hair. Her unpredictable temper. Her sassy ways. And how much he would love to see her again. But he kept veering off to thinking about how he could get hold of some money and was no nearer to finding a solution. He left the hostel and set off in the direction of the station.

He didn't consciously think about it until he saw the pub. It was called the Farmer's Arms and when he heard the cash register pinging out a warning like an old school bell it made him think of the pub near home. It was a warm morning, the rain had dried up and the door to the lounge bar had been propped open. When he looked up at the sound of the familiar tinkle, he saw the till was just inside the open door. He couldn't believe his eyes when he saw the landlord disappear, leaving the cash drawer open. As far as he could see, there was no one else about. A quick glance told him the landlord had been filling the drawer with change, ready for the lunchtime punters.

Stan was immediately alert. He glanced around and could still see nobody, the pub was not yet open for business. Without thinking about what he was doing or what the consequences might be, he stepped inside the open door and grabbed the fistful of notes he could see sticking out of the drawer. What he couldn't see was the landlord, bending down behind the counter, so he was shocked when the florid-looking man suddenly popped up with a bellow, 'Oi! What the hell do you think you're doing?'

For a split second Stan froze. But then he caught the man's eye and he knew at that moment he had no choice but to run.

He could hear the old man yelling, 'Stop, you thieving magpie. Get your sodding mitts off my money!' and he was afraid someone might step across his path and try to trip him up. But there was no one but the landlord chasing after him and Stan had a head start. He ran as fast as he could, though the coughing had begun again in earnest. Fortunately, the older man was in worse shape, puffing and groaning within the first few yards, his overhanging belly bouncing up and down. Stan took the first side street he came to, stuffing the notes into his pocket as he ran. He twisted and turned down as many narrow cobbled streets as he could, pausing briefly for breath when he thought his lungs were about to burst. To his relief, he realized he was almost at the train station and he stepped into a nearby shop doorway so that he could make sure he wasn't still being pursued.

Steam billowed out from a newly arrived train as he entered the station. The smell of smoke and bad eggs caught the back of his throat. He was overtaken by a coughing fit and it took several minutes for him to recover, but he was pleased he hadn't heard any shouting or the piping of police whistles. He headed for a dark corner where he could catch his breath. His lungs were heaving and it took some time before his breathing stilled and his heart stopped pounding. He was feeling faint but he knew he had to push on. It was important to catch a train tonight. Keeping close to the walls, his face turned away out of sight, he edged towards the ticket office.

He walked slowly so as not to attract attention and to his relief no one seemed to notice as he climbed aboard the train. He found an empty compartment and sat down. He was aware of his heart still beating faster than normal and he dropped his head into his hands. Then he pulled down the blinds. He reached into his pocket and took out the notes and slowly counted them, handling each one with care. He had never had so much money in all his life. He allowed himself a smile, picturing his mother's face if he arrived in a black cab at the other end. He would tell her that the money was the spoils of war.

But his arrival was not the pleasant surprise he had hoped, although his mother was both shocked and excited to see him. For as he stumbled from the taxi cab he fell coughing into the front room, covering the threadbare carpet with his blood.

Chapter 17

Lily Walsh had seen enough death and disease in her time to know at once what was wrong with her son. She had seen the symptoms of tuberculosis first-hand when her own mother had died from it and she felt a chill of fear strike her heart as she helped her son into the one armchair in the back parlour. She immediately sent one of the neighbour's children off to fetch her other son, Charlie, home from the pub.

'What on earth shall we do, Charlie? She relied on him for everything. 'We've no money put by for the doctor.'

'We'll have to get someone to come and see him, Mam. The local voluntary hospital have a doctor who'll come for a penny.'

'I don't want to be going to no doctor,' Stan gasped

from the armchair. 'There's nowt to be done and they'll want to put us all in quarantine or God knows what.'

'It's such a shock, finding you on the doorstep like that. It was the last thing I expected. And then all that blood.' Lily began to cry.

'Don't take on so,' said Charlie, though his own eyes were brimming with tears as he looked down at Stan, his gaunt features and sunken cheeks barely recognizable from the young man in ruddy health that had left Weatherfield just a matter of months ago. 'Who'd have thought our Stan would be one to swan off to fight in a bloody foreign war.'

Lily sniffed. 'Without so much as a by-your-leave.'

'Do you need a hand getting him into bed, Mam?'

Lily nodded and together they helped Stan out of the armchair in the living room and up the steep stairs.

Stan knew he was dying. Charlie had discreetly put the word out and with a whip-round from the locals had pulled together enough funds for a visit from the local doctor. The army doctors had been right, after all; his condition had gone downhill rapidly.

'If he could be treated in a sanatorium, there might be chance for him, Mrs Walsh, but I fear even now that would be too little, too late,' the doctor told them as he packed up his case

His mother and Charlie cried bitter tears, knowing that there was no money for such expensive treatment, but Stan had at least made it home and that meant a lot to all of them, though the doctor had insisted that he be kept in strict isolation.

For Stan himself it was good to see his mother and brother again. They'd made him as comfortable as they could. Charlie had said he could have the bed all to himself, while he would take himself off to kip on the old couch downstairs.

There was only one thing Stan needed now. He would die a happy man if he could only see Elsie again.

'I'm not sure as she'd come, love,' Stan's mother said sadly when he asked her the next day. 'You know what folk think to TB. No one even wants to mention the word. They're dead scared of getting it thyselves. Not that you can blame them . . . '

But Stan was insistent. 'Maybe you could find a way to ask her. Give her a chance,' he begged. 'You know she has a mind of her own, that lass.' He lay back on the pillow Lily had managed to find to prop him up on when the coughing got bad. 'She'll come – I'd take a bet on it. She's not scared of what other folk think.'

Lily began to sniffle. 'I'm only sorry we can't afford to send you to a sanatorium.'

'Nay. Pay no mind to that.'

Suddenly Lily's face brightened. 'What about that money you brought back?'

'No, I've told you, it's not nearly enough. But it will do to get some decent food for the three of us.' Stan's voice was not strong but he was adamant.

Lily burst into fresh tears.

'Mam, don't go on so. It's too late for me. There's nowt much anyone can do anyway, you heard what the doc said.'

The effort of talking started another coughing fit. He signalled for her to give him a rag from the pile of torn-up sheeting beside the bed and then his head fell back against the pillow, his thoughts turning to Elsie again and his yearning to see her once more.

It was a few days later when a notice went up asking all Weatherfield residents to pick up their gas masks at the town hall. Elsie was taken aback when she saw it. There had been much talk in the factory about the possibilities of a German invasion, with some of the girls saying it could happen that summer, but Elsie hadn't taken it seriously until now. She'd chosen to believe that, no matter what Mr Hitler might say and do, there wouldn't actually be a war in Europe and certainly not in Weatherfield. Wasn't that what poor Stan had gone over to Spain to ensure? But this made it sound like war really was on the cards, and soon.

Even so, she didn't believe they had anything to worry about on Back Gas Street. Still, if free gas masks were on offer, then why shouldn't her family have them? So, she joined the locals heading into the town centre, some of whom had survived the Great War of 1914 and knew all about the importance of gas masks. The young kids on the street were anxious to get their hands on the masks for a different reason: to them, it was all a great game. They thought gas masks would make terrific playthings and couldn't wait to put them on and start scaring each other.

Elsie had told her mother she would pick up masks for the whole family, taking Jack with her so that she could be sure they gave her one to fit his small face. Her mother's response had been: 'I don't know what you're bothering for. I'll certainly never wear one of them things and I doubt anyone else in this family will either.'

Now Elsie was making her way back from the town hall, having let Jack run on ahead. At the sound of a voice calling 'Hey, you!' she turned to see an older woman waving at her. The woman was enveloped in a clean print overall and had a scarf covering her headful of curlers like a turban.

Though she couldn't recall ever having seen the woman before, Elsie stopped to let her catch up. Moments later she found herself staring into a lined face with the saddest brown eyes she had ever seen. She wondered what such an old woman could want with her.

'I'm told you're Elsie Grimshaw. Is that right?' the woman said.

Elsie raised her eyebrows. 'Depends who wants to know.'

Lily hated backchat and was ready with a putdown for this cheeky young redhead but then remembered Stan's face as he had begged her to find Elsie and thought better of it. 'My name's Lily Walsh,' she said firmly. Elsie looked surprised. 'I'm Stan Walsh's mam.'

'Oh yes?' Elsie said. Memories of Stan and the way he'd abandoned her came flooding back as she realized that Lily's sad eyes reminded her of him. 'And have you heard from him lately? I suppose you know by now where he went to when he disappeared all them months back?'

'Yes, I know. And I've not only heard from him, I've seen him. He's at home with me and our Charlie right now.'

Elsie was shocked. 'What? You mean he's back?' She wasn't sure whether to believe her. 'Has he been wounded?' she asked cautiously.

'In a manner of speaking. You can come and see him for yourself, if you've a mind.'

This was not what Elsie had expected to hear and she was thrown into confusion, unsure how to answer. She'd long since regretted her harsh words when Stan had come to say goodbye and had often thought about what she might say if ever she saw him again. But she didn't want to appear too eager. She'd thought of writing to him, if she'd known where to write. But now it seemed she was being offered a chance to make her apology to his face and yet here she was, dithering. Was it Stan that really wanted to see her, or was it just the wishful thinking of his mam?

She emerged from her thoughts to discover that the old woman was still talking.

'I've got to warn you, though: you mustn't tell anyone that I've asked you. And you can't tell anyone if you decide to come.'

'Whyever not?' Elsie didn't know what to make of the strange request.

Lily didn't answer immediately, then seemed to make up her mind saying in a low voice, 'He's got TB, so it's up to you to decide whether you want to see him.'

Elsie felt sick at the dreaded words. 'Is he bad?' She hardly dared to ask.

Lilly snuffled and pulled a rag from her pocket to wipe her running nose. 'Yes, he's bad. You might not have the stomach for it – he's a shadow of the lad you'll remember.'

Now Elsie's only thought was to be there for Stan. 'But are you sure he wants me there? We didn't part on the best of terms,' she admitted. 'Though I want to come, very much,' she added with feeling.

Lily smiled sadly through her tears. 'I was hoping you'd say that, lass. He so wants to see you, but I didn't want to pressure you.' She linked arms with Elsie then and told her where and when to come.

'Elsie, is that you?' Stan wondered if he was hallucinating again, like he had done in Spain. He could see this vision at the bedroom door that looked like Elsie in a print dress, her flame-red hair brushed back off her face and a posy of flowers in her hand. But he couldn't be sure it was real.

The young girl stepped into the room. 'Yes, it's really me,' said the voice he knew so well. 'I wanted to bring you summat, but I didn't know what to bring.'

'You've brought you. That's enough,' Stan said, still not entirely convinced she wasn't an illusion. 'And it's good to see you. But don't come too close.'

'Why not? I want to see you proper, like.' Elsie was prepared with a hanky to cover her mouth, but all she could do was squeeze it tightly as she took in the sight of the invalid in the bed. She could barely believe that the Stan Walsh in front of her was the same person. His once-strapping frame was painfully thin and the bedshirt he wore hung loosely from his drooping shoulders. There was a bead of sweat across his brow and he seemed to be struggling for each breath. She sat down on the corner of the bed, put the daisies down and clutched his clammy hand in her own. 'Oh, Stan, I'm so sorry for what I said. I just wish I could take it all back.' She paused. 'I was sorry even then, but didn't get the chance to tell you.'

'You don't have to fret about that now.' Stan smiled. 'I don't. Not any more.'

'If I'd said sorry and we'd made up, I could have persuaded you not to go and then you wouldn't be ill now.'

'Wild horses couldn't have stopped me going, Elsie. And even after everything that's happened, I'm still not sorry I went. We didn't win, but at least I tried. I did my bit.'

Elsie regarded Stan with fresh eyes. She'd always known that he was a man of high ideals, but only now could she see how much they meant to him. She was overwhelmed at his bravery and sacrifice. 'All you should be worried about is getting better now, Stan.'

'I'll not be doing that, lass, let's be honest. We both know that. I bet you've seen better haunting a house.' He tried to laugh at his own joke, but all he could manage was a cough.

For once Elsie was at a loss for words. She pushed the daisies towards him. 'Here, I brought you these. Sorry I couldn't wrap them up.'

He picked one up and put it to his nose. 'No matter. They're right lovely. Thanks.'

She smiled, then started talking about anything she could think of. Soon she had him laughing with her stories about the little 'uns and their latest antics. She told him that when he was better they would borrow Charlie's bike again and ride out together on to the moors. 'We'll take our sarnies and maybe a bar of chocolate and—'

Stan was smiling as he cut in, shaking his head: 'I'm afraid you'll have to do that on your own.'

'Tell me,' Elsie asked, desperate to change the subject, 'did Charlie ever find out about the bike?'

'He did ask me how the paint got scraped, so I think he guessed. But promise me you'll not stop riding a bike. In fact, you can have mine. I'll tell me mam I said so. And then all you'll have to do will be to find someone else to ride with.'

Elsie stared at him. 'There'll never be anyone like you, Stan.' She had been struggling to hold back the tears, but now she lost her battle and they began to flow in earnest. 'I wish I was going to marry you, Stan,' she sobbed. 'I'd be so proud to be your wife.'

'And I'd be the luckiest man in the world to be your husband, Elsie. But luck isn't on our side this time.'

'Oh, Stan.' Elsie gripped his hand and tried to control her emotions. She could see he was flagging, his face was grey and his eyes sunk back into their sockets. She didn't want to tire him out. 'I tell you what,' she said, clutching his hand, 'I'll come again tomorrow and I'll come again every day, every day until . . . ' she hesitated, aware of what her words would mean.

'Until I don't need you any more, Elsie.' Stan held her gaze and Elsie knew she would never love anyone the way she loved Stan in that moment.

'That's right, Stan.' Leaning over the bed, Elsie planted a tender kiss on his forehead, not caring about the TB or anything else. He managed to give her a nod, then his fingers fluttered and the daisy he'd been holding fell back on to the grey blanket.

'Goodbye, Stan,' Elsie whispered. 'I'll be seeing you.'

'Goodbye.' His voice was merely a whisper.

The following day, Lily Walsh sent word to Elsie at the

factory that Stan was dead. That whispered goodbye was the last word she would ever hear him say.

Elsie shed her tears for Stan in private. She felt as if her heart was breaking and cried like she had never done before. How was she ever going to replace him? Her first love had come to a cruel and tragic end and Elsie wondered if something in her had died along with him.

Christmas 1938

Chapter 18

Elsie stared at the newsagent's window, finding it difficult to believe it would soon be Christmas again. It was cold and damp as there had been lots of rain, though there had been no sign of any snow yet. Elsie usually liked Christmas time. Regardless of the miserable conditions outside, people on the whole seemed more jolly and friendly at that time of year. But this year was different. People were scurrying about with anxious looks on their faces, for no one was sure whether or not there was going to be a war. Only a couple of months ago the prime minister had come back from a meeting with Mr Hitler and had talked about 'peace in our time'. Elsie had been relieved to hear he had signed a special agreement so there couldn't possibly be a war now.

'They've found a way to settle things,' she'd assured her little sisters. 'So there's no need to worry. We already had the war to end all wars before you and I were born.'

But then the other week, when she and Fay had sneaked into the cinema, she'd seen the Pathé News showing trains filled with children leaving Germany for England. They were waving goodbye to their parents. Everyone was crying and jostling as soldiers with rifles were herding little ones with tiny suitcases and badges with their names on their coats on to the trains. The newsman said they were escaping the war that was waging in Europe. Was that true? And if so, was it really coming to Britain? Some said that even if things were all right now, by Christmas next year it could be very different, with England being overrun with Germans. Elsie no longer knew what to believe.

She turned her attention back to the window. In the corner, as always, stood the Christmas tree. But it was looking tired and old now. Its branches were no longer green, and the fairy with the wand that used to look like she was flying from the topmost branch had disappeared. Some tinsel still hung across the branches but it didn't seem to glitter any more and the cotton-wool puffs of pretend snow were grey instead of white. None of the other decorations had changed much from last year and all the years before. There were washed-out paper chains and what seemed to be the same boxes of chocolates in their faded wrappings. She dreaded to think what the chocolate inside would be like by now. That made her think of her own precious bar of chocolate that Stan had given her for her birthday and an unexpected tear ran down her cheek. She left it unchecked as she closed her eyes. She could see Stan as he was walking by the Field. Stopping to chat. Her first boyfriend. The first person apart from Fay and little Jack who had shown her any real affection. He had been her first love and it was hard to accept he had been gone for three months already.

She opened her eyes and stepped closer to the glass, trying to see her reflection. She still looked the same as she had last year when she stopped to admire the Christmas tree. Her pale and sickly face hadn't changed much in the last twelve months. She never had been able to get hold of any make-up after that dreadful business at Woolies, and she had no beetroot juice so there was no way to brighten up her lips. She sighed. The only thing that had changed was that Fay had hacked at her hair recently when they came across an old pair of scissors in the Field. But the blades had been almost blunt and Fay had not been able to do much with her fringe. It was still uneven and the flyaway bits that reached down to her shoulders were all different lengths too.

She was so engrossed in looking at the window, wishing she could change her image, she didn't hear the footsteps. It gave her a fright when a voice interrupted her thoughts.

'What are you gawping at in there, eh?' It was a man's voice, deep and strong. 'I could show you far better Christmas trees than that,' he said.

Elsie whipped round. A huge man was standing there, looking even taller because of his hat. His open overcoat showed he was dressed in a suit, and it wasn't even Sunday. Her mouth gaped open but she didn't feel able to speak. Not that it mattered, for he was talking again.

'Oh, my goodness,' he said, 'and we have real tears too. Now what are those all about? Crying because Santa didn't come?'

Elsie felt anger flare; how dare he make fun of her! 'No, I'm not,' she snapped. 'There's no such thing as Santa Claus. I'm not a child.' She paused then and added under her breath, 'Not that he'd know where I bloody live anyway.'

The man held his large hands up in surrender like John Wayne did in her favourite cowboy films. In fact, she thought he looked a bit like John Wayne. Very tall, with broad shoulders, big feet and hands. But this man's fingers were scrubbed clean with no dirt under the nails. His face was darker than the film star, like he needed a good shave, and thick dark hair curled out from under his trilby. She couldn't see his eyes until he bent down to look at her face, but then she saw that they were dark as well.

'Oops, sorry,' he said. His eyes had laughter in them. 'Only joking. Maybe it's just the rain. Anyway, you look half-frozen. How do you fancy a hot cup of coffee?'

Elsie screwed up her nose, she'd never had coffee.

'OK, tea then,' he said. 'There's a café down the road.'

'Do you mean the Milk Bar?' Elsie asked.

He nodded.

'Aye, I know it. Though I've never been inside.'

'Well, now's your chance. What do you say? Warm us both up?'

Elsie felt a rush of excitement. She wasn't going to pass up the opportunity of going to a café, even if it was with a complete stranger. The offer of a hot drink and a warm place to sit down with an attractive man, without one of the kids mithering at her skirt, was very tempting indeed. It was obvious he was quite a bit older than her, and no doubt a hell of a lot more worldly wise, but it was only a cup of tea. Besides, she was going to be sixteen next birthday. Old enough to look after herself.

Despite the large window overlooking the street, it was impossible to see into the Milk Bar from outside because the glass was all steamed up. As she walked in, Elsie was hit by the smell of strong coffee and sweet sticky buns. It seemed to hang on the blast of warm air that greeted them. There were people sitting at almost all the tables and there was a steady low buzz of noise. A young girl in a white apron was ferrying drinks and cakes to the tables and clearing up the dirty cups and saucers as she went.

'Morning, Arnold,' a tired-looking woman behind the counter greeted him as soon as he walked in. 'The usual? Cup of tea, is it?'

'Morning, Lizzie. Make that two, if you please.' He took his trilby hat off and tossed it on to the hat stand in the corner.

'Right y'are,' she said. 'Coming up.' Elsie was aware the woman was eyeing her up and down. Her cheeks suddenly felt warm and she hoped she wasn't blushing.

Arnold walked over to an empty table by the window and pulling out a chair sat down. Elsie sat down too, though the solid wooden chair was heavier to move than it looked. She gazed round the small room. It was the first time she had been inside any café, not just this one, and it all seemed very different from the pubs she was used to. The tables were smaller, the chairs bigger. There was no sign of sawdust on the floor but the large diamond-patterned tiles made it look bright and stylish at the same time. The walls had originally been painted yellow over wallpaper but where the steam had made contact the paper was now peeling away and there were stains and marks on the ceiling which looked like something had carelessly been tossed up there and never come down.

As people came in, they gave their orders to the woman behind the counter and she speared a copy on to a hook as they paid their bill. Then a little while later the extremely young-looking little waitress served the orders on a tray.

But it was all the equipment that fascinated Elsie, even though she was no stranger to machinery, working in the factory. But she had never seen apparatus like the array of gleaming metal lined up behind the counter. One machine was making a series of gurgling noises before some extremely dark coffee began to drip into a cup. Another was whipping up a head of steam that sounded like the engine on a train she'd once seen at Exchange Station.

'Are you going to tell me who you are, and do you make a habit of picking up stray girls and buying them a cup of tea?' she demanded as soon as he sat down. 'And ta very much, by the way.'

'Arnold Tanner,' the rather gruff voice told her. 'And who are you?'

'I'm Elsie Grimshaw.' She didn't know why, but she put out her hand. He looked slightly surprised but he wiped his hand on his trouser leg before taking hold of it and shaking it.

'And where do you live, Elsie Grimshaw, that Santa and his reindeer didn't bother stopping on his way past?' The teasing note was back in his voice and she grimaced as he mentioned Santa again. But this time she held on to her temper.

'Back Gas Street,' she said, with equal emphasis on each word, and she looked him directly in the face as if offering a challenge.

If she was hoping for a reaction she was disappointed, for he didn't flicker so much as an eyelid. All he said was, 'Do you now?' as if that explained everything.

'Where do you live?' she asked, and sat back folding her arms across her chest.

'Good question,' he said.

They were interrupted by the arrival of the waitress and a tray loaded with two thick-lipped cups of steaming brew.

'Two teas with milk and extra sugar,' she said, slapping them down so hard that the strong brown liquid spilled over into the saucer. She also brought a large bun on a plate with a thick layer of a shiny white something smeared on the top. She put that down in front of Arnold. Elsie could hear her stomach growling but he didn't seem to notice. He bit into the bun and didn't offer her any.

'Why's that then? What's so good about it?' Elsie persisted.

He laughed. 'Because officially I'm not really living anywhere at the moment. I'm kipping down at my friend Joe's. But I'll soon be on the move.'

Elsie sipped her tea even though it was still scalding hot and wondered if she dare ask for a bite of the sticky-looking cake. She hadn't realized she was so hungry. He looked at her without smiling as he took another bite and put the remaining piece back on his plate.

'I collect rents for one of the landlords and he's about to fit me up in a new place all on my own.'

Elsie was amazed. What kind of a place would that be, she wanted to know. And where had he been living before he moved in with Joe? But she bit back the questions; it sounded too forward to ask so much at once. Instead she said, 'So where's your new place going to be then?'

'In Coronation Street,' he said.

'Blimey, that's posh,' she couldn't stop herself exclaiming. 'Anywhere near the viaduct? I learned to cycle there.'

He nodded. 'Not far.'

'How d'you manage to get a place there?' she blurted out.

He laughed. 'Well, I suppose it is posh, compared to Back Gas Street.'

She was aware of his eyes studying her face and was determined not to give him the satisfaction of a reaction. 'Young man like me needs 'is own place, see. Only losers and mummy's boys still live at 'ome.'

He leaned forward then, his eyes narrowing as he said, 'And in answer to your other question, I deserve it because I work bloody hard.'

So do I, she wanted to retort, but nobody gives me owt like that. She thought it best not to say a word though.

He sat back, resting his chunky arms on the curved wings of the chair and Elsie looked down at the table. It was freshly scrubbed wood, stained with heat rings from cups and glasses that obviously couldn't be rubbed off.

'I bet you're not even old enough to work,' he said.

Once again, anger nearly got the better of Elsie, but when she looked at him a slight smile was twitching at his lips. So she told him about the factory and that she had once worked in a bar as well.

'How old are you?' he asked. 'Working in a bar and all.'

'I'm eighteen,' she said and smiled, but disbelief was written across his face.

'Get out of it! You must think I was born yesterday – you're just a kid,' he said, his bushy eyebrows knitting together in a frown.

'Well, you're hardly much older than me, acting flash, bragging about getting your own place.' Elsie hated being called a kid; she'd seen more life in her almost-sixteen years than most people did in their entire lives.

At that his hand shot out and he grasped hold of her arm, his fleshy fingers holding it in a vice-like clamp. Elsie had to stop herself from crying out.

'Don't you come that lip with me, lady,' he snarled. His eyes flashed, his grip was strong and painful and for a brief moment Elsie felt afraid. The switch from fun to anger had been so sudden.

Bloody hell, she thought, there's just no getting away from the bullies in this world. But he was different to her dad, she could tell. There was a confidence about him, and you could see he wanted to go places, unlike her lazy parents.

As quickly as he'd grabbed it, he let go of her arm and patted her hand lightly as he laid it down on the table. She was as much amazed at the gentleness of his touch as she had been by his anger. At the same time she was aware of butterflies in the pit of her stomach and a warm glow filtering through her body. There was something mild yet wild about this man that sent thoughts of Douglas Fairbanks and Clark Gable flashing through her mind. She hadn't felt so excited in months.

But the excitement didn't last. She was disappointed when they were ready to leave the café and he didn't suggest another time for them to meet. After he had collected his hat from the stand and seen her out of the door and safely across the road, he walked away in the opposite direction without so much as a word or a backward glance. Elsie had seen enough films to know that lovers never parted like that. They wandered off hand in hand into the mist, stopping every now and then to kiss. What would it be like to hold Arnold's hand, she wondered, his huge fingers closing entirely around hers? Would she ever be able to reach up close enough to test out the warmth of his lips and tongue that had looked so inviting as they had talked? One thing was for sure: if she was ever to see him again, she would have to raid the Sally Army shop for some high-heeled shoes.

As she wandered slowly home, Elsie pondered on how much she had enjoyed being treated like a lady, if only for a few brief moments. It had felt wonderful to have someone actually buy her something. It didn't matter it was only a cup of tea. Arnold had bought it especially for her, the same way Stan had once bought her a bar of chocolate. Both times, it had made her feel very special indeed. She sighed. Perhaps now was the time to put Stan into the background and to stop living in the past. There had been a time when she'd looked to him to help lift her out of Back Gas Street, but that dream was well and truly over now. It was time to stop looking back.

Elsie stopped dead in her tracks as a new thought struck her. She patted her hair and pouted her lips as if she were in front of a mirror, making herself laugh. She had always been determined to have a boyfriend by her sixteenth birthday and time was running out as she would be reaching that grand old age next March. Not for her the kind of boyfriend who was only interested in a quick grope in the bushes – she was already too worldly-wise for that. No, she wanted someone more serious, someone who acted like a grown-up.

What with Stan's death and people gloomily predicting that the world would soon be coming to an end if Hitler had his way, Elsie was more determined than ever to make the most of whatever time she had left. She didn't want to die having never known anything but the squalor of Back Gas Street and the drudgery of the factory. She wanted to die happy. And what would make her the happiest would be to find someone who would take her away from Back Gas Street.

Arnold, it seemed to her, fitted the bill perfectly. He looked to be the sort of man who could help her to thumb her nose at her father – and her mother, for that matter. If she threw in her lot with him, she'd leave them and the slums behind. She clapped her hands and chuckled out loud at the prospect, then looked round to make sure no one had heard her. But there was no one else on the street right now, so she did a little skip and a jump. She knew exactly what she must do. If Arnold Tanner collected the rent from properties around Coronation Street, then she knew where she had to go to make sure she would 'accidentally' bump into him.

As she rounded the familiar corner of Back Gas Street, she started to count down in her mind the number of times she would have to see the front door of number 18 again.

Chapter 19

Elsie remembered well the smooth cobbled streets of Coronation Street, even though it seemed a lifetime ago that Stan had brought her here so he could teach her to ride Charlie's bike. Though she smiled at the memory, it was one she was determined to put behind her. As she walked along the pavement she wished she had a bike with her now so she wouldn't feel so exposed. Maybe Stan forgot to mention the bike to Charlie, or Charlie thought the bike too precious to give to her but it had never materialised. Anyway, it seemed to her that all the locals were watching her, thinking she didn't belong. It was obvious from the state of her clothes and her too-tight shoes that she had no place here. If she'd had a bike, she could have whizzed up and down the road and no one would have tried to stop her to ask what she was doing there. Not that anyone had stopped her, yet. The few people who were out and about seemed too intent on their own business to worry about what she was doing there. She was grateful for that, because she had no idea what her response would be, if challenged. She hadn't even decided what she would say if she actually ran into Arnold Tanner.

It wasn't like her to feel nervous about such things, but she had to admit she was feeling completely out of her depth. Not that she was about to let that stop her. You had to seize your chances in this life, and once Elsie had made up her mind to do something she wasn't one to give up until it was done.

The one advantage of walking over riding a bike was that it gave her a chance to take a closer look at all the houses. She walked slowly down one side of the street until she could go no further, then up the other side, admiring the neat houses with their sparkling windows and donkey-stoned steps. And most of the windowsills and front doors looked like they had been freshly painted too. Some of the chimney pots were belching out a considerable amount of smoke and she imagined hearty fires burning in the grates.

She stopped in front of one house where the gleaming brightness of the brass doorknocker caught her eye. Even the brickwork looked like it had been scrubbed. She longed to take a peek inside, but it was impossible to see directly into the front room because there were lacy curtains blocking the view. It was a homely looking house, with green paintwork on the windows and door. Standing back, she saw braids of smoke curling out of the chimney pot. She pictured the occupants warming themselves in front of a cosy fire. What wouldn't she give to live in a house like that! She wondered what the reaction would be if she knocked on the door and asked to have a look around. But she knew that couldn't happen, so she carried on walking.

Several other houses had the same type of lace over the windows and a couple of times she thought she saw the curtains twitching, yet no one accosted her and no one banged on their window shouting for her to bugger off. She had never seen curtains like that in Back Gas Street, where many of the windows were broken and boarded up, and the sills and doors were badly in need of a lick of paint.

These houses looked much bigger than anything she had ever seen in her neck of the woods, yet there were far fewer children playing in the street. They must have smaller families than what I'm used to, she decided, and she wondered how many people lived in each house and how many bedrooms there were. From the looks of it, she guessed there was more than one bedroom to every house and they probably had either an indoor privy or a private outdoor one. She knew of only one family in Back Gas Street who had a bathtub indoors, and that was where they kept their coal.

What did people do with so much space? Maybe they filled it with other people? Maybe more than one family lived in each house? Or did they have lots of 'things' like she'd seen in some houses she had been to. At her friend Aggie's, they had a separate gas cooker in the kitchen that meant they didn't have to cook on the open fire. And they also had so many chairs that everyone who lived there could be sitting down at the same time.

At one end of the street was a pub called the Rovers Return, and that too looked neat and tidy on the outside, though of course she couldn't see in through the frosted-glass windows. It had a green facade that looked fresh and the windows had been polished to within an inch of their lives. The sign said it was a Newton and Ridley pub – same owners as the Butcher's Arms. She wondered if the layout was the same inside.

When she passed the pub for the second time, she paused. A wind had whipped up and the bitter cold was striking through her thin clothing. Snow had been threatened by the end of the afternoon, too. She would have loved to go in and get warm, but she had no money and didn't want to risk being thrown out of the pub. She could hardly rely on some stranger buying her a drink again and Arnold Tanner was nowhere to be seen. Dispirited, she decided to go home. She obviously wasn't going to bump into Arnold here.

She was about to turn away when the door to number 9 opened and an old man's voice could be heard yelling all manner of curses.

'Don't you come mithering us again, Mr Bloody Rent Collector!' she heard the voice yell from inside the house at the same time as a large male figure appeared on the doorstep.

'I'm only doing my job, Mr Todd,' the figure called back.

His hat brim was well pulled down and his chin and mouth were muffled by a scarf so she couldn't see his face, but she would have recognized the huge frame of Arnold Tanner anywhere. His tone sounded threatening as he went on: 'There's people queueing up for houses like these and Mr Wormold won't tolerate late payments, you know that.'

A grunting laugh came from within. 'Tell 'im 'e can come and whistle for it.'

'You won't be feeling quite so cocky when I show you that we mean business,' Arnold yelled. 'You've been given fair warning that if you don't have the rent money together by the next time I come, you'll be turfed out. We'll soon see who's whistling then. Remember, Todd, one week is all you've got.' And with that he stepped out into the street. Arnold touched the edge of his hat and nodded towards the short stocky man who had followed him out on to the doorstep. Despite the cold, the old man's collar was off his shirt and his sleeves were rolled up as if he were spoiling for a fight.

At that point Elsie thought it best to slip away, but she stopped when she realized Arnold had seen her. He ignored Mr Todd, who was shaking his fist after him, and hurried over the road to where she stood shivering.

'What the hell are you doing here?' he said, but he didn't sound angry.

'Oh, I often have a wander down Coronation Street,' she lied. 'I've got a bit of a soft spot for the place. I learned to cycle here.' She gave him her practised line, even though she knew he wasn't in the least interested in cycling. In fact, when they had been together in the café he had told her he hankered after driving a car and had his eye on either an Austen 10 or a Ford 8. She could certainly see him driving rather than riding a bike, for she couldn't imagine him cycling across the moors. Though she couldn't help feeling that his wish for a car was as much to make the neighbours green with envy as it was about wanting to get behind the wheel.

'What happened there?' she asked, interested in learning more about the altercation she had just witnessed.

'He's a stubborn old bugger, but he'll cough up – they always do. Either that or he'll get chucked out on the street, and not gently either.' Arnold flexed his arms, as if imagining the violent encounter. Then, to Elsie's surprise, he put his arm across her shoulders. His overcoat felt thick and warm and she snuggled up as close as she dared.

'Isn't that the house you said you were after?' she asked.

'Number 9,' he said. 'That's the one. And I'll get it

too, if the old fool doesn't pay his rent. Mr Wormold has promised me. These people don't seem to realize you don't get owt for nowt.'

'Has he got a family? Or does he live on his own?' Elsie wanted to know.

'I've no idea. Anyway, never mind him – you're a sight for sore eyes.' He sounded sincere, but it was hard to tell as his moods seemed to shift so quickly. 'Here, you look half-starved with cold. Let's be getting you out of this wind.' He steered Elsie towards the Rovers Return and she knew any resistance would have been useless.

The inside of the pub was as neat and tidy as the outside. The pub was split into three parts and Arnold directed her to one of the comfortable seats in the public bar. The woman behind the bar had the air of a landlady. Her hair was blonde, pinned up in the latest fashion, and her neat blouse and skirt looked like they had cost a bob or two. She gave Arnold a haughty look as he approached the bar.

'Arnold, what can I get you and your . . .' the woman pursed her lips and regarded Elsie disdainfully, ' . . . lady friend?'

Who the hell did she think she was? Elsie huffed. Bloody woman, looking down on her in that way. She raised her chin and eyed the landlady saucily.

'That's Elsie, Mrs Walker. She's all right,' he answered, nodding his head in Elsie's direction.

'That's as maybe, Arnold Tanner, but I hope you

won't be harassing my customers for their rents while you're in here?' She gave him a cold stare.

'Nay, don't fret, I'm off duty.'

'I sincerely hope so. And that young lady is too young to be drinking alcohol.'

He bought a pint for himself and a lemonade for Elsie. He didn't ask what she wanted, which was just as well for despite having worked in a pub she still didn't have a favourite tipple and wasn't sure she liked the taste of alcohol yet. He indicated he would bring them to one of the booths where he'd told Elsie to go and sit.

'Sorry it took so long,' he apologized when he finally carried the drinks through. 'Annie Walker's the landlady here – her and her husband Jack run the place. She's a snooty cow, and they don't like me coming in. But my money's as good as anyone else's. Better, in fact.'

'Why don't they like you?'

He gave a laugh. 'Come on, you know what I do, can't you use your imagination?'

Now she laughed. 'I suppose you and I would make a good pair then,' she said without thinking, 'because it would make me want to dig my heels in too. No one would get rid of me that easily.'

'Attagirl!' he said. 'That's the kind of spirit I like to hear. They say redheads have lots of fire and go about them.'

'Na, I don't think it's anything to do with that. One of my sisters has the same hair as me and when she found summat she really didn't like, she ran away.' Elsie sighed. She didn't know what had made her think of Phyllis right now. No one had heard from her since the day that thieving Harry had moved in, and she'd long since given up any hope of finding her.

'Shame. How long did she sulk before she came back?'

'She hasn't come back,' said Elsie and she found herself telling him the story.

'I bet I could find her for you, if you really wanted to know where she is,' Arnold said unexpectedly.

'What makes you think you could do that?' Elsie was all agog.

He tapped the side of his nose. 'Because I've got lots of contacts in all sorts of secret places. They can find out anything you want to know.'

Elsie stared at him, not sure whether to believe him. But he looked as if he meant what he was saying. 'OK,' she said. 'You're on.'

'I'll let you know next time I see you.' Elsie's stomach did a sort of somersault when he said that. Was there really going to be a next time?

'How about you and me go to the Plex next week?' Arnold said casually. 'I could tell you then.'

'What's on?' Elsie asked. It was unusual for her not to know, but his invitation had taken her so much by surprise all thoughts of what was showing at the pictures had gone clean out of her head.

Arnold laughed. 'I've no idea – 'appen, we won't be

doing much watching anyway. I'm hoping we might get to know each other a little better, if you know what I mean.'

Elsie grinned. She knew exactly what he meant, and if he could help her find Phyllis, then she wouldn't put up a struggle.

Chapter 20

When Arnold Tanner had come out of number 9 to find Elsie standing there, he couldn't believe his luck. After doing battle over non-payment with 'odd sod Todd', as he called him, he'd worked himself up into a fair old lather. The sight of a pretty face had lifted his mood in an instant. And she looked familiar too. Wasn't that the young lass he'd taken to the Milk Bar for a cup of tea the other day? Well, well, well, had she been chasing after him all this time? He had regretted letting her go without finding out where on Back Gas Street she lived, and he certainly hadn't expected to see her again so soon. Yet here she was, turning up almost at his own front door.

He'd never had a problem attracting young ladies and persuading them to do whatever he wanted. Most of them were afraid of him and he never minded that for when they got to the final post that seemed to help them enjoy it all the more. But this one was different. She didn't look scared at all. Mind you, he was sure she was far too young for him, no matter what age she had claimed to be. But the fact that she had come to him on his home turf in Coronation Street was now making him think she might be easier pickings than he could have dreamed.

He wasn't sure he believed all that nonsense about bikes. It was him she was really after. And if that was what she wanted, then that was what she would have. Mind, he would have to be careful in case she wasn't as streetwise as she might like to think. But with a bit of caution, things could turn out very well indeed. He would even put a bet on it. He would have a wager with his mate Joe tonight about how long it would take him to get her into his bed.

But not looking like she did right now. It was one thing taking her to the pictures where it was dark and it didn't matter much if he was seen. Besides, the back row of the flicks was always a good barometer of how far a girl was prepared to go. But he would have to do something about her appearance. Living on Back Gas Street, it was easy to understand why she looked the way she did, like a waif and stray, but if he started stepping out with her everyone would laugh at him. She was definitely not the sort of girl he usually had hanging on to his arm. When he'd first met her, that had been enough to make him think maybe she wasn't worth the effort. Now he'd had a chance to look at her more closely, he was beginning to change his mind. It was the flame-red hair that clinched it. At the moment, it was about as attractive as an untidy doormat. But he'd caught glimpses of the pretty young thing hidden underneath, and she certainly had curves in all of the right places; seemed like she might have a bit of fire in her belly too which was always good when you were in the sack. It would require a bit of work, but he reckoned she might be worth it.

He didn't know any woman who would object to having her hair done and a bit of make-up slapped on. Girls would do anything for a pair of nylons and some new lippy; they were daft like that. And he did like his women to add a touch to nature on their lips and cheeks – he wanted his girls to make the effort for him. He was sure that, with a little help, Elsie could turn out to be quite something.

Perhaps he should have a word with his mother. See if she had any suggestions. She usually had a good eye for that sort of thing.

On Saturday night they met in front of the cinema by the box office entrance. Elsie knew where it was, though she had never been into the theatre that way before. Arnold was already standing in the queue for tickets. Elsie was amazed how many people were waiting patiently in an orderly line, all prepared to pay for their tickets. She joined him when he reached the till and was handing over the money, and she was thrilled to see he was buying the most expensive seats at the back. It was somewhere she had never sat before. She was walking on a cloud as they were shown into the large cinema. But then she felt too embarrassed to accept Arnold's offer of orange juice and chocolate as the young usherette held up a small flashlight to point out where they might sit. Arnold wanted the two seats that were right in the middle of the back row and they had to interrupt several young couples as they made their way along.

'At least we won't be disturbed,' Arnold muttered, grinning at Elsie as he held down her seat.

She smiled back as she sank into it, amazed to find she couldn't feel any springs or stuffing pushing their way through the plush red velvet.

Arnold offered her a cigarette and they both puffed away until the end of the adverts. Then he put his arm round her and she felt his fingers drumming gently on her breast. She didn't say anything but she settled her head back and turned her body so that she was snuggled up against him. The drumming changed to stroking as the B film began and she felt so warm and cosy she almost fell asleep. But when he began to rub her breast harder and to squeeze her already erect nipple she found it difficult to concentrate. She was barely aware of what was going on as an old detective in a bowler hat slowly unravelled the second-rate murder mystery. When the lights went up at the interval, Elsie hastily straightened her clothes. Arnold removed his arm and smiled at her, though neither said anything.

The usherette wandered up and down the aisles with her tray as Elsie had watched her do many times before, but this time to her delight Arnold bought them a choc ice each. When they settled down again to watch the main feature – *The Lady Vanishes*, with Margaret Lockwood and Michael Redgrave – Arnold gave her a short but forceful kiss, using his tongue as the lights dimmed. She kissed him back, wondering how much of the film they might actually see. She loved watching the glamorous actresses in these kind of films and daydreaming that one day she might have a nice dress or fancy make-up like they did. The cast list had hardly finished rolling when she felt his hand grasping her knee and switching quickly to caressing the soft flesh of her inner thigh. They both slid down in their seats as his lips covered hers and his hands began to explore between her legs. As his fingers probed so she twisted and turned so many times she was glad there was no one behind them to complain. She wasn't too upset to miss most of the action of the film, for she had had the pleasure of her own action. And she could always sneak in one evening with Fay to see the rest.

They emerged into the chilly evening and Elsie fastened up her coat as quickly as she could. She had enjoyed herself more than she would have thought possible and she hoped they would be able to do it again soon.

'I'll walk you home,' Arnold offered, 'or maybe we can get the bus.'

Elsie suddenly felt ashamed. She realized she didn't want him to see where she lived and admitted truthfully that she didn't know what buses might go there.

'Why don't you walk me as far as the Field,' she said. 'You don't have to come out all the way.'

Elsie stopped when they reached the Field to give him the opportunity to turn back. She looked across the empty waste ground and was surprised to see several mounds had appeared with corrugated sides and proper doors with locks.

'Blimey,' Arnold said, for he had seen them too. 'There really is going to be a war. Those look like the Anderson shelters I was reading about.'

Elsie shook her head. 'God help us all,' she muttered. 'I don't even want to think about it.'

'That's as maybe. But things are really hotting up,' Arnold said. 'C'mon, I'd better get you home,' and he insisted on seeing her to the front door.

As they rounded the corner into Back Gas Street, Elsie stopped, not wanting him to see the actual house.

'Bit of a step down from Coronation Street, eh?' She felt she had to make some comment.

Arnold clasped her by the arms and lowered his head so he could look her in the face. 'Makes no difference to me,' he said. 'It's what you do next that counts.'

Then his tone changed and he laughed as he said, 'I reckon it's time you met my mother.'

Elsie crinkled her forehead. 'Any special reason?' she asked, taken aback by the change of subject.

Arnold nodded. 'Yes, there is. But I'm going to keep that a secret. It won't be owt bad. In fact, I think you'll like it when you find out what it is. You'll just have to wait and see . . . '

Chapter 21

Amy Tanner lived in a small village close to Weatherfield and Arnold said a trolley bus would drop them right outside her house. Elsie was nervous on the evening they'd arranged to go. She'd agreed to meet up with him at the Rovers Return first.

'Are you going to tell me what this is all about?' Elsie asked him as they sat together on the bus.

'Yes, I will. But as I say, you'll like me mam, so there's no reason to get in a lather about it.'

'What's all the mystery then?'

'No mystery. Not now. In fact, the whole world will know all about it very soon. For you, my dear, are going to have your hair done.'

Elsie's hand flew up to her head. She felt along the edges of her uneven fringe and, as if to protect the curling strands that were straddling her shoulders, she began to wind them round her fingers. 'What exactly do you mean by "done"?'

'Don't look so scared. I thought you'd be pleased. My mother is a hairdresser. It's what she does for a living.'

Elsie stared at him. 'You mean she has a shop?' She had never been in one in her life, though she had seen plenty of hairdressers' shops in town.

'No. She couldn't afford to set up a shop close enough to home. So women come to the house. There's a bathroom upstairs and that's where she does their hair. She washes and sets and cuts and perms and whatever else women like to have done to their hair.' He waved his arms vaguely in the air.

Now Elsie giggled with relief. 'And she wants to have a go at mine?'

He nodded. 'That's the idea.'

'You told her what it's like?'

'I did indeed.'

'But I don't want any of that . . .' She was thinking of the dreadful smell and the humiliation whenever her mother had rubbed paraffin into her hair to kill off the lice. 'Besides, I can't afford it,' she said, frowning. She'd heard all sorts of stories about trips to the hairdresser's from the girls at the factory, and as a result she had a good idea what these things cost.

'Oh, forget about paying,' Arnold said. 'It's my treat.'

'But you can't . . . ' Elsie began.

'I'm not just doing it for you. I like my girls to look good.'

Elsie bristled. 'What are you trying to say?'

'Come off it. You're a looker, Elsie, but you're a bit shabby. Take what's on offer and don't grumble, that would be my advice.'

Elsie looked down at herself. He was right. She felt deflated.

'When's your birthday?' he asked, more kindly now.

'It's coming up soon – in March.'

'Good, an early birthday present then,' he said.

'But you can't do that for me,' Elsie protested, momentarily overwhelmed by the gesture.

'Why not?'

'Because it's too much. It's . . . ' She thought she was going to cry.

'Let me worry about that. She's my mother.' He laughed. 'She won't overcharge me. She wouldn't dare.'

Elsie didn't know what to say, so she asked, 'What does she know about me?'

'She knows that you've got hair and that it's red – what else does she need to know, for crying out loud?'

Elsie wanted to know how he had referred to her. As his girlfriend? Or what? But she decided it was better not to ask.

'So what will she do to it?' she asked.

'I never hang around long enough to find out. All I know is, it's not like going to the barber.'

Elsie was learning that looking a gift horse in the

mouth got you nowhere. An early birthday present sounded like just the thing she needed, so she laughed out loud and said, 'I should hope so.'

When they arrived, Arnold introduced her simply as 'Elsie'. Mrs Tanner smiled at her but eyed her curiously. 'I'll leave you two to it,' Arnold said, and he disappeared into the front room with the evening paper while Mrs Tanner directed Elsie to the upstairs bathroom.

She settled into the chair and tipped her head forward. It felt strange having someone she didn't know wash her hair. She couldn't remember anyone else, other than her mother, touching it until Fay was old enough to join her at the pump. She closed her eyes against the soap as instructed and tried to imagine what it might look like when it was all finished. She thought she could smell paraffin at one point, but Mrs Tanner didn't speak much and Elsie didn't ask. She felt her hair being wrapped in a towel and she followed Mrs Tanner back to the bedroom that served as the salon, feeling strangely vulnerable with her wet hair clinging to her head.

Elsie asked her tentatively, 'What exactly do you plan to do?'

'No need to look so worried, my love,' Mrs Tanner assured her. 'Now that I've washed it and got it really clean I'll cut and style it properly and maybe put in some marcel waves. I'll need to see how it falls naturally. Then once it's set, I'll pop you under the dryer for a bit. That sound all right?'

Elsie nodded.

As Amy Tanner worked on her hair, she asked Elsie lots of questions. Elsie, despite her natural defensiveness, found herself opening up to Mrs Tanner, telling her all about Back Gas Street and her big, chaotic family. She told her all about Stan and about losing her job at the pub. She wouldn't have believed she had so much to say.

All the while, Mrs Tanner listened patiently, gently encouraging Elsie to reveal more about herself than she was used to doing, making encouraging noises and looking at her now and again with kind and curious eyes.

There was no mirror on any of the walls so she had nothing to look at while her hair was being 'done'. Elsie closed her eyes tightly as she saw the sharp scissors coming her way and could only feel the cold metal against her forehead as Mrs Tanner began to tackle her fringe. Then she sat as calmly as she could, listening to the snip, snip as the scissors roamed her head, feeling the tug of a complete stranger trying to disentangle her curls. She had no idea what the woman was doing, she could only hope that she wouldn't turn her into a freak.

Afterwards, when she saw the great chunks of hair on the sheet that had been spread under her chair, she gulped nervously. Mrs Tanner was busy brushing and running her fingers through whatever was left. Then Elsie felt the clamp of the metal teeth of the marcel wave clips. She had seen these fierce-looking tools at

Aggie's, but had never used them on her own head. She couldn't wait to tell her friend about this, and the girls she worked with at the factory. But what if she didn't like the end result? She might end up having to cover her head with a headscarf until it grew back into its familiar tangled mess.

She didn't enjoy sitting under the dryer with the metal clips burning hot against her scalp, but she didn't feel she was in a position to complain when the woman was doing her a favour. At least, she hoped that was the case. Elsie wouldn't know whether it was a favour or not until she saw the end result.

When the drying ordeal was over and she had suffered more brushing and more tugging, her head certainly felt lighter and she shook it from side to side, amazed at how her hair sprang back and forth with every twist. Mrs Tanner had been watching her, but now she busied herself rolling up the cut hair into the sheet. When Elsie stood up, she stared admiringly at her new creation, touching it lightly, letting the straightened edges bounce against her hands.

'A lot of the women I serve would give their eye teeth to have hair like yours. And they spend good money getting a colour as rich as this,' Mrs Tanner said. It was the first time anyone had complimented Elsie on something she was born with.

Finally, she brought Elsie a small hand mirror so that she might see for herself. Almost afraid to look, she took a moment before she opened her eyes. But what she saw was truly amazing and she looked round, wondering where the old Elsie had gone.

'Is that really me?' She touched the image. 'Arnold said I'd look different, and I really do, don't I?' Now she really did look like Maureen O'Hara.

'Aye, you do, lass – and a whole lot better, if you don't mind my saying. What do you think to it, love? Do you like it?'

'I think it's . . . it's lovely,' Elsie said.

'Then no doubt his nibs will think so too.'

'Do you really think Arnold will like it.'

'He bloody well will. And with good reason, too. He's very particular about the girls he steps out with,' Amy said.

Elsie was startled. 'Stepping out with'; was that what he had told his mother?

'You know,' Mrs Tanner said, 'you've got really nice skin, considering . . . ' She didn't finish the sentence as she hurried away to the room next door. She came back with a little white pot of Pond's cold cream. 'Here, why don't you finish this out. It'll make your skin feel nice. And I've got an old lipstick somewhere.' She rummaged on the table in the corner and produced a couple of red lipsticks in metal cases. 'You can have these. They were odd samples. There's not a lot left in them, but they'll help to brighten up your face a bit. There's a spot of rouge in that little pot as well. Happen you could rub some into your cheeks. Give them a touch of colour too. It'll help to show off your best bits. You've got very pretty eyes, I'm sorry I don't have any kohl.'

Elsie couldn't believe the woman's generosity and friendliness. When she thought of all the fuss she'd had, trying to get some make-up from Woolworth's. No one had ever been this nice to Elsie in her entire life and she couldn't work out why. She said as much to Mrs Tanner.

'I can't thank you enough, but why would you do all this for me?'

'You know, Elsie, my life wasn't always as it looks now. I come from a place just like Back Gas Street – not very far from it, in fact. It was a slum then, just like yours is a slum now, and I was lucky to meet a good fella, my husband Wally.' Amy Tanner's eyes flitted to a photograph on the dresser. Elsie saw a younger version of Amy linking arms with a man. She presumed it was Arnold's parents on their wedding day. In the photograph, Wally had a look of Arnold about him, but he was thinner with kindly eyes and was smiling fit to burst. Amy followed Elsie's eyes and smiled tenderly at the picture. 'He looks right proud, doesn't he! Always says I made him the happiest fella in the world that day. My Wally is a chimney sweep, like his own father — that's where is is now and he'll come back covered in soot as always, but he'll come into the house through the back door, wash himself at the sink and won't step over the threshold of the parlour until he's scrubbed clean. That's the sort of man he is. His mother was a hairdresser and she taught me. Since then, even when things have been tight, we've done all right, the three of us.'

Elsie found it hard to believe Amy Tanner could ever have come from somewhere like Back Gas Street, she seemed so refined and elegant.

'Everyone needs a bit of help in life and if I can help someone, then I will. I like you, Elsie. Arnold is a handful and he can wrap me around his little finger, like most sons can their mothers and his father thinks he's the bee's knees too, but there's something about you, love. You might just have what it takes to make a real man of him – if anyone can.'

Elsie was touched by the woman's generosity. When she was finished, she found Arnold downstairs waiting to take her home. His face lit up when she entered the room.

'What do you think, son?' Mrs Tanner was close behind. 'Isn't she lovely?'

'Bloody 'ell, Mam,' he said. 'You've done me proud there. Thanks.'

Elsie couldn't believe her ears.

'You're a right smasher,' Arnold said. 'Do you know that?' He planted a wet kiss on her lips. 'Now I've got to take you to meet Joe.'

Elsie looked puzzled.

'I told you I'm living in his flat near Coronation Street till the house is sorted and bloody hell I want to show him what a knockout you are.'

'And you can come back here any time,' Mrs Tanner cut in, bundling him out of the way so she could link her arm through Elsie's. 'If I'm not busy, I'll see if I can squeeze you in. I'm sure Mr Tanner would love to meet you too.' She gave Elsie a wink. 'I can always send the bill to him,' she added, jerking her head in Arnold's direction.

'Thanks so much.' Elsie clasped the old woman's hand.

'My pleasure. And Arnold's too, if the look on his face is anything to go by,' she cackled. 'Oh, but hang on a minute—'

She disappeared upstairs and returned a moment later with a cotton dress over her arm. 'I nearly forgot. I meant to give you this. It's an old thing I don't wear any more. But it might just do you.' She held it up against Elsie.

'I've no use for it no more,' she said. The flowered print was pretty – green with lots of flowers – even if the style was a bit old-fashioned.

'I don't know how handy you are with a needle, but I thought maybe you could do something with it,' the old woman said.

Elsie looked at it and grinned. As it was now, the style was too old for her and the dress was far too big, but she knew Aggie could soon fix that.

Chapter 22

They took the same trolley bus on the way back and Elsie kept catching sight of herself in the window. Each time she saw her reflection, she couldn't help smiling and touching her hair. She'd also given her face a bit of colour with the make-up Mrs Tanner had kindly given her, and she had to remind herself she didn't have to keep biting her lips to turn them pink.

'Feel different?' Arnold asked her.

She nodded. 'Completely. I never would have thought it possible.' And she looked down at the brown paper bag in her lap wondering how quickly Aggie might be able to get on and sort out her new dress.

The flat where Arnold was temporarily living was in a block much taller than any Elsie had ever seen before. The building was five floors high and Joe's flat was at the top. Arnold pressed a buzzer to warn Joe they were on their way and they walked up the stone steps to the fifth floor. Joe greeted them at the door with a beer in each hand and he thrust one at Arnold as he took a swig from the other.

'Here you are, pal,' he said. 'I've been keeping it warm.' He looked as though he had been drinking all night and the childlike chuckle and the slurred greeting confirmed that. They followed Joe into the living room where a haze of cigarette smoke seemed to hang in the air. There were several ashtrays overflowing on to a large Bakelite tray that rested on a rickety stand, but the windows were tightly shut and there was nowhere for the fug or the stale tar smell to go. Some chipped plates and cups that had obviously been there a while added to the chaos. Joe looked as though he wouldn't be able to stand up much longer and he sat down quickly on the badly stained couch. He patted the cushion beside him for Elsie to sit down too. But it had lost most of its stuffing and didn't look very inviting. He seemed to be having trouble focusing his eyes as he looked her up and down and he complimented her on her hair like he had been rehearsing the words all day.

Not that it would have mattered to her if he had. She still felt a thrill. She never tired of hearing such praise. She picked up a framed photograph from where it was standing on a small cupboard and used it as a mirror. The picture was of a woman about the same age as Amy Tanner and she would have guessed it was Joe's mother. But she didn't look long at the photograph for it was her own reflection in the glass that smiled back at her. Elsie felt a rush of happiness and gratitude to Arnold. He might be rough and ready, but no other man had ever put this effort in on her behalf.

Elsie wasn't stupid, though. She knew that a man like Arnold wasn't doing this for purely selfless reasons; no doubt she'd be expected to repay him at some point – in a way that suited him – but that thought didn't trouble her like it would most girls of her age.

'Sorry,' she said, putting the picture frame down. 'I'm still getting used to my new hair.' She was embarrassed and felt the need to explain, not realizing Joe was not listening and Arnold was no longer in the room.

It was a large room with only a few pieces of furniture but they were over-sized and made of such heavy wood that the table, chairs and sideboard seemed to fill the entire space. The cabbage roses on the wallpaper made the walls look crowded too, so that the room seemed smaller than it was. There was a gas fire in the only wall that wasn't broken up by windows, doors or furniture, but it was not lit.

When Arnold came in from the kitchen he was carrying another bottle of beer. 'Where's your manners then?' He kicked Joe's foot hard as he spoke and handed the beer to Elsie. 'Here, get this down you,' he said. 'Sorry my so-called pal there didn't think to offer you one. But if the empties in the kitchen are owt to go by, he's been on a bender all night.' He made a tutting sound. 'It's no wonder he's already looking the worse for wear.'

When Joe's bottle slipped on to the floor and the remaining beer trickled out on to the carpet, Arnold stood up. 'Enough. Time for you to go to bed, my lad,' and he roughly shook his friend awake. Joe came to with a start.

'What's up?'

'What's up is that it's past your bedtime, chum,' Arnold said.

'Oh, OK. Thanks.' Joe got up and tottered uncertainly towards what Elsie assumed was his bedroom.

'That's better,' Arnold said, reaching his arms up to the ceiling, which he could almost touch. Then he stretched out on the couch as far as he could, though it meant that his feet hung over one end. He didn't seem to care, for he beckoned Elsie to come and join him. There was barely enough room on the narrow cushions but he encouraged her to snuggle up as close as she could. She felt the hardness of him even before he kissed her and she allowed him to guide her hand to touch it. But then his hands began fondling her breasts with such ferocity that it quite took her breath away and left her unable to move. He was exploring her mouth with his tongue in the way that she liked when suddenly he stopped and got up. Just as suddenly he pulled Elsie to her feet.

'We'd be far more comfortable in my bed,' he said

huskily. He pulled her down a short corridor past the rumbling and whistling noises coming from Joe's room to what was obviously his bedroom and he shut the door behind them. Of course, Elsie thought as he wrapped his arms round her and then began to fumble under her skirt, this is the bit where I pay for that haircut.

And with that thought firmly planted, even when he lay heavily on top of her and began to handle her much more roughly, she didn't even try to resist. Stan had always said that he'd been careful when they were making love, though Elsie wasn't entirely sure where the careful bit came in. Arnold certainly knew how to please her in all of the right places and she realized only afterwards that he hadn't mentioned anything about being careful at all.

With both of them gratified, she drifted off to sleep. When she woke up, it was morning. She was struggling to remember where she was and it came as a shock to realize she had been there all night. It was the first time she had stayed away from Back Gas Street a whole night without warning Fay in advance.

She doubted that anyone would really notice but if her father was on the warpath then he'd use any excuse to give her hell.

Fay would have missed her if no one else did and hopefully would have covered for her, but Elsie knew she needed to get home to let her sister know she was all right.

She had been sleeping on her side in the narrow bed. That was all there was room for as Arnold was lying flat on his back. He was still sleeping and she didn't want to wake him, but she had to clock in at a set time at the factory in order to start work. She tried to slip out of bed unnoticed but as soon as she moved she heard him grunt.

'What? Eh?' he muttered, and she knew it was too late. She wanted to laugh at his nakedness, his willy all soft and floppy. Elsie thought he looked quite vulnerable for once and felt a surge of affection. It wasn't like she'd felt with Stan, but it was good enough. Her neck felt bare and when she put her hand up she remembered what had happened to her hair. But the joy and excitement of yesterday seemed to have been blown away on the wind. She had told no one of her meetings with Arnold and now she was worried about how she was going to explain the sudden change in her appearance. No one would believe a hairdresser had done it for free. The first people she'd have to face would be the girls at the factory, though she could hide it from them underneath her headscarf. Then again, if she didn't get a move on, her hair would be the least of her worries for she was going to be late.

Chapter 23

Fay was concerned when Elsie didn't come home, she had never stayed out all night without telling her before. No matter how late it had been when she was going out with Stan, she always came home at some point so that she could get the children off to school in the morning. When Fay thought about it, Elsie had been rather secretive of late. It hurt to think her sister might have a new boyfriend that she hadn't told her anything about. Surely Elsie knew she could trust her? Her big sister always confided in her, but if she had taken up with somebody new, for some reason this time Elsie had not said a thing.

Fay couldn't share her worries with any of her other sisters, they were far too young to understand, but her main concern was that everything was all right and

Elsie was safe. Anything else was unthinkable. She had to believe that at the age of nearly sixteen Elsie was able to look after herself. Hadn't she been doing so already for many years?

The problem was keeping Elsie's absence from her father. The fact was, she was probably safer out on the streets than she was at home. Fortunately, last night he had come in even more drunk than usual and had fallen into a deep sleep as soon as he'd undressed and got into bed. Fay thought it would be straightforward to cover for Elsie's morning chores. Her mother, of course, would say nothing even if she noticed Elsie wasn't there. And the younger girls knew better than to comment.

Jack was the one who was liable to get Elsie into trouble without even realizing it, because he was too young to know any better. Most mornings he nagged for his eldest sister to look after him and it wasn't always easy to fob him off. Fay knew she would have to think of some story today that would keep him happy so that he wouldn't keep asking for Elsie in front of their father.

If she was honest, Fay was put out at having to stay behind to cover Elsie's chores. Recently, things had changed in her life too, and she didn't have as much time as she once did to do her sister's jobs as well as her own. Thankfully the weather was a little warmer now so it was easier to get through all the tasks first thing, and when she felt really pushed she could rope in Iris and Nancy – who at ten and eight years of age were old enough to help out more, even if they didn't like it. She would have asked Phyllis too, had she not gone missing. But Freda and the other little ones were still too young.

Things had changed for Fay after Harry had left. Not that she was sorry he had disappeared, never to be seen by anyone in the family again. She never could forgive him for stealing Elsie's money. But it had taken her a while to get over her infatuation with a man she had once thought might save her from her doleful life. She, as well as Elsie, had taken a beating from her father over it, as he believed they were both responsible for scaring away a foolproof source of income. But worse than that, it had spoiled her once-rosy view of men and as a result she was no longer interested in finding a boyfriend. Thanks to Harry, she felt she could never trust a man again.

The only good thing he'd done was to suggest a way she could raise enough money to go to secretarial college. Having taken his advice to heart and acted upon it, she'd been hired as a cleaner in the college. It meant she had to start work while most people were still asleep, then creep back home for a few hours' sleep so she could be ready for the free classes she had earned. That had all worked very well at first, and Fay had been very excited to find she was finally able to fulfil her dream. But when she had to start covering for Elsie more and more, it became impossible to keep up with her cleaning job. Even though she was being paid with lessons rather than in cash, she knew they were growing impatient with her at this new unreliability.

She had told Elsie, but her sister seemed to have so many problems of her own she had either forgotten or chosen to ignore the warning. Fay was upset. She was sure Elsie didn't mean to be so heartless. She would have to talk to her again. In the meantime she would cover for her today and give the cleaning job a miss. She still had enough credit in the lessons' bank for another week's worth of classes and now she had the hang of the thing she could at least continue to practise her shorthand on her own.

After her typing class that morning she was gazing at the noticeboard where opportunities for certificated students were advertised. There was a whole array of jobs, exactly as the college had promised would be available once she had passed all the examinations. She looked with longing at the kinds of places she might work. In the top corner of the board was a handwritten notice, 'Cafeteria waitress wanted. To work lunch and coffee breaks only.' Fay couldn't believe her luck and she hurried along to the administrator's office to present her case.

The college manager and the chief course tutor were deep in conversation when she arrived and a look passed between them when she explained why she had come. 'Unfortunately, I wouldn't be able to keep the cleaning job going as well,' she apologized, 'but the hours for this job would suit me much better.'

The manager pulled out her file from the metal cabinet behind her and shook her head as she began to read. She passed it to the tutor.

'Tell me, Miss Grimshaw,' the manager said, staring at Fay over the top of her half-moon glasses, 'Why should we give you such a demanding job when you have proved to be so unreliable as a cleaner?'

Fay was ready for this, for she had thought about it on her way to the office and had decided to be honest. 'Because at lunch and coffee break times I won't have to cover for my sister at home.' She hoped she wouldn't have to explain any further. The two behind the desk looked at each other and raised their eyebrows.

'I cannot pretend this will be an easier job,' the tutor said, 'on top of all your classwork and homework. And I hope you realize the difficulties you will face when everyone in the college requires lunch and breaks at the same time.'

'I'm not afraid of hard work.' Fay lifted her head proudly and looked directly at the tutor. 'It was only the timing that was the problem.' Then she softened her gaze. 'But please, it would mean so much to me to be able to finish this course.'

'Hm,' the tutor said, leafing through the file. 'You have been keeping up with both your shorthand and your typing speeds. And I see you have been doing some bookkeeping as well.' She looked at the manager and nodded.

'Very well,' the manager said, 'we will give you a

month's trial. We can see how hard you work when you are here, but I warn you: if your work or time-keeping are not satisfactory, then your lessons and the job will have to terminate at the same time.'

Fay wanted to hug and kiss them both but she made do with thanking them sincerely for their time, then she bobbed a curtsy and ran from the room to her next class.

After college that day, Fay, still anxious about Elsie, went to the factory in the hope of seeing her sister there. If she had gone from wherever she'd spent the night straight to work, she should be finished for the day about now. Sure enough, soon after the hooter sounded and everyone rushed to be first out of the gate, to her relief she saw Elsie among the crowd, looking as jolly and bouncy as ever. Fay ran up to her sister and they hugged and linked arms before setting off down the road.

'Did the old bugger notice?' was Elsie's first question, and Fay was able to assure her that he hadn't.

'But where were you, Else? I need to know. We've got to talk about this because I can't keep—' She stopped talking because Elsie had whipped off her headscarf.

Fay's jaw dropped. 'Good God,' she said. It took her a few moments to recover from her astonishment and then she demanded a full explanation.

'Promise on your life you won't tell a soul,' Elsie said. Fay took hold of her sister's hand. 'Cross my heart and hope to die,' she said solemnly. Elsie began to tell her about Arnold, but she couldn't help interrupting.

'Where did you meet him? What's he like?' Fay couldn't ask her questions fast enough. Eventually, Elsie told her everything. Everything except the most intimate details. On those she refused to be drawn.

'Do you like him? Do you love him? Does he love you?' Fay was still full of questions.

Elsie laughed. 'Not sure how to answer any of those.'

Then another thought struck Fay. 'Do you think he might marry you?'

'I don't know,' Elsie answered honestly. 'I know he likes me. He must do, to spend so much money on me. The thing is, he's hoping to move soon, into Coronation Street.'

'Wow!' Fay was impressed. 'On his own?'

Elsie shrugged. 'Much too early to say.'

They had come to the end of the Back Gas Street terrace and they both instinctively stopped.

'I would put your scarf back on.' Fay suddenly felt anxious. 'You can say you've got earache or something, otherwise the old man won't let it rest.'

Elsie agreed, flattening her curls as she tied the woollen scarf over her hair once more. She sighed. 'You know, Fay, I've got to get out of this place. I'm almost sixteen now and I can't be living with that vicious old bugger much longer. You've got to help me. Then I can help you.'

Fay bit her lip. She wanted to go as much as Elsie

did, she was sure, but she understood that as the eldest Elsie had a right to go first.

'Do you think this Arnold could be the one to help you do that?' she asked.

'I don't know yet. But if I play my cards right, he could be.'

'What does that mean? What do you have to do?' Fay was curious.

'Not sure yet. It's risky, so I don't want to say anything I might regret.'

'You can trust me, Else. You know that,' Fay pleaded, not wanting to be left out of her sister's plans.

'I know. It's not that.' Elsie put her hand up to Fay's cheek and for a moment Fay wanted to cry. 'It's just that, if you know too much, the old man could beat it out of you, so I won't tell you for now – but I promise you'll be the first one I tell.'

'Are you going to be seeing him again?' Fay said.

'Oh yes.' Elsie's eyes brightened. 'Oh, and by the way, he says he can help us find Phyllis.'

Fay perked up at that. 'Do you think he really can do that? It would be wonderful if he could. How will he do it?'

'He wouldn't say, but I think he has lots of contacts who might be able to find out. It's been keeping me awake at night, worrying what's happened to her. There's nothing worse than not knowing.'

'I suppose she wouldn't really want to come home, would she?' Fay felt saddened again.

'True, but it must be safer than stopping out on the streets, mixing with who knows what sort of people and putting herself in danger,' Elsie said. 'I know we both envy her a bit being smart enough to get out before we did, but she's still just a kid.'

At that, Fay smiled. 'I know. And I would like to see her again. Is that selfish of me?'

Elsie gave her quick hug. 'Nah. It's just being Fay-like.' And they both laughed.

They had reached their front door and Elsie took Fay by the shoulders. 'Listen, about the other thing. I will try to come home most nights, but you must understand it isn't always possible. You know, one thing follows another and it's easy to get carried away.'

Fay didn't know about any of those things beyond feeling warm butterflies in her stomach. But she didn't want to tell Elsie that.

Chapter 24

It wasn't difficult for Arnold to guess where Elsie's sister Phyllis might be, for there was only one place that all the young kids from around the Weatherfield area gravitated to when they ran away from home, and that was under the arches at Manchester's Exchange station.

The station was close to the River Irwell, where some of them ended their sorry lives, no one ever being able to say exactly how or why. As for the rest, they tried to keep going as best they could. They'd sleep on old sacks and light fires to try and keep warm. They'd forage for food and generally do whatever they had to in order to stay alive. The boys could earn a few bob's worth of crusts running errands, and taking and fetching messages, but the girls tended to be taken under a questionably kind man's wing and shown how to earn some 'easy money', though most of it would end up in their so-called benefactor's pocket and the poor girls would be ruined, often stuck in a life on the game. Arnold had never liked to use pimps, but he knew others in Wormold's gang who threw an odd coin or two their way. So it was easy enough for him to put the word out that he was searching for a redhead about thirteen years old, though he pretended it was on behalf of a mate. It didn't take long before he received a report of one such lass living the rough life down there. He didn't say anything to Elsie but decided to go and see for himself.

As soon as he saw her, he had no doubt it was Phyllis. She was the spitting image of Elsie, before she'd had her hair cleaned up. But the moment she clapped eyes on him and realized he was looking for her, she tried to run away. Fortunately, it didn't take him long to catch her and he held on to her bony wrist so she couldn't escape.

'What do you want, mister?' she asked, trying to wriggle free of his grasp. 'I ain't done owt. Get your hands off me!'

'I'm not taking you anywhere, don't worry,' Arnold said. He wondered why her parents hadn't tried to find her. He'd met some callous people in his time and was a hard bugger himself, but even he was shocked at just how neglectful the Grimshaws were of their children. 'I just want to know your name. That's all. I'm not here to hurt you.'

'Why are you here then?' She peered at him curiously.

'I told you. Now, how about you tell me what I want to know. What's your name?'

'What would you like it to be?' She lifted her head in defiance. She certainly had Elsie's spirit.

'How about . . . ' Arnold hesitated. 'How about, Phyllis?' he said.

She laughed. 'That's a daft name. My name's Mattie.'

'Well, Mattie, I've got a message for you. It's from your big sister Elsie.'

He saw her eyes flicker for a moment when he said Elsie's name, but then she looked away.

'I 'aven't got a big sister,' she mumbled as she tried again to shake her hand free.

'She's worried about you,' Arnold persisted, as if she hadn't spoken.

She looked at him out of the corner of her eye.

'She'd like you to go home.'

'I'm not going anywhere,' the girl insisted. 'Let me go or I'll tell Rogers about you.'

Arnold stood up when she said that. Rogers was the leader of a rival local gang and he didn't think Mr Wormold would thank him for causing trouble over the likes of the young scruffian he had here.

'Fair enough,' he said. 'But I'll tell Elsie I've seen you. You're lucky someone gives a monkey's about you – it was her that sent me looking.'

'You can tell her what you like,' the young girl whispered. She rubbed her wrist as he let her go and

239

then ran off into the dark recess underneath one of the arches.

Elsie had taken to seeing Arnold most evenings after she had seen to the family's needs. She would go to Joe's flat, where he was usually ready and waiting for her. They didn't see much of Joe as he was generally out drinking, so she and Arnold had the place to themselves. They had fallen into a pattern which Elsie had no objections to, though she tried not to stay the whole night. It caused less trouble that way at home.

Another reason she loved to be with Arnold was all the titbits of food he seemed to collect, despite all the scaremongering about shortages. The threat of war was definitely hotting up and although no one could be certain yet what was going to happen, there was talk of men having to sign up for a conscription register. Arnold was convinced he would have to undertake some basic training courses too. Officially, no food was rationed, but chocolate, fruits, like bananas and oranges, even sugar began to disappear from the grocers' shelves. Elsie had never had enough money for such luxuries anyway but since she'd met Arnold he had given her lots of little extras that she was able to take home. Even now, he always managed to find things she knew were no longer in the shops.

One night they were lying together on the couch listening to the latest news on Arnold's radio about

Hitler's march into Europe. He suddenly sat up and switched the radio off.

'Never mind all that bloody doom and gloom,' he said. 'I've got something better to tell you.' He tickled her playfully as he said, 'Although you lost your bet, I'm afraid.'

'Gerroff.' Elsie tried to fend him off. 'So what was that?' She didn't remember placing a bet. 'Good news, I hope?' She was in a good mood because she'd managed to avoid her father for several days now.

'I think I may have found your sister Phyllis.' Arnold waited for her reaction.

Elsie's face lit up immediately. 'Where is she? How is she? What's she up to?'

'It's all pretty much as you might expect for a runaway, given that she's living under the arches at Exchange Station.'

Elsie's face fell. 'Are you sure it was her?'

Arnold laughed. 'With hair like that? It's a dead giveaway. Besides, she looks exactly like you.'

'Did she say her name was Phyllis?'

'No, she's bright enough to have changed her name. Said she was called Mattie. But I didn't believe her and I'm sure she knew that.'

'So what happened? What did she say? Why didn't you bring her home with you?' Elsie was eager for information.

'She made it quite clear she wasn't going anywhere. I'm afraid you're wasting your time fretting about her.'

'Maybe I should have gone too.' Elsie suddenly jumped up and pulled at Arnold's arm. 'We could go down there now. I'll come with you. I can talk to her. I'm sure I could persuade her to come home.'

Arnold gave her a look which told her the subject was at an end. 'Look, love, I bet even if you went down there right this minute you wouldn't find her. She'd be long gone. Believe me, she doesn't want to be found. C'mon, enough bleating about that little ragamuffin, she'll be all right, she's in with the Rogers gang.'

Tears trickled down Elsie's face when he said that, for she knew he was right.

'Anyway, I fancy a bit of slap and tickle after I've been tramping round Weatherfield all day. Stop thinking about her and come and look after me instead.' He roughly pushed her towards the bedroom. Elsie went, somewhat reluctantly for once. She felt sad that one so young should be lost to the family. But she knew Arnold was right and there was nothing she could do. All that she could hope was that Phyllis would remain safe. Young as she was, Elsie would have to leave her to live her own life in her own way.

Chapter 25

Fay found working as a waitress was very hard on the feet and required different skills from sitting at a typewriter or taking down dictation. As the tutor had warned her, everyone wanted to be served at once and she spent her shift rushing back and forth trying to remember any orders she hadn't had time to write down. There was little opportunity for her to find food for herself and by the end of the day she felt too tired to carry on with the homework they were given by each class tutor. Somehow she did find the energy though and she continued her studies at home taking special care of the second-hand workbook she had managed to buy from the tips she made. It was harder when Elsie wasn't there, but as soon as she had finished with tea and before the younger girls went to bed, she found some time to hide herself in the bedroom to practise her shorthand and swat up on what she had been told she would need to know for the examinations. She was determined to pass all her courses first attempt, without having to fit in extra sessions.

When she was finally presented with her full secretarial certificate there was no happier student than Fay Grimshaw and she invited Elsie to join her at the little presentation ceremony they held at the college.

'I'm so thrilled for you, Sis!' Elsie hugged Fay hard.

'Now we'll both be able to get out of Back Gas Street,' Fay whispered in her sister's ear. At this, both girls had tears in their eyes.

'What will you do about getting a job?' Elsie wanted to know.

'That shouldn't be too difficult,' Fay said. 'Here, let me show you.' Taking Elsie's hand, she led her to the noticeboard outside the manager's office. The manager was just returning from the hall where the ceremony had been held.

'Ah, Miss Grimshaw!' she accosted Fay. 'I see you managed to juggle it all in the end, well done.'

'Thank you, Miss Shepherd.' Fay bobbed a curtsy. 'And thank you for giving me the opportunity.'

Miss Shepherd looked at Elsie, who stared back at her, unblinking.

'I'm her sister,' Elsie said.

'You should be proud of her.' The manager nodded towards Fay.

'Oh, but I am,' Elsie said and beamed.

'I think you should find something there to suit you.' Miss Shepherd glanced at the noticeboard. 'I would actually recommend this one.' She pointed to a job that was being advertised in a solicitors' office in Manchester.

'Really?' Fay was astonished the woman seemed to be taking such a personal interest.

'Yes, really.' The manager gave a little smile. 'And I should be delighted to write a reference for you.'

Fay opened her mouth to say thank you but Miss Shepherd had already swept into her office and shut the door.

'Gosh, I don't know how she knows this one would suit me,' Fay said, reading the notice carefully. 'Only problem is, it means travelling into the centre of town every day.'

'You'd have to take the tram.' Elsie shrugged. 'It still might be worth it. Depends what wages they're offering.'

'It doesn't say. I've got enough money for the tram to get me to the interview, so maybe I should apply and see what I make of it.'

'Definitely,' Elsie said.

'That's decided then: I'll write to them,' Fay said, and she linked Elsie's arm and gave it a squeeze as the two set off, delighted with the day's work.

The tram dropped Fay in the centre of town and from there it was a short walk across the square and into the arcade. The offices were on the third floor; after listening to the clanging metal of the iron lift gates, Fay decided to walk up the stone staircase. The name Talbot and Jones was printed in black lettering on the frosted glass of the door. Fay knocked timidly, unsure what to do. She thought she heard a reedy voice call, 'Come in,' so she turned the handle and poked her head inside the room.

A woman about the age of Miss Shepherd was sitting behind a large wooden desk. The thin voice didn't match the sturdiness of her features. The nameplate that stood in front of the blotter said Miss Turner.

'Miss Grimshaw?' she queried.

'Yes,' said Fay. 'I hope I'm not late.'

'Mr Talbot asked for you to be shown in straight away.'

She pressed a button on her desk and Fay heard a faint buzzer in another room. Miss Turner opened a door behind her that was marked, 'Private' and announcing, 'Miss Grimshaw,' ushered Fay in.

She had never had an interview before so she didn't know what to expect. But she began to relax as Mr Talbot asked her questions about her skills and her certificates and she realized there was nothing she couldn't handle. But she was thrilled and amazed when he finally said that he would be pleased to offer her the job.

'Would you be available to start straight away?' he wanted to know. 'Only my previous secretary is too ill to continue.' And when Fay said yes, he stood up immediately and shook her hand.

He called in Miss Turner, who agreed to show Fay which desk would be hers.

She left Mr Talbot's office with her head spinning, unable to take in what had just happened. She had landed her first secretarial job within days of finishing at college. Now she knew she was on her way out of Back Gas Street.

There were two other desks in the large front office, set at angles to Miss Turner's desk. The empty one would be hers, and Miss Turner said she would order a nameplate as soon as she could. The other one was now occupied by a young man who Miss Turner introduced as Mr Butler, a junior clerk. He was a pleasant-looking man, not much older than Fay was and he smiled shyly at her as he extended his hand.

'Hope you'll be as happy here as I am,' he said, smiling.

Fay barely had time to hang up her jacket before a buzzer sounded on Miss Turner's desk. The receptionist hurried into Mr Talbot's room. There was the sound of raised voices, though the words were not clear. When she came back, her cheeks were scarlet. She pulled out several of her desk drawers in quick succession and looked relieved when she picked out a new shorthand pad and a stubby pencil. She thrust them both at Fay. 'Here,' she said, 'take this. Sorry there's no time to show you around, but Mr Talbot expects you to take some dictation now. He has some urgent letters that must go in the post tonight.'

Mr Butler gave a snort and hid his face behind his hand as he scurried back behind his desk. Bewildered, Fay took the notebook and pencil and hurried into Mr Talbot's office. It wasn't what she had been expecting, but she had worked too hard to fail now. She would have to show them that whatever they threw at her, she was more than capable of doing the job.

Chapter 26

Elsie didn't know whether to laugh or cry when she realized she had missed her monthly again. She had never been very regular, so when the first month went by she'd not worried. By the end of the third month she still wasn't ready to entertain the possibility that she was pregnant, even though she was sick most mornings. Sometimes Stan had used rubber johnnies but Arnold never did, just told her that he knew what he was doing. She knew enough about the birds and the bees by now to know the risks they were taking, but when Arnold was in his drink he didn't care about being careful. In fact, over the last couple of months, Elsie had seen a different side to Arnold Tanner. He could still be thoughtful on occasion but now she was 'his' he could often be brutal and harsh. Especially when he'd had a few drinks. She was learning to read his moods but the shine had definitely come off whatever feelings she'd had for him in the beginning. Now she'd missed for the third month in a row, she didn't know what to do. It was not her imagination that her waistline was beginning to expand. Let's face it, she thought, anyone as scarecrow thin as me can't really miss it when their belly suddenly begins to bulge.

So here she was, most likely up the duff, and too terrified to tell Arnold for she had no idea how he would react. When the drink had hold of him he was no better than her father. He had a mean streak and was liable to turn nasty for no particular reason, and then he would really hurt her. She'd had plenty of bruises to show for that. But she couldn't always predict what would bring out his cruel side, so she had no idea how he would take it when he found out she was pregnant. It wasn't as though he'd ever mentioned marriage or said he wanted kids of his own. When she'd talked about her brother and sisters, he'd never shown much interest, apart from going to look for Phyllis. As far as she knew, he had no siblings of his own. She, on the other hand, was used to kids. She loved them – so long as there weren't too many babies without a breathing space between.

On the plus side, Arnold was great in bed, They had fun and she enjoyed what he had to offer more than she would have thought possible. He could be kind too, like when he paid for her hair, or when he bought her things. But she had to be honest, she didn't really love him, not like she had Stan. And she was damned sure he didn't love her.

Did she really want to be trapped like her mother in a loveless marriage? Especially when she was only sixteen. Then again, could she afford to pass up the chance that pregnancy could offer her a way out of Back Gas Street? All she needed was to persuade him to do the honourable thing. She could do worse than marry Arnold, and he was after all the father of her child. Even so, she couldn't make up her mind how or when to tell him.

The person she most had to fear was her father, for she'd always known how he would take such news. The first thing he would do was throw her out. Then he'd probably set about persuading the baby's father to become a bridegroom, assuming he seemed to be unwilling. But when she thought of Arthur trying to take his belt to the six feet and however many inches there was of Arnold Tanner, a little smile crept on to her face. Arnold was built like a prizefighter, which was why he was such a valuable part of Wormold's gang. He certainly wouldn't be afraid of Arthur Grimshaw.

Knowing she couldn't put it off any longer, Elsie made her mind up to go to Arnold's flat straight from work. She didn't usually go so early, but she didn't want to go home first to sort out the children's tea, even though she knew Fay had a special evening planned with Terry Butler. It will do them no harm to fend for themselves for once, she muttered under her breath as she walked to the flat. After all, if things went as she hoped, they might have to do without her altogether very soon.

She rang the bell as she always did then trudged up the stairs to the fifth floor, pleased that she could see a light on in the flat. She found the climb harder than usual and was out of breath when Arnold opened the door. She threw herself at him in a giant hug and could tell from his face he hadn't expected such a greeting.

'How did you know I'd be here so early?' he said.

'I didn't. I took a chance, that's all. Thought I could always wait with Joe if you weren't here yet.' She threw her jacket over the armchair.

Arnold gave a laugh. 'It's Joe who's not here yet,' he said, and he disappeared into the kitchen. 'I didn't think we were meeting up tonight so I was planning on going out later on,' he shouted to her.

'That's all right,' Elsie said. 'I won't be stopping long.'

Arnold came back as usual with two beers. Elsie took a long gulp; she needed Dutch courage tonight.

Arnold sat down on the sofa. 'It's good that you've come,' he said between sips of beer. 'I've something to tell you.'

'Yes? And what's that?'

'I'll not be moving into number 9 Coronation Street after all.'

Elsie was surprised.

'Would you believe the old bugger came up with all

the rent money just as things were about to get interesting.' Arnold balled his fist as though he was sorry he had missed a fight.

'That's a shame,' Elsie said, not sure how much this might affect her.

'No, it's not,' Arnold sniggered. 'Because I shall be moving into number 11 instead!' His look was triumphant and Elsie too was pleased. At least he was definitely moving into Coronation Street, which in the long run might be a good thing for her.

'Congratulations.' She raised her bottle. 'I'll drink to that.'

'I think we both will,' Arnold said, and he clinked his beer with hers.

Arnold looked round the room and his gaze came back to rest on Elsie. 'Well, that's my news. How about you? What's the reason you're here so early?'

Elsie was trying to gather her thoughts but her stomach was flipping back and forth. Suddenly she took the plunge and said, 'I may as well tell you straight out . . . '

This is it, she told herself, now I'm committed. There's no way out now.

'What?' Arnold prompted.

Elsie took another gulp of beer then blurted out, 'I'm up the duff.'

Arnold's eyes widened and he stared alternately at her face and then her stomach. 'Are you sure? How do you know it's mine?'

'What do you mean, you rotten bugger? Of course it's yours!'

He looked at her belligerently. 'It didn't take me long to get into your knickers. How do I know you haven't been at it with anyone else?'

Elsie could tell he was goading her. 'Don't you try any of that with me, Arnold Tanner! You know bloody well this sprog is yours.'

Arnold gulped and Elsie could see the panic in his eyes. 'How can you be sure? Have you seen a doctor?'

'Of course I haven't seen a doctor, I've no money for that. Women just know and that's all there is to it.'

'But how far gone are you?'

'Three months.' She looked down and patted her swollen stomach. 'That's how I know.'

'I see.' He sank back into the couch and stared into the neck of the bottle. 'When's it due? Any idea?'

She shrugged. 'I'd be guessing around January.'

He gave a grim laugh. 'We should be well into the war by then.'

Elsie looked alarmed. 'Do you really think so?'

She felt so relieved he hadn't flown into a rage, she was almost tempted to hug him. But then she realized that he hadn't suggested they get married.

'Here, finish your drink,' he said, tipping her bottle. 'I'll fetch you another. I know I could sure do with one.' He went into the kitchen with a dazed look on his face.

Just then Elsie heard the bedroom door being pulled

open and a woman's voice shouted, 'Arnold? Arnold, are you there?'

Elsie stared as a blonde she had never seen before emerged from Arnold's bedroom. It was like being in a B film. The woman popped her head round the kitchen door and said to Arnold, 'I'm off. You seem a bit busy with other "things" right now.'

Then she glided into the living room and retrieved her coat from the back of the door. Elsie felt an uncontrollable rage rise up inside her. How could Arnold muck about with some tart, especially at a time like this? As the woman passed by, Elsie grabbed her by the shoulder. 'Oh, please don't leave without something to remember me by—' And with that she gave the woman an almighty slap across her cheek.

''Ere, who the 'ell do you think you are?' the blonde screeched. She went to slap Elsie back, but Arnold jumped in and bundled the woman out of the flat, telling her that he'd see her later.

Elsie's eyes flashed with anger. 'You rotten bastard.'

'Bastard, am I?' he shot back, and before Elsie could see it coming, he thumped her hard across her skull. 'That'll teach you to come in here throwing your weight around. No one tells me what to do, right? No one.'

Elsie clutched her head. So this was the sort of man she was going to have a child with, possibly even get saddled with forever. Now she wasn't sure if she wanted him to do the right thing by her or not – that could be the worse option.

Not trusting herself to speak, she picked up her cotton jacket that had fallen on to the floor and walked out quickly with as much dignity as she could muster.

When she got home, all the kids were out playing. Her mother was sitting at the table staring down at a cup of cold tea.

'You're late.' Alice looked up briefly. 'Or are you early? I never can tell when you're going to turn up these days. Always out gallivanting, always with some bloke or another – giving the family a bad name.'

Elsie gave a bitter laugh. 'You're kidding? It's not like we had a good name to start with.'

She drank some milk from the bottle, realized too late it was on the turn and almost retched. The moment she sat down at the table, she burst into tears, unable to contain herself any longer.

Her mother sat back in the creaking chair and looked at her intently. 'You got anything to tell me?' she asked.

'Like what?' Elsie tried her best to sound defiant.

'Like how far gone you are,' Alice said.

Elsie stopped crying as if by magic and stared at her mother.

'No point trying to lie your way out of it, Elsie. I've had too many myself not to see it on you. Surely you don't think I didn't know?'

'Three months,' Elsie said.

Her mother nodded. 'That's about what I guessed. Are you all right?'

Elsie nodded. It was the first time she could remember her mother had asked her such a question.

'Good,' was all Alice said. 'You'll need to be, for I don't know what'll happen when your father wakes up to the fact.

'He doesn't know?'

'Not yet.' Alice struggled up from the table.

'Then you won't tell him?' Elsie said.

Alice coughed her usual thick phlegmy cough. 'I won't have to, you stupid lass. It'll be there plain as plain, soon as he chooses to see.'

Chapter 27

'You don't have to worry,' Elsie yelled, 'that's the last you'll ever see of me. I can't wait to get out of this hellhole.' She could see her father reaching for his belt, but she was determined he had thrashed her for the last time. No matter what she had to do to escape, she wasn't going to let him raise a hand to her again.

She raced upstairs out of his reach and began to scrabble together her few precious bits and pieces. She blew off the dust from a small cardboard box she'd kept under the bed where she still had the chocolate bar wrapper from her first-ever present, some bits of make-up and the few coppers she'd managed to save from her wages since all her pub tips had been stolen.

Her father had spotted her condition sooner than

she had bargained for. Predictably, his first reaction had been to order her out of the house.

'You're a bloody whore and no daughter of mine, I tell you.' He swayed drunkenly as he sneered at her and pointed towards the door.

'No daughter with half a brain cell would want you for a father! You've done nowt for any of this family, just drunk away my hard-earned wages while watching us half starve. You're not a real man – a real man would take care of his kin.'

'How bloody dare you!' Arthur lunged towards her clumsily, but Elsie was too fast for him and dodged out of the way.

'You'll never lay a finger on me again. And if you do, Arnold Tanner will thrash the life out of you.'

At this, her father faltered and looked at her unsteadily. 'What's that you say?'

'That's right – you heard. You're not the only one who can use his fists, and maybe it's time you were brought down a peg or two. See how you like it when it's someone your own size – or bigger.'

'You're talking crap,' he said, but he was wary this time and his belt stayed where it was.

Looking around at the shabby, rundown house that she'd laughingly called home for one last time, Elsie now vowed to no one in particular: 'I'll not set foot inside this place again, never you mind.' Then she grabbed the dress Aggie had put together for her from Amy Tanner's cast-off and put it with the rest of her prized bits in a paper bag she'd found, tucked it under her arm and ran downstairs.

Her younger sisters were clustered at the bottom of the stairs crying.

'You can't go, Elsie! How will we manage without you?' Iris wailed.

'Where will you go?' Connie wept.

'Now Dad'll go after us,' Freda snivelled, while little Polly just howled.

Baby Jack managed to creep in between them all and tugged at Elsie's skirt, bawling and begging her not to leave him. Only Fay was missing, but Elsie knew she had gone walking with Terry Butler, the young man she'd met at the office. She hoped she was having a good time. Her father was busy searching in the cupboard for another bottle of beer and for the moment seemed to have forgotten her. Her mother was sitting in her usual spot at the table and Elsie saw she was sobbing too. 'Where will you go,' Alice wept, 'with no man to look after you?'

Elsie couldn't answer that question but still she dismissed Alice's tears. It was too late for her to be crying over her daughter's fate now. After years of neglect, Elsie had no time for her mother. It was only the children she hated to leave like this, but it had reached the point where she had no choice. Her father had made that very clear.

Besides, this was what she'd wanted, wasn't it? The only problem was, now that it had come to the crunch, she didn't know where she was going to go. She hadn't heard anything from Arnold since she had fled his flat. And if she had learned one thing from all this it was that, whatever happened next, she was on her own.

'I've told you not to fret about me, Mam,' Elsie said boldly, expressing courage she didn't really feel. 'It's time I went. I can't stay here any longer. Then she whispered, 'I'll be at Aggie's, for a short while at least. Tell Fay, will you?'

Her mother nodded. 'Take care of yourself, chuck. Best you can.'

'I'll be all right, Mam.' And as she watched her father drunkenly trying to detach his belt from his trousers, she used the opportunity to slip out of his grasp for the last time.

This is it, she thought as she pulled open the front door, but before she could step outside she felt a sharp pain in the centre of her back as her father's boot connected and she was catapulted over the front doorstep and on to the slippery cobbled street. Her hand went protectively to her stomach. That was the final straw. From this moment she knew her life would never be the same.

Anxious in case her father decided to follow her out into the street, she picked herself up as quickly as she could. But she needn't have worried, for he'd disappeared inside and there was a thud as the front door banged shut behind him.

'Not got much to show for me sixteen years, have

I?' Elsie muttered as she hastily gathered up her few belongings before they got soaked by the drizzle that had started to fall. She gave a wry smile as she patted her stomach again. 'But I soon will have.'

She pushed the items once more into the soggy paper bag, tucked it awkwardly under her arm and struggled off down the road.

Fay had settled well into working at Talbot and Jones. She had worked for Mr Talbot for a few weeks before she found out that it was his idea that the two names should appear together on the letterhead rather than one, although there was no actual Mr Jones. He thought it looked better that way. The work was extremely demanding and Mr Talbot was a difficult man to please. But to Fay, the harshness of his temper and his attention to detail in every aspect of her work did not compare to the physical beatings she'd received over the years from her father. The worst she experienced from Mr Talbot was a tongue-lashing and she usually managed to let that pass over her head.

'Don't mind him, Miss Grimshaw,' Terry Butler had consoled her the first time it had happened. 'His bark's worse than his bite.'

'I won't,' Fay assured him. 'Believe me, I've suffered far worse. A few names and cross words won't mither me.' Fay regretted speaking so openly as soon as she saw the concerned look on Mr Butler's face, so she didn't elaborate even when he asked her direct questions until thankfully he let the matter drop.

Terry Butler was a quiet, shy sort of man. Over those first few weeks, Fay had taken to having a cup of coffee and lunchtime sandwich with him. When it was just the two of them, she invited him to call her Fay and he insisted she called him Terry. But they addressed each other more formally in the office, having seen Miss Turner's disapproving frown whenever a Christian name accidentally slipped out. Fay found she enjoyed talking to him, even about such serious matters as all the killings in Europe as the Germans invaded. They talked about the effects of the impending war on Britain such as the shortages and rationing that people were already suffering, but at all costs she avoided discussing her family and home.

On the day that Elsie left home, Fay had no idea about the drama that was unfolding in Back Gas Street. She was late back, having agreed to go for a walk with Terry after work. There was a brass band playing in a nearby park and at his suggestion they strolled arm in arm around the bandstand, enjoying the music and the light summer evening. The earlier rain had cleared the air and Fay loved the smell of the newly opening flowers and the fresh-cut grass.

'We won't stay long, as I know you have chores to do at home,' Terry said. 'And I don't want to leave my mother too long on her own,' he sighed. 'Though I may soon have to, because it's a long bus journey from

Saddleworth and it really is too far for me to travel in each day. I've started looking for lodgings where I could stay during the week and go home only at the week-ends.'

Fay wished she could offer him a room. How pleasant it would be to travel in to work together each day. But remembering the chaos caused by the last lodger they had put up in Back Gas Street, she shuddered and said nothing. Besides, she was ashamed of how the Grimshaws lived and she never wanted him to see it.

'Is there just the two of you?' she ventured to ask after a moment or two's silence.

'Yes. My father had a heart attack soon after my younger sister was born. And then she died of scarlet fever when she was still a child.'

'I'm sorry to hear that,' Fay said, thinking how grateful she was that, despite the frightful conditions in which they lived, all her siblings, apart from the stillborn baby, had somehow managed to survive.

Chapter 28

Aggie Farrell lived only a few streets away from Back Gas Street but it might as well have been another town. As Elsie walked down the row of neatly fronted houses she thought how much like Coronation Street it was, and what she would give to be able to live in a house like that herself. She stopped at Aggie's front door and took a deep breath. She was soaked through, even though the rain had stopped, and she felt wretched. But she was here now so there was nothing for it but to go ahead with the first part of her plan while she thought about what to do next. She rapped at the door with the shiny brass knocker and gazed up at the house. The windowsills were freshly painted, the doorstep freshly scrubbed. Green shoots were pushing through between the cobbles beneath the window in the tiny front yard. They looked so pretty, even if they were weeds.

Elsie felt a rush of warmth hit her as the front door opened and Aggie stood in the doorway, a look of concern on her face.

'Elsie!' Aggie exclaimed. 'You're the last person I expected. What are you doing here? What on earth has happened?'

'Sorry, Aggs. It's been raining and I'm fair fit to be put through the mangle. But I didn't know where else to go.'

Aggie's brow creased.

'The old man's finally chucked me out,' Elsie said, angry that she couldn't prevent a tear escaping down her cheek.

'You don't have to apologize. Come on in, lass, and tell me all about it.' Aggie welcomed her sincerely and she stood aside to let Elsie into the narrow hallway.

'If me dad's anything, he's a man of his word.' Elsie tried to make a joke of it. 'Always one to keep his promises.'

Aggie snorted. She put her hand up to examine Elsie's face.

'Nah, no need to fret, he didn't take the belt to me this time,' Elsie said. 'Though he bloody well tried.' She put her hand to her stomach.

'He found out?' Aggie said. 'I suppose he had to.'

Elsie nodded. 'He guessed. Mam was right. I couldn't keep it hid much longer.'

'Do you need to stop here for a bit, then? Aggie asked.

Elsie looked anxiously at her friend. 'Could I? It won't be for long, I promise.'

''Course you can. With our Stella gone, there's room in my bed. I'll just tell my mam.' Then she called down the hallway: 'Mam! It's Elsie – she needs a bed for a few nights, all right?'

A faint voice mumbled from somewhere at the back of the house. Elsie couldn't make out the words but Aggie seemed to take it as approval, for she led the way down the passage and into the kitchen. Despite the warmth of the summer's day, a small fire glowed in the range. A kettle hung over the glowing coals and two flat irons were warming in the side cubbyhole.

'Thanks ever so much, Mrs Farrell,' Elsie said. 'You won't even know I'm here. And I promise it won't be for long,' she added, with a reassurance she didn't feel.

'Have you heard the news? About the war?'

Elsie looked at Mrs Farrell in confusion. 'What do you mean?'

'It been on the radio and all over the *Gazette*. The Prime Minister announced that we're at war with Germany!'

'Blimey.' With everything else that had been going on over the last few weeks, with her pregnancy and all the business with Arnold, Elsie had barely been aware of the changes that had been taking place over Weatherfield way and beyond. But she thought of them now and began to realise what it all meant. Some of the bigger houses and parks had lost their railings, big carts came in the night and removed them. Elsie swallowed, thinking about who was going to look after the little ones if there was a raid now that she wouldn't be there. *Thank God for Fay*, Elsie thought. She was sensible, unlike her feckless parents. 'What do you think will happen now?

'They say there's going to be conscription, but already some of the men at the factory are queueing to join up.'

It was so much to take in. After the many months of talk about war, it had finally arrived. All Stan's sacrifice had been for nothing.

'Anyway, what the 'ell is going on with you? Is all this because of what I've been hearing about you and young Arnold Tanner?' Mrs Farrell looked down at Elsie's waistline. 'Is that what set your dad off?'

'Depends what you've heard.' Elsie gave a rueful smile. 'It certainly didn't help. Things have never been good with him and me. He never thought I was up to much. So whatever I did, he was not best pleased.'

'I heard that you and Arnold Tanner have been stepping out. Word gets round these parts, you should know that by now.'

'Bit more than stepping out, I'd say,' Aggie put in. 'More like regular courting, eh, Else, wouldn't you agree?'

Elsie nodded. 'I was beginning to think so, but you never can tell with men.'

'And now you're in the club. Is that it?' Mrs Farrell raised her eyebrows.

''Fraid so.' Elsie lowered her gaze.

'And what does young Arnold say about it?' Mrs Farrell asked.

Elsie shrugged. 'Not much.' She kept her head bent forward and refused to look at Mrs Farrell. She couldn't bring herself to tell anyone about the incident with the woman at the flat.

'I reckon someone should put a rocket behind him now you're in this condition. After all, it took two to get you this way. He needs reminding where his responsibilities lie and I've a good mind to do it myself.'

Elsie giggled, imagining the older woman doing just that. 'My dad would love to do it if ever he got hold of him, I'm right sure of that,' she said. 'But I still wouldn't want to go back home.'

'What did your mam have to say about it all?'

'Oh, you know how it is. It's not easy for her,' Elsie said defensively. Then her face clouded over and she stared into the fire. 'It's the little 'uns as I feel sorry for. With me gone, I reckon they're going to be feeling the broadside of that belt from now on.'

For a few moments nobody spoke.

'Well, you're welcome to stop here, lass, long as you need. Till Arnold comes to his senses – with or without help. And to hell with what the other neighbours think,' Mrs Farrell said.

'Have you thought what you might do if he doesn't come to his senses?' Aggie asked quietly.

Elsie hesitated. Nobody spoke. Then, 'Yes, I've

thought,' Elsie said eventually. 'But I need to wait a while, not rush in and do something I might regret.'

Fay had had a very pleasant evening and spent the journey home considering the possibility of Terry becoming her new boyfriend. He was far too serious-minded to be thought dashing or exciting, preferring to mull over everything carefully before he made any kind of move. But he was respectful and although he was not always much fun he was very kind and considerate. After Harry, Fay wasn't sure she wanted someone too exciting, though it did bother her that people like Elsie might find him dull. The important thing was, he was a steady bloke, dependable and reliable, and his looks were agreeable if not handsome. He didn't set her heart pounding like she'd read about in books, but she found him comfortable to be with. What with all the turmoil at home and the war threatening the country, she had to admit it was good to spend time with someone as calm as Terry. And amid all the talk of conscription and army training, with his poor eyesight and fallen arches it was unlikely he would be eligible for service.

Above all, she wondered whether it might be possible that Terry could be her ticket out.

As she turned into Back Gas Street she was shocked to see all her siblings swarm towards her, each one wanting to be the first to tell her what had happened to ie. And when she entered the front door she was d to hear her father muttering, 'That girl is dead to me,' and to have her mother confirm that what the children had been telling her was true: her big sister had indeed gone.

'What happened? Where is she? Fay demanded to know, her boldness bolstered by her fear for Elsie's welfare.

Her father banged his fist down on the table. 'I won't hear mention of her name in this house ever again.' But when he went off to fetch another bottle from the cupboard, her mother whispered, 'She told me to tell you she'll be stopping at her friend Aggie's for a bit. Till she sorts out what to do . . . you know what I mean.'

'What can she do?' Fay whispered back, horrified by what her mother might be implying.

Alice Grimshaw shrugged. 'Marriage isn't the only way,' she said darkly.

Fay shivered. 'You don't mean she should see one of them women – you know – the ones who'll help . . . get rid of it?

'Aye, sometimes that's the only choice left when a man leaves you high and dry. She wouldn't be the first.'

'Oh, Mam, I hope it doesn't come to that.'

'Maybe not, perhaps she'll think of something. She usually does.' And that was all her mother would say.

Elsie had decided that the one person who might be able to help her was Amy Tanner. There was always a danger that talking to his mam would be more likely to push Arnold the other way, but she didn't have a

273

lot of choices left to her. What if Arnold wouldn't do right by her? She could give the baby up for adoption, but she'd still have to go through with the pregnancy and wouldn't be able to keep it secret. There was no convenient aunt living in the country where she could sit it out till the baby was born and then palm the poor mite off to a local farmer's wife. The only other option was too horrible to contemplate. She'd heard whispers in the factory; horror stories about women who tried to get rid of their babies with knitting needles and bottles of gin – of the things that could go wrong and invariably did. Elsie was adamant this was not for her – she'd rather have the poor little bugger than run the risk of throwing both of their lives away.

This was why she found herself outside Amy Tanner's house, nervously wondering whether to knock on the door or not.

Before she could pluck up the courage, she saw Amy at the window, smiling and waving at her. Within a few moments she found herself sitting at Amy's homely kitchen table with a pot of tea in front of her.

'It's lovely to see you, Elsie. You look smashing, like you've filled out a bit – it suits you.'

'Well, that's the thing,' Elsie said awkwardly and then hesitated.

Amy looked at her quizzically over the teacup as she was pouring the hot brew, and when Elsie's hand moved to her stomach, the penny dropped.

'Oh, I see.' Amy's smile had faded, but her eyes had

the same kindness in them. 'Well, that's a pretty pickle you've both got into. Does Arnold know?'

Elsie nodded.

'And is he trying to avoid all responsibility?'

Elsie nodded again.

'This isn't an ideal beginning to a marriage, Elsie,' Amy said, 'but there have been worse ways to start 'n' all. Do you love him and does he love you?'

Elsie didn't speak but looked down at her shoes. To her surprise, Amy laughed.

'Hearts and flowers only last so long, Elsie love. There's many a marriage that doesn't start with love but can work its way up to it. The country is at war now and who knows what the future holds. No doubt both you and Arnold have got some growing up to do, but if you can put your best feet forwards then you've as much chance as any other couple.'

'Do you really think so, Mrs Tanner?' Elsie asked uncertainly.

Amy Tanner sighed. 'I'm not rightly sure, lass, but leave Arnold to me.'

The next evening, at home time, Elsie was surprised to see Arnold waiting by the factory gates. Aggie saw him first and slipped her arm out of Elsie's. 'I think it's you he wants to talk to, and you'd be better off without me there,' Aggie said, and before Elsie could say anything she disappeared into the crowd. For once Elsie felt a flutter of fear in her chest as she looked at her burly boyfriend.

'I heard your old man kicked you out.' Arnold grasped her hand and pulled her towards him, leading her in the opposite direction than they normally took.

'News certainly does travel fast,' Elsie said without looking at him.

'So where are you living now?'

'I'm stopping at Aggie's, if you must know – in Kimball Street, down by the gasworks.'

'Look,' Arnold stopped and turned to face her. 'About what happened the other day . . . '

'Go on,' Elsie said, 'I'm listening, though I really don't know why I should.'

'That girl, she's nothing to me. Just someone I bumped into in the pub. I didn't even know her name. I'd had a few, we got to talking. You know how it is.'

'No, I don't know,' Elsie said. 'Not when I thought we had something between us.' She wasn't sure how far she should push it and tried to catch a glimpse of his face. But even when she did, his eyes as usual were shielded by the brim of his hat.

'Yeah, well, I'm very fond of you, that's right. And the thing is, I've been thinking over what you said.' He suddenly put his palm flat on her belly and Elsie gave a start. Then she covered his hand with hers and held it there for a few moments.

'Poor bugger,' Arnold said, taking his hand away. 'I feel sorry for the little sod already. It's not fair on him. He didn't ask to be born. So I think we should get wed. Give the unfortunate bastard a name. What do you think?'

Elsie gasped. She couldn't think. Her heart was hammering so loudly it seemed the whole street must hear. This was exactly what she'd wanted. But now she must tread carefully so she didn't upset him. It was not the most romantic proposal she'd ever heard. But what the heck. The last thing she wanted was for him to change his mind. She was scratching around trying to think what she should say when the words popped out of her mouth before she could stop them. 'Have you been talking to your mother?' she said. Now she felt anxious, wondering if she had said the wrong thing. But to her surprise he smiled at her.

'Happen I have,' he said. 'And she says you've to go live with her and me dad until the wedding.'

Elsie couldn't believe what she was hearing, but Arnold persisted.

'What do you say then, shall we tie the knot?'

This was it. The chance she had been waiting for and Elsie wasn't going to let it pass her by.

'Yes,' she said. 'Yes, I will.' Then she giggled. 'Am I saying those words too soon?'

Arnold tilted his hat back from his face for once and he grinned as he took her arm and linked it through his.

There's no reason why we can't make a go of it, Elsie thought. He's not half bad and I'll do my best to make it work.

'The licence will probably take a few weeks,' Arnold said. 'I'll go down to the registry office tomorrow and see what's what. I'll let you know. Meantime, I'd best take you back to Kimball Street.'

He left her at the corner of the street and when Elsie walked into the house she was beaming. Aggie ran into the hallway to greet her. 'What was all that about? What happened?'

Before she could reply, Mrs Farrell called out from the kitchen: 'Don't you dare say a word. Come in here and tell us both. I take it from the sound of Aggie's voice it's summat good.'

'We're getting wed,' Elsie announced, not even attempting to keep the excitement from her voice. 'In the meantime, I'm to go and live with his mother and father.'

There was a delighted scream and a shout and both mother and daughter swamped Elsie with hugs and kisses.

'So, when is it to be, then?' Mrs Farrell said.

'As soon as the licence comes through. He's going to get us a slot at the registry office as quickly as he can. It might not be for a few weeks, but I don't care about that.' She clapped her hands in delight and did a little skip around the room. 'I'm going to get wed and I'll never have to go back to Back Gas Street. That's all I need to know.'

'I don't suppose you'll be wanting to tell your dad,' Mrs Farrell asked.

'Will you be telling your mam?' Aggie wanted to know.

'No.' Elsie was adamant. 'I shan't tell them. They'll not care. I don't want either of them at my wedding, any road. Though you two are invited.'

'Arnold's not a bad lad, despite what some folk round here think,' Mrs Farrell said.

'He can't be that bad because he's actually asked me to marry him.' Elsie laughed.

Aggie chuckled too. 'Not that it sounded very romantic.'

'Give over, what did you expect? It's Arnold Tanner we're talking about here, not Clark Gable.'

'So you think he might turn out to be all right, after all?'

'Some men can, you know,' Mrs Farrell chipped in. 'I'm glad to see he's taking his responsibilities seriously.'

'True. And guess what, as soon as we're wed I'm going to live with him in Coronation Street. He's just moved into number 11, so I won't have to live with his mother any longer than necessary. Not that I'll mind that. She's been really nice to me.'

'Maybe she'll give you some more clothes,' Aggie said. 'But make sure they don't need so much altering this time.'

'It's not just clothes you'll be wanting,' Mrs Farrell chipped in. 'You never know what else you might need. You're having her grandchild and you can't predict anything where babies are concerned.'

'True enough,' Aggie said. 'I mean, what with this blasted war, anything could happen. Arnold and the like could be called up into the army at any moment.'

'No, surely not?' Mrs Farrell sounded shocked. 'Our Johnny says it'll all be over soon.'

'That's what they said about the Great War. That it would be over by Christmas. And look what happened there,' Aggie chipped in. 'And now with that bloody creep Hitler poking his nose into everyone's business and trying to take over, there's no knowing where it'll end.'

'At least he won't be coming here – unless he can swim,' Mrs Farrell said.

'Let him try! We'll soon show him.' Elsie sounded defiant.

'Do you really think lads like Arnold and our Johnny could be called up?' Mrs Farrell asked, suddenly fearful.

Elsie laughed. 'I don't think I've anything to worry about. Arnold won't have to go into the army. Not with a baby coming. He'll be . . . what's the word?'

'Exempt?' Aggie said.

'Yes, exempt.' And Elsie dismissed the thought from her mind.

Chapter 29

By the time the wedding licence had come through and the official date of 4 October 1939 had been set, Great Britain was firmly on a war footing. But Elsie cared nothing for any of that for now. All she was concerned about was that she should be married before she got any bigger, as she was already over six months gone. Arnold had said she should buy a new dress or a suit for the wedding and had offered her some money. But Elsie had never had new clothes before, nor had she been to a wedding, and she was worried she wouldn't know what to look for that would be right for the occasion. Besides, although there was still no official rationing it was becoming more difficult to find many items in the shops.

Once again Amy Tanner came to her rescue. Not only

did she look after Elsie while they were waiting for the official date but she had one of her customers make a special wedding outfit for her. She said she had a bolt of really nice material she had been given by her husband at the time of her own wedding. So within a few weeks Elsie had a new two-piece suit of beige linen and had found a cream pair of shoes at the charity shop to go with it. Amy also gave her a pale pink blouse to wear underneath the jacket as well as a blue garter to wear with the fine pair of silk stockings that were Arnold's contribution to the affair. And on the day of the wedding Amy once again set Elsie's hair and combed it up, then helped her put make-up on her face and eyes.

'There now,' Amy said, standing back to admire her handiwork, 'that takes care of the old, new, borrowed and blue bits of the rhyme. And you look pretty as a picture.'

Elsie stared into the mirror Amy had provided and couldn't believe her eyes. She'd never dreamed she could look like that. Her face and hair almost made her look pretty. And the new clothes were very flattering. The skirt had elastic in the waist and the jacket wasn't meant to fasten, so unless she stood sideways on she looked a little chubby rather than pregnant.

She clasped hold of Amy. 'I really can't thank you enough for all you've done for me,' she gasped, trying not to cry.

'Give o'er, lass, or you'll be spoiling all your make-up,' Amy said with a laugh.

As they came downstairs, Wally Tanner gave a wolf whistle at his soon-to-be daughter-in-law. 'Eee, our Arnold's got a right treat waiting for him tonight!' he teased, eyes twinkling.

Amy told her husband to give over, punching his arm playfully and Elsie blushed uncharacteristically, but she felt buoyed up as they went out together to the taxi that Arnold had ordered to take them into Weatherfield for the ceremony. Elsie had grown very fond of the Tanners over the last few weeks; she could see that Wally was a bit of an old rogue, but their kindness and good humour couldn't be further away from the misery and ill-feeling at Back Gas Street.

As they drove through town, Elsie thought she knew how the king and queen must feel, waving to everyone they passed, and when they came to the town hall she said to Amy, breathless with excitement, 'Do you think all those long lines of men are here to see me get married?'

'Wouldn't that be lovely!' Amy sounded equally excited. 'Like you're a famous film star or something.'

Elsie nodded but the serious looks on their faces told her that couldn't be so.

'What are they there for?' Elsie peered out of the cab.

'I expect they're waiting to enlist,' Amy said.

Elsie shuddered. Thank God Arnold wouldn't have to do that. 'A newly-wed with a baby on the way can hardly be expected to go off to fight a war.'

Amy laughed. 'No, I suppose not,' she said, as Elsie sat back, patting her belly and smiling.

Fay was waiting outside the registry office, pacing up and down on her own. She had hoped to bring Jack with her – she knew Elsie would have loved that – but her father was on the prowl and she knew he would have stopped her. Trying to explain it all to Jack would have been impossible; he was still far too young to understand.

Elsie had obviously not arrived yet and neither had her husband-to-be. There was a part of Fay that hoped he wouldn't come. Fay didn't like Arnold Tanner much. Yes, she knew he had done some nice things for Elsie, but that didn't make up for the fact he was a bully. And from what she'd heard, he was likely to be unfaithful before long. But her sister seemed to accept him as he was, so she'd said nothing. The best thing about him was that he was taking Elsie out of Back Gas Street. It was just a pity she'd had to get knocked up first. Fay also dreamed of getting out. Now that Elsie had left the house, things were worse than ever and she was finding it difficult to stand up to her bullying father. Like Elsie, he'd insisted that Fay give over most of her wages; luckily, the firm didn't write how much her wages were on the envelope but gave her a separate slip with it written on instead, so she was able to keep some of it back. She secretly hoped that Terry Butler might be the one to help her get away from all that, but she definitely did not want a baby in her belly before they'd had time to get married.

Fay missed her sister – not only for the protection she'd tried to offer but for the fun times they used to have. Like late at night when they'd giggle together in bed while the little 'uns slept.

When the taxi arrived, Fay dashed forward to greet the bride and stopped before kissing her to admire the new two-piece.

'Wow, you look smart!' Fay said. She was clutching a posy of flowers and she thrust them at Elsie. 'Here, I saved up for them. I thought you should have some flowers.'

'Ah, thanks, Sis, they're lovely.' Elsie gave her a kiss. 'And thanks for coming. Glad the old man didn't stop you.'

Now Fay clasped hold of her sister. 'I wouldn't have missed it for the world.'

The large reception area of the building was filled with couples with the same idea as Elsie and Arnold, most of them in the same plight. Some of the lads, however, were already in uniform and it was plain to see that one or two of the lasses were much further on than she was. Elsie panicked for a moment when she didn't see Arnold, but then she relaxed when she spotted Joe, sober for once. He was to be their best man.

'We're number 4 in line,' Joe said. 'Arnold will be back in a minute. '

Aggie and Mrs Farrell arrived in time, but true to form Arnold appeared barely seconds before they were called in for the ceremony, his mother and father scowling at him as he came into the corridor. The wedding was conducted by a rather fierce-looking man who introduced himself as Mr Hutchins the registrar. He took his time clearing his throat and finding the page in his book, and for a brief moment Elsie thought she was going to be sick. But then the butterflies settled and she had no more time left to wonder what it might be like to be a married lady. All it took was a few sentences, the flip of a page, a greeting, and a good wish, and she was Mrs Elsie Tanner.

When they came out it was Joe who said, 'The Dog and Duck's down the road, shall we go and toast the happy couple there?' Everyone agreed and the small wedding party began to move away. It was then that Elsie saw her mother, hanging back in the shadows of an archway in the grand hall.

'You go on without me, I'll catch you up in a minute,' Elsie said to Arnold and she slipped her arm out of his. Her mother had moved away but Elsie caught up with her.

'Mam, how come you . . . ?' she began, but she couldn't bring herself to say that she hadn't been invited.

Alice stopped and said softly, 'I'm right sorry your dad's not here too, but you know how it is.'

Elsie was staring at the fresh bruise on her mother's face. Yes, she certainly knew how it was.

Alice put her hand up to her face self-consciously. 'You mustn't think too badly of your dad. He wasn't always like this, you know.'

'It's the only side of him we've ever seen,' Elsie seethed, and she could feel her anger rising.

But looking from the purple bruise to her mother's sad eyes, she realized that deep down she felt nothing but pity. 'I'm glad you came,' she said, and patted her mother's arm.

Alice's eyes shone with tears. 'You look lovely, chuck. I'm right proud of you. You and that man you were linking arms with. I presume he's your new husband. I'm pleased he's done right by you.'

Husband. Elsie liked the sound of that. At sixteen years old she was now a respectable married lady, about to become a mother herself. She was no longer the little girl to be knocked about by her drunken father. It was up to her to make the most of her new life.

'Are you coming with us down to the pub?' Elsie felt she had to ask though it had been her intention to put every one of her family – apart from Fay and Jack – behind her.

'No, chuck,' Alice said. 'You go and enjoy yourself. I'll be thinking of you.' And with a little wave of her hand, she melted into the crowd.

Arnold was generous getting his rounds in after the wedding. They toasted Elsie and the baby so many times that by closing time Elsie realized even she was drunk. Arnold splashed out on a taxi to take them back to Coronation Street and she was grateful because her new shoes had cramped up her toes till she could hardly walk.

'So long as you don't expect this kind of treatment all the time,' he said grumpily as he pushed her into the cab. 'I'm not made of money, you know, so you'd best get yourself some shoes for once that don't cripple your feet.'

When the taxi pulled up outside number 11, Fay insisted she was all right walking the rest of the way on her own and refused Joe's offer to see her home.

'I'd feel more obliged to see you home,' she said and she shied away as he reached out towards her and almost fell over.

As Elsie watched her sister go she felt a sudden moment of regret. She'd got what she wanted, now she had to hope everything would turn out all right like in the children's fairy tales she used to read at school. Then on the evening breeze she caught the sound of hymn-singing floating up from the bottom of the street. Good grief, she thought, I hope I'm not going to have a bunch of religious nuts for neighbours.

She looked at Arnold as he paid the driver. She really wasn't sure whether she had done the right thing. Whatever she was caught up in, it was all a new adventure. And true to her nature she looked forward to seeing what was going to happen next.

Chapter 30

Elsie had not actually seen the inside of her new home yet. Arnold had stopped her visiting before they were married saying he wanted time to do it up first. But when he opened the front door and switched on the light, her first feelings were of disappointment for he didn't seem to have done much at all. He picked up the small bag which held everything she owned that she had brought with her from his mother's house. As he carried it inside she was about to say that he should have carried her over the threshold, not the bag. But when she saw the peeling paint and the darkly papered walls, all fantasies in her head of her husband being anything like Clark Gable or Laurence Olivier were driven from her mind.

Arnold went straight up the stairs and she followed.

They were much wider stairs than in Back Gas Street and to her amazement at the top there were two doors doors leading off the tiny landing. Arnold kicked one of them open and threw her bag down beside the unmade bed. Elsie stared at the bed, not caring about the rumpled sheets or the bare patches where the wallpaper had been stripped off the ceiling and the walls. She was just delighted to see that it was so big and she threw herself down on it without waiting to be asked.

Arnold flopped down beside her and immediately rolled over and planted his mouth firmly over hers. His hand automatically moved up to the top of her legs and she began to wonder how she was going to get her skirt off so that it wouldn't be ruined. But then she realized his hands had stilled and his mouth had unlocked from hers. Before she could say anything she heard loud snores as he rolled away on to his back.

She didn't know what time it was when she was woken by the feel of his hands roaming her body once more. The smell of beer was still strong on his breath as he pressed himself to her, mean and hard. She hardly had time to realize what was happening before he was deep inside her and she was lit up momentarily by a flash of joy. Then with a grunt and a sigh his desire had shrivelled and she could only lie there in the dark with her own thoughts, listening to a baby screaming next door.

The next morning they hardly spoke at breakfast time as they sat opposite each other at the kitchen table. Despite being dressed in his smart suit, he looked terrible. His eyes were bloodshot and his hair stuck up in spikes in all directions and he looked like he hadn't shaved for a week. Elsie herself wasn't any better, for the kohl with which Amy had carefully outlined her eyes for the wedding had now rubbed on to her face and all the pins had fallen from her hair. She was going to put on her coat over her nightdress but then, remembering a film she'd once seen with James Stewart, grabbed something she thought looked like a dressing gown from a nail on the back of the bedroom door. She'd wrapped it around her like she had seen the film star do, but even with her protruding belly she could have fitted someone else inside with her.

She had come down early, woken by the noise of the screaming baby next door. She'd tried to shut it out by focusing on what she might make for breakfast. She'd looked carefully into all the cupboards in the back room and kitchen for there were quite a few, but the only thing she could find to eat was in a metal bread bin in the scullery, home to a crust of mouldy-looking bread. Elsie looked around to see if she could heat some water for coffee and Arnold pointed to the range while he helped himself to a beer. Needless to say, only ashes were left in the grate, but there were a few lumps of coal in the scuttle on the hearth and some kindling and Elsie set about trying to light a new fire.

'If you leave me some money I can get a few things from the corner shop for our tea,' she said. Arnold looked at her as if she had spoken a foreign language, then he reluctantly threw a ten-bob note and a few coins on to the table.

'You'd better make that last,' he said. 'I'm not made of money, you know. There's a war on. Fun time's over.'

'No, but you do like to eat,' Elsie snapped back, 'same as me.' As she said it, his hand lashed out and he slapped her hard across the face. Astonished, she put her own hand to her cheek to sooth the stinging.

'Yes, of course I bloody like to eat,' he yelled. 'And I expect my tea to be on the table when I get home.'

'You rotten bully, fine way to treat a woman that's expecting.' She nursed her fast-swelling mouth but she tried to keep her voice strong, determined not to show her tears. 'If I don't know what time you're getting in, how can I know when to cook?'

'How the hell should I know? Just have it ready. I'll eat at whatever time I get in.'

Elsie stared at him. Where had the generous young man gone so quickly? Who was this monster who was no better than the father she thought she'd left behind?

She didn't speak again while she made them both coffee and she wasn't sorry that he didn't bother to drink his but picked up his hat and left to go to work.

Elsie pulled the dressing gown as close as she could round her. She was determined not to let his shocking behaviour get her down, so she set about exploring the house, a cigarette dangling from her lips.

The back room, kitchen and scullery she'd already

seen first thing this morning. They were a decent size and took up half of the ground floor. There wasn't much furniture apart from two battered armchairs, a table and some chairs with green padded seats. The seats had darned patches but what was left of the original material matched the faded curtains framing the window on the back wall. All the walls had once been some shade of green too with the trimmings picked out in dark brown. But now everywhere looked like it could do with a fresh lick of paint.

The scullery had the luxury of a large Belfast sink with its own tap of fresh running water. Even more exciting, there was a separate back door that led out to a small cobbled yard and the privy – a privy that was for her and Arnold's use alone. Someone had strung a small line from the privy to a hook buried in the wall of the house. She presumed it was for washing but nothing hung from it. A rusty-looking mangle stood in one corner of the yard with a washboard and wooden washing dolly beside it.

Elsie went into the house again and shut the back door, turning the key with delight. She was pleased she wouldn't have to walk all the way around the outside of the building with a bucket. The floorboards were not as cold to her bare feet as the outside cobblestones as she made her way down the dark passageway to the front of the house, to the only door she hadn't yet tried. When she opened it, she was pleasantly surprised to see that the front parlour was actually quite bright as it looked out on to the street. The two-seater couch and matching armchair had seen better days and so had the threadbare square of carpet that covered most of the linoleum on the floor. But it was not an unpleasant room. Elsie quietly closed the door then laughed, remembering she was on her own in the house and she could make as much noise as she liked. Though she doubted she could match the noise of the screaming child she could still hear through the wall. She thought about trying to use the tin bath she'd seen hanging on the nail in the scullery but felt it might take too long to fill. It was thrilling enough to have an indoor tap. She filled a small bowl with water and had a stand-up wash by the sink instead.

She had finished getting dressed and was putting on a dab of lipstick when she heard the air-raid siren wailing for the first time. It was so loud it might as well have been in the room and for the first time since the war had begun she felt afraid. Elsie grabbed her gas mask, glad she had kept it with her, and ran to the front door, realizing that she wasn't sure where to go.

Several people were already in the street. They seemed to be heading towards the large building down by the viaduct where she'd seen a sign saying The Mission of Glad Tidings. That was where she'd heard all the bloody hymn singing yesterday and to her disgust there were strains of hymns coming from there now. She was wondering if there was another shelter she could go to when a voice called 'Good morning.' Elsie turned to see an older woman emerging from number 9. 'You're new to the street, aren't you? My name's Vi.'

'Yes, that's right,' Elsie said. 'My name's Elsie.' She slammed her front door shut and fell into step with her neighbour. 'Are we headed for that Mission?' Elsie asked. 'Is there a shelter there, do we know what's going on, is it a drill?'

'Aye, it must be, but you can't be too sure. I hate it, all that bloody singing, but folk reckon the Mission basement is as safe as anywhere to hide, and pray that the Germans won't ever find us there.' Vi gave a shudder. 'I'm not long back from a stay at the seaside. I went there for my health, so I don't want to be spending my last days in a damp basement, thank you very much.'

'Are you still poorly, then?' Elsie asked.

'No, I'm much better now, thank God. But if I do get sick again I'll know who to blame. It'll be those bloody Germans' fault.' She shook her fist in the air and gave a hoarse cough. 'My daughter's about your age. She's out at work right now but happen you two should get to know each other. Are you married then?'

'Yes, I am,' Elsie said proudly, holding out her finger with its narrow brass ring.

'Oh, you're the one as wedded Arnold Tanner.'

'Yes, that's right.' Elsie smiled.

'Pleased to meet you, Elsie Tanner,' said Vi with a giggle.

Elsie followed her new friend into the double-fronted

foyer of the Mission and down the stairs. There she was stopped by a stout woman wearing a dark coat fastened to the top. She had a scarf tied at her neck and a hairnet covering her greying hair.

'You're new around here.' The woman with the hairnet stopped her. 'I've not seen you before. My name's Mrs Ena Sharples.' The woman's tone was as sharp as her name. 'I'm the caretaker here.' She didn't put out her hand but stood with her arms folded across her bosom, eyeing Elsie up and down. 'Aren't you the one who's moved into number 11?'

Elsie nodded. That was all she could do for the woman didn't stop talking long enough for her to reply.

'So, Arnold Tanner finally got caught,' Mrs Sharples cackled.

'As a matter of fact, Arnold Tanner is me husband. What of it?' Elsie said, trying to hang on to her dignity. 'We got married yesterday.'

Mrs Sharples looked down pointedly. 'Looks like you only just made it in time an' all,' she said.

Elsie was shocked that the woman could be so rude and she opened her mouth to say something, but Mrs Sharples hadn't finished. 'You can tell him from me, just because he tried to make an honest woman out of you, it doesn't suddenly all become respectable. And none of that changes the fact that his like is not wanted round here. He's nothing but a bully boy who likes to throw his weight around, but that doesn't wash with me. I remember him when he was this high.' She held her hand out, palm down, not far from the ground. 'He might look big and strong when it comes to fighting with weakling pensioners, but them Germans won't bother to pick out the heroes from the cowards when they drop their bombs.'

Elsie was fuming. She stood as tall as she could, glad she'd taken time to pin her hair up as it made her look taller. 'He might be a bully boy, but he's my bully boy. Why don't you keep your lousy opinions to yourself.'

Mrs Sharples came sharply back at her. 'I make the rules here. This is my Mission and I can say anything I like. But I think you'll find I'm well known for plain speaking. And what's more, for speaking the truth.' She looked round the large basement room. 'You can ask anyone, they'll tell you. A spade is a spade as far as I'm concerned, and it chucks up muck, no matter whether you like it or not.'

Elsie thought that Ena Sharples was an interfering old cow. Welcome to Coronation Street, Mrs Bloody Arnold Tanner, she thought. What a great way to get to know the neighbours! She gritted her teeth as she tried to think up some retort. But then she was aware of being jostled as other people were trying to get past her into the safety of the shelter and she had to move away.

As she went further into the basement she was aware that Mrs Sharples had left her post by the entrance and was now sitting down at the harmonium. She was playing a medley of well-known hymns and encouraging everyone to join in. 'Come on, folks, let's hope for the best and have a singsong while we wait for the all-clear,' she ordered.

'What about something a bit more jolly than a hymn?' someone shouted.

'Yes, "Run, Rabbit, Run",' said another.

There was a faint titter of laughter. But Ena Sharples ignored this request as the strains of 'Onward Christian Soldiers' belted out of the harmonium. Before long a few people began to sing and the voices gradually started to swell.

Elsie didn't join in, she was too angry. She found a chair next to a young woman who wasn't singing either. She was rubbing her enormous pregnant belly with one hand and mopping her brow with the other. Elsie thought the woman looked like a ripe peach.

'I'm Elsie Tanner,' she said as she sat down. 'You look ready to drop.'

'I'm Ida Barlow,' the woman said. 'Aye, you're right n'all, they tell me it could 'appen any minute.'

'Bloody 'ell, let's hope it's not tonight.'

'It can't come quick enough for me, I'm fed up carrying this canonball around.'

'That air-raid siren was almost as bad as my bloody neighbours,' Elsie said. 'Noisy buggers.'

'Oh, and who's that?' Ida asked.

'I don't know. I haven't met them yet. But I sure as heck can hear them. The walls must be paper thin.'

Ida laughed. 'You can say that again. So long as you don't try saying owt like that to the landlord.'

Elsie stiffened when she heard that word. It seemed everyone here hated anything to do with their rent. But she knew she'd get nowhere if she were too thin-skinned, so she ignored the jibe.

'I've moved into number 11. I'm talking about the people at number 13,' she said.

'Oh dear, that will be May Hardman's lass, Christine. All day and all night I believe she can scream sometimes. I wish you the best of luck. Poor mite's got chronic colic. I hear they've been at their wits' end. Not that you'll see much of May. Keeps herself to herself. But Madge, her sister, has been helping out, so maybe if it gets too much you could have a word with her. Not that she'll be able to do much about it, mind.'

'No, I suppose not.' Elsie thought about Jack. When he got in a paddy there was no stopping him. He could scream for hours on end. Not even his teddy helped. A lump rose in her throat and she had to look away.

Ida suddenly put her hand to her mouth and looked apologetic. 'Gosh, I'm sorry, I've only just realized. Is it you that's married to Wormold's man, the one who lives at number 11?'

'Yes, that's right,' Elsie said, trying to sound confident.

Ida nodded without saying anything further and Elsie was glad when at that moment she heard the 'all clear' blasting into the street above. The residents were shaken up but glad it had been just a drill.

Elsie took her time walking home. At least, she was trying to think of it as home, though she'd not been there long. Suddenly she felt a wave of loneliness wash over her and realized one of the things about Back Gas Street was, you were never on your own. Maybe once she'd got to know more of the neighbours it would be the same here. She reached number 11 and pushed at the front door but it remained tight shut.

'Is there a problem?' Vi from number 9 called over to her.

'I don't know. The door won't open. It seems to have got locked somehow.'

'Yes, they all do that. Did you not put it on the latch?'

'No.' Elsie had never heard of a door that locked itself without you having to turn the key.

'Have you got a spare key?' Vi asked.

She didn't like to say she didn't have any key at all because Arnold had forgotten to give her one. That wasn't the sort of thing she wanted to admit to any of her new neighbours.

'Ah well, my husband will be home soon,' Elsie sighed. And she sat down on the front step and lit a cigarette.

'By the way,' Vi called over. 'Next time there's an air raid, you should know you can always take shelter in the cellar at the Rovers Return,' and without another word she disappeared inside her house.

Chapter 31

When Arnold came back, it was much later than she had expected and she was still waiting on the doorstep surrounded by cigarette butts. She'd just finished the last one in the packet.

'Where've you been?' she asked without thinking, for she could smell the booze on him from a distance. She was surprised when he answered civilly: 'I've been out with Joe to thank him properly for being best man.'

'Then you've eaten,' Elsie said with relief.

'No, I've not,' Arnold barked.

'Well, I'm sorry but the shops will be closed so it's too late now to buy anything for tea. Next time you'll have to make sure to leave me a key,' Elsie snapped.

'Oh, so it's my fault now, is it? Because you're so careless as to slam the door shut without checking it was on the latch.' This time Elsie saw the slap coming and she managed to dodge it.

'We'll have to go to the Rovers. Don't they serve pies there or summat?' she said.

'You can count yourself lucky this time because I'm starving, so we'll have to go over there and see what we can get. But don't think of pulling this stunt on me again.'

'How was I supposed to know bloody doors lock themselves?' she muttered.

'I can see there's lots of things I still have to teach you,' Arnold said angrily. And he slapped her bottom hard as he followed her into the house.

It was busy when they arrived at the Rovers and they struggled to find a seat. Elsie could see that the windows of the pub were coverd by heavy blackout blinds. All of the houses had been ordered to cover up with paint or heavy curtains in order to minimise the light that might help the expected German bombers hit their targets.

Arnold ordered them both a meat-and-potato pie and they ate it hungrily under the watchful stare of Annie Walker. By the time they walked back from the Rovers, aided only by the light of the moon as the streetlights had been extinguished, Elsie was feeling extremely tired but there was something about Arnold's mood following the several beers he'd downed in quick succession that told her the night was not ending yet. Not that she minded his attentions; most times she felt flattered to think that he desired her, which in her book was far better than being ignored. And most of the time she enjoyed it, so she was happy to play along. What she didn't like was when his whole attitude suddenly flipped in a way she couldn't predict, for then he could really hurt her.

As they'd walked home from the pub he seemed to be in a jolly mood, but she was alerted by the way he kept nuzzling into her neck and reaching out to painfully tweak at her breasts because he thought no one could see. He was still laughing when she joined him in the double bed and he kissed her in the way that she liked and then he sat astride her body as he fooled around with her breasts. It wasn't until she realized that in his drunken state his sausage-like fingers couldn't manage the buttons of her pretty nightdress that she saw the dangerous flash in his eyes. She felt and heard the rip of the delicate material as he cleared the last obstacle out of his way and she knew then this was going to be one of those painful nights. The more she struggled, the more he forced himself on her, finally pushing so hard into her that she actually feared for the baby. And she knew she'd have bruises in the morning in places she couldn't even see.

At the end of her first week in Coronation Street Elsie decided it was up to her to set to work smartening up the bedroom in the way that she wanted and she didn't care what Arnold thought of her choice. He'd made it quite clear there was no money for such luxuries, using the war and the shortage of materials as his excuse. But Elsie wasn't bothered for she had her own kind of decoration in mind. She stripped off the old floral wallpaper, replacing it with pictures she'd cut out of the picture-goer magazines of her heroes and heroines from the silver screen. She planned to buy a small pot of paint that would add colour to the picture rails, window sill and door. It was a painstaking job but as she worked her way up the first wall she realized how much she was enjoying it. When she stood back to look at it, she was impressed with her work, although Arnold had so far made no comment. But she hoped that by the weekend he would actually have something nice to say.

On the Friday night after he'd been on a pub crawl with the rest of Wormold's gang, Elsie knew better than to imagine he would say anything sensible, so she didn't expect him to remark on the fact that she had managed to finish an entire wall. And on the Saturday morning she crept out of bed, careful not to disturb him in case he had a sore head. It never occurred to her that he might be up before her so she was shocked when she tiptoed into the kitchen to find him sitting at the table with the fire lit and the water already hot enough for coffee.

'What happened to you?' She looked at him anxiously. 'Couldn't you sleep?'

'Sleep was no problem. I slept like a log,' he said, and poured himself another coffee.

It was then she noticed the small suitcase by the door.

'What's that?' she said.

'What's it look like?' he sneered.

'Never mind playing silly buggers, Arnold. I'm asking what it's doing there.'

'It's the bag I've packed to take with me. I'm going into the navy today. I've enlisted and I'm off to camp for basic training. There's a war on, in case you hadn't noticed.'

Elsie had to sit down quickly. 'Navy? What are you talking about? You've not been called up. You don't have to enlist.'

'True. I don't have to – not yet, anyway. But I wanted to do it now, while I've still got a choice.'

'But you're . . . whatever they call a special case. You've got a wife with a baby on the way.'

'That must describe half the population.' Arnold laughed. 'I'm not eligible for any exemptions. But by signing up before I'm sent for, I reckon I'll get to call the shots.'

'Shots on what?'

'On which service I go into, for a start. I don't want to be one of those army mugs on foot. Cannon-fodder they used to call them, because that's all they are. I'd rather go into the navy. Me dad was a seaman and I reckon it'll suit me just fine.'

Elsie stared at him. 'So how long will you be away on this basic training?'

'I don't know. A few months, maybe more.'

'Months?' Elsie repeated. 'And then you'll be back?' She was struggling to understand.

'No. Then I'll be posted, most likely somewhere overseas.'

'This is Joe's work, isn't it? He's put you up to this.'

'No one's put me up to anything.' Arnold was beginning to raise his voice. 'But if you must know, Joe's enlisted too.'

'I still don't get it. Why do you have to go so soon before they even send for you? I don't understand.'

'Because conscription is just around the corner and I don't want to wait for that. Don't you see? If I go early, I get what I want.'

Arnold finished his coffee and went to collect his case.

Elsie could feel panic rising in her throat and felt more hopeless than she had ever felt. 'And what about me? What am I supposed to do while you're gone?' she asked. Elsie had tried not to say it but she couldn't avoid the question now.

'You'll have the baby to keep you occupied.'

'Bugger the baby. I've been here a week. How will I pay the rent? I've no money . . . '

'You don't have to fret about that. The rent will be taken care of. And I've settled my navy salary on you, so they'll be sending money to you regular.'

'When will you be back?' Her voice was not as strong as she would have liked.

Arnold shrugged. 'That's not up to me.' He gave her

a full kiss, thrusting his tongue deep into her mouth. Then, without a backward glance, left the house.

Elsie sat there for some time without moving, trying to absorb the fact that she was now all alone.

Chapter 32

Elsie sat up in bed and stared round the room. Arnold had been gone a few weeks, but she still couldn't get used to the idea of having the whole bed to herself. To her relief, the baby next door had stopped crying all night and she wondered if perhaps the family had gone away. If she was honest, now that there was no crying during the day either, she missed the reassuring feeling of knowing someone was on the other side of the wall. She didn't feel any more comfortable with the empty silence.

She had tried to put up a brave front after Arnold had left, but she couldn't get away from the fact that she had no one else to think about now, no one to prepare a meal for and when she was cold there was no one to snuggle up to in bed. She battled constant angry thoughts about Arnold and his abandonment and thought back to Amy's words about getting off to a good start. She couldn't think of a worse one. She also thought of the family in Back Gas Street and the overcrowded bed they had slept in at home. Did they ever think of her, she wondered. She wished she could see little Jack again. Did he still remember her? But the person she missed most was Fay, for here there was no one to talk to any more. Not like she talked to Fay.

She had been so desperate to get away and she knew she could never go back there, not even for a visit. She'd burned her boats, made her own bed, whatever the sayings were, so she couldn't go back to the old house to see how they were getting on. Although maybe there was some other way she could get to see Fay.

The truth was, she was bored with her own company, bored with having nobody else to care for. Whatever she had been up to before, at least there had always been other people around and things had just happened. Whereas now she was having trouble thinking of ways to fill her time. She never would have believed it, but she missed work. She missed her friend Aggie and all their old routines. And it wasn't as though the house needed cleaning, she'd tidied the place only last week.

She looked down at her stomach that was bulging out worse than ever, and knew she was also fed up with heaving such a heavy lump wherever she went. It felt like months since she had been able to see her own feet. But there wasn't much she could do about that. It would soon disappear once the baby came along.

She had decided on a girl's name some time ago when she had first seen her favourite actress the glamorous Linda Darnell in the film *Hotel for Women*. If it was a boy, he would be called Clark after Clark Gable, the sexiest man on two legs. That needed no explanation as far as she was concerned.

She was trying her best to get on with her neighbours and had gone for a drink to the Rovers Return with Jim Todd, Vi's son from next door. He'd popped in to hammer in some nails when she'd had trouble hanging up a picture, and she felt it would be rude to refuse his invitation. Neither did he refuse when she offered to extend the evening to something more than a couple of glasses of gin. Now that Arnold had left her, Elsie decided that if he thought she was going to keep to her wedding vows he had another thing coming. For better or worse . . . Arnold hadn't even given their marriage a chance before he'd joined up. She didn't believe for a minute it was because he'd had a sudden attack of patriotism. She'd learned enough about him now to know that soiled terry nappies, colic and midnight feeds would be the last thing he'd want to get caught up in.

Anyway, there was always a price to be paid. She'd had to put up with the snide comments from that sharp-tongued, evil witch Ena Sharples, who seemed to have her eagle eyes everywhere. She sat with her cronies in a corner of the snug that they'd claimed as theirs.

One milk stout and she could sit there all night, muckraking, pulling everyone in the street to pieces. Elsie hated the thought of what she called 'that nosy bugger' poking her nose into places where it wasn't wanted, but it was a price she'd have to pay. She'd almost been thankful when Jim was called up into the army and their little fling was over.

The old witch had had less to say when Elsie had gone to the Rovers with Alice Burgess from number 7. Alice was also a new bride whose husband had gone off soon after their wedding, so they had a lot to share.

And Elsie found she liked Jim's sister Sally, who worked at the Rovers. Unfortunately she didn't take to the pub's snooty landlady, Annie Walker, who looked down her nose at her each time she approached the bar. It was as if she'd brought in a bad smell on her shoes. Whenever she could, Elsie tried to get Sally to serve her at the bar as she let her have her favourite tipple of gin. Lady Walker, on the other hand, insisted Elsie was underage and would only serve her lemonade.

She'd been treated with more politeness when she'd gone to register at the local shop where the shopkeeper was also called Elsie – Elsie Foyle. She was a small woman with blonde hair that was obviously from a bottle and she'd once been on the stage.

'It's good you've registered early,' Mrs Foyle said. 'That way I know who my regulars are and I can make sure you get your proper rations when rationing books are handed out in the new year.'

'We'll all be having one, won't we?' Elsie said.

'Indeed we will. And I shall have to be very strict measuring correct portions.' Elsie couldn't imagine this woman being strict with anybody, but she was glad she was on her own, for her needs wouldn't be so great once the government started to decree how much or how little everyone could eat.

Elsie sighed. How the world was changing – and her world seemed to be changing more than most. She thought again of Back Gas Street as she lay back on her pillows and admired her handiwork on the walls. Maybe things weren't looking so bad after all. Certainly she was pleased with the changes she had made in her new bedroom. She'd got the place looking quite different and in her eyes so much better than before. She loved the way the pictures of all her favourite stars went from the floor right up to the ceiling. That project had taken up quite a bit of her time and she'd really enjoyed doing it. Maybe she should think about decorating some of the other rooms too.

She heard the noise of children outside calling to each other as they ran up and down over the cobbles and she looked over to the window. From the bed she couldn't see out but when she stood up she noticed the small advertising poster for the latest epic, *Gone with the Wind* which had opened the previous week. Yes, she thought. That's how I'll fill the day today. I'll go to the pictures. She stared a little longer at Vivian Leigh and then at her favourite, Clark Gable, and to her surprise felt her nipples stiffen and her insides flip a summersault for the first time in ages. She put her hand on the lump that was her stomach, her fingers almost reaching the tops of her legs. That's what was missing, she suddenly realized. For all his rough ways and the bruises and the slapping, Arnold had brought her a lot of pleasure too. A pleasure that the puny lad from next door had hardly been able to match.

Suddenly the noise outside swelled and she got up and went to the window. The street was filled with children who were gathering outside the Rovers. They were milling about as a young woman, possibly their teacher, was barking instructions as she tried to bring them to order. They each carried a suitcase and had a badge stuck to their coats. Elsie was reminded of the Pathé News item when she had seen German children on the station platform as their train was getting ready to depart for England. She doubted these children were leaving the country, though she had heard about youngsters being evacuated to live with families in the countryside, away from all the danger of falling bombs. She looked as hard as she could at the unruly group and a lump rose in her throat as she wondered if any of her sisters or Jack were being sent away.

As she watched, the children were being told to hold hands in pairs, then to form a long line as they began to march down the street towards the train station. Thinking so much about the family made Elsie suddenly sad. She gave herself a shake and said out loud, 'Come on, Elsie, not like you to feel sorry for yourself,' and she got up and dressed and went off into town.

The shop windows reminded her it was almost Christmas, although there were no Christmas lights anywhere. But most of the shops had some kind of seasonal display. It was the toy shop window that caught her eye and she pressed her nose against the pane. The Christmas tree in the corner reminded her of the newsagent's window she used to admire each year. But this one was so much bigger. The tree glittered and sparkled in the winter sun and its shining green branches filled one side of the window from top to bottom. And in the other corner were little Christmas stockings, though to Elsie they looked more like giant socks, filled with oranges and nuts. There were no surprise packages, for all the gifts were openly displayed on a bed of brightly coloured wrapping paper, covered in snow scenes and robins. There was no mystery about the dolls, the doll's houses, the trains and cars or the books. They were there for all to see. In the front of the window there was a small nativity scene like Elsie had seen at school. The whole thing took her breath away. The difference was that this time she had a little money in her pocket so she could have bought something small. But that didn't really matter, for there was still no one else around to buy a present specially for her. The last person to do that had been Stan, with his bar of chocolate, but that seemed like a lifetime ago.

* * *

Fay had told her where she worked in the centre of town but as Elsie walked along admiring all the Christmas displays in the shop windows she wondered if her sister would appreciate being disturbed during the day, especially in the light of everything Fay had told her about Miss Turner's insistence on strict time-keeping, and Mr Talbot's demands on her skills. Much as she would have loved to meet Terry Butler, maybe this was not the best time to pay her sister a visit.

She was still thinking about Fay when she realized she had reached the cinema where *Gone with the Wind* was showing. She wanted to be home before nightfall and there was a show about to start that would enable her to do that. She didn't like walking home in the dark any more, she didn't feel safe in the blackout. With no street lights or car headlights and all the traffic lights dimmed, it wasn't easy for cars to see her or for her to see any kind of obstacle on the pavement or in the road. She could easily trip over something or fall down a hole and she was so close to giving birth she didn't want to be taking any chances.

She walked up to the box office and smiled to herself as she paid for the ticket. It was a good job she wasn't relying on sneaking in through the fire door this time. She would never have been able to squeeze through the narrow gap. It felt like a long time since she had been slim enough to do that. The usherette showed her to a seat near the back and she settled down to enjoy the next few hours in the company of her favourite star.

Elsie was carried away with the whole story of the life and loves of the southern belle Scarlett O'Hara and at the end she gasped and sobbed out loud when Rhett Butler announced his intention to leave. She wasn't even aware that she had grabbed hold of the hand of the person in the next seat when the tension grew too much to bear. It wasn't until the lights went up and the young man beside her smiled and made a play of putting her hand back in her lap that she realized what she had done. She turned to apologize to him.

'Not a problem,' he said. 'My pleasure, in fact.' And he grinned at her, his blue eyes twinkling. He was wearing the blue uniform of an airman that made his eyes look even bluer and she asked him whether he had liked the film.

'Not really my sort of thing, I must admit,' he said. 'I was just killing a few hours. I thought it would cheer me up. But now I'm not so sure. Are you all right?'

'I will be, when I finally calm down,' Elsie said. 'I'm a big romantic softy. And I adore Clark Gable, so I'm not really a good judge where the film's concerned.'

She struggled to get out of the seat and patted her stomach as she stood up. 'From the way it was kicking, I think the baby enjoyed it.' She gave a rueful laugh.

The man looked down at her belly as if seeing it for the first time. 'Oh golly,' he said. 'Would you like me to see you home?'

Elsie turned to look at him properly. His fair hair had been clipped very short, to fit under his cap no doubt, and his mouth seemed to be set in a permanent boyish grin. When he made his offer he looked so eager she hardly liked to turn him down.

'It's quite a long way. We'd have to take a tram,' she said, giving him the chance to change his mind.

'That's OK,' he said. 'I don't have to get back to base till late tonight.'

'Then thank you very much,' Elsie accepted.

'Just show me the way,' he said, and he offered her his arm.

Elsie was amazed when they reached Coronation Street that they had found so much to talk about but he was very easy to be with. By the time they reached her front door it was getting quite dark and she was glad she wasn't on her own.

He followed her into the house and only hesitated for a moment when she began to climb the stairs. 'I didn't mean . . . ' he began.

'Neither did I,' Elsie said, 'but things change.' And she held out her hand towards him.

Now that's more like it, Elsie thought afterwards as they lay side by side sharing a cigarette. I like a strong man who knows what he wants and doesn't beat about the bush. He's got a helluva lot more to offer than the skinny little lad from next door. I'll think of it as my contribution to the war effort, bringing comfort to some poor airman, like what someone else is no doubt bringing to my husband right now. She took a long draw from the cigarette and then stubbed it out, feeling more contented than she had done for ages. She closed her eyes for a moment but then to her delight she felt his hands pulling her towards him and the pleasure began all over again.

It was a beautiful night with frost beginning to attach to the trees and she would have thought no more of her adventure once he had gone, for she knew no more about him than that his name was Tim. But when she opened the door to finally say goodbye she saw Ena Sharples snap her head in her direction with sudden interest as she trudged her way to the Rovers Return. She was wearing her ARP warden's helmet and shouted, 'Get that bloody light off and close the door, you fool,' before Elsie had pulled the door fully open. It was Tim who quickly stepped back inside and pulled the door shut behind him.

'Bugger!' Elsie said as she switched out the light. 'It would have to be the dragon who happened to be walking past,' and for an extra moment the two of them collapsed with laughter in the dark into each other's arms.

Chapter 33

Elsie had never known what it was to celebrate Christmas. At home, there had been no money to buy presents or do anything special for the kids. So no one at Back Gas Street had ever encouraged her or her siblings to think about it as a special time of year. But this year, when there was the opportunity, Elsie thought she would join in the fun with everyone else. Rumour had it that over New Year there was to be singing and maybe even some dancing at the Rovers with most of the street promising to go.

The weather was the coldest it had been for years and on New Year's Eve it began to snow. Elsie wrapped up warm in the new shawl she had bought from the market and a pair of boots that actually fitted her from the charity shop. Despite her anger at Arnold and his absence, the rent, thank goodness, was covered and the fourteen shillings that she got from his navy salary was more than she'd ever had in her life. It didn't stretch that far after the bills were paid but there was always something left for her to put by each week. She was able to afford little treats and to start filling her wardrobe with clothes – but more importantly, it meant she didn't have to go back to the factory, which was definitely a freedom worth having.

The snow was beginning to settle when she came out of the house and the cobbles were so slippery she was terrified of falling. It took her a while, but she made it safely to the Rovers with only the light of the moon to guide her.

Once inside, despite the blackout, the place looked surprisingly jolly. Tinsel, glittering baubles, paper chains and other homemade decorations had been hung in each of the rooms for Christmas and as Elsie arrived the men were dragging the old piano from the select into the public bar. Her namesake, Elsie Foyle, was preparing to play. Elsie was relieved. At least there wouldn't be hymns and songs from the Great War, which was all Ena Sharples seemed to know.

New Year's Eve had brought out many of the locals and Elsie found herself chatting to a few of her neighbours.

Mrs Sharples didn't come into the public bar, preferring instead to stay with her cronies in the snug, but she had positioned her seat in such a way that she could see everything that was going on.

In her short time at the pub, Elsie was managing to work out what was what and more to the point, who was who. Elsie Foyle ran the local shop and apart from their names, the other thing they had in common was not being backward in coming forward. Mrs Foyle could often be heard loudly berating her husband out the back of the shop or be found singing at the top of her voice to the piano in the Rovers – looked on disapprovingly by Annie Walker, of course.

Sally Todd did a few shifts at the Rovers and tonight it was so busy, she was barely able to snatch a few words with her friends at the bar. Elsie sat with Vi and Sally's sister Dot, who worked with Sally over at the factory during the day.

'Who are those old cronies that Ena Sharples is in the snug with? They look like witches around a cauldron.' Elsie smiled at her own joke.

Dot laughed along. 'That's Minnie Caldwell and Martha Longhurst she's sat with – more like dragons with all that cigarette smoke billowing around them.' The girls laughed.

'Ena's a right interfering old bag,' Dot continued. 'Her husband died a couple of years ago and she moved into the mission then. Drives everyone crackers, with her "God's everywhere" claptrap. It's especially hard on her two daughters, Madge and Vera. I feel right sorry for them.'

''Appen I've already felt her fiery breath on me collar,' said Elsie, thinking of their run-ins on the street.

'Now, now, ladies, I do hope you're not indulging in idle tittle-tattle?' Annie Walker appeared at the bar, looking at them critically over the top of her nose.

'Evening, Mrs Walker,' Elsie said, giving the landlady a cheeky smirk.

'I hope you're not drinking alcohol, Elsie Tanner, I've no intention of risking my licence on a young whippersnapper like you. I'd say you were old enough to know better, but that wouldn't be true, would it?' Annie eyed Elsie's bump accusingly. 'Arnold Tanner left you high and dry has he?'

'High but not dry.' Elsie took a sip of her lemonade knowing Dot had slipped a shot of gin into it, and raised her glass to the Rovers' landlady. 'Anyway, he's doing 'is bit for King and Country, saving the likes of you from the Jerrys.'

Annie looked about to respond when Elsie heard a voice over her shoulder. 'I hope you're getting into the festive spirit, ladies. Nothing I like to see more of at this time of year than a group of happy faces and people enjoying themselves.' It was Jack Todd, Vi's husband from number 9. Smiling and avuncular he beamed at the trio. He's full of more than festive spirit Elsie thought, but who was she to care?

'Annie, give all the girls a sherry on me.' That's more like it, thought Elsie.

Annie's face was like thunder, but she beckoned Sally over and instructed her to pour the girls a drink, though Elsie only got a fingerful. Grateful for the kind gesture all the same and settling in to listen to Mrs Foyle raise her voice and exhort the whole pub to jig along to 'Hands, Knees and Boomps-A-Daisy,' the girls laughed and wished each other, and Annie, a Happy New Year.

Later, as the clock struck midnight, Elsie thought of Arnold and what he might be doing. *Got 'is hands up some woman's skirt, no doubt*, she thought. She thought briefly of Stan too but she wasn't one to dwell on the past. She downed another couple of glasses of gin out of sight of Annie Walker and sang along lustily with everyone else.

She was still feeling merry as she walked home with Vi, Sally and Dot after closing time and stopped to admire the Christmas-card scene that greeted them as they stepped out of the pub. The snow had continued to fall all evening and theirs were the first footprints to break up the perfect white sheet that covered the pavement and the road. It looked so smooth it was hard to tell where one ended and the other began. Elsie was glad of her new boots but still had to walk carefully as she tried to pick her way through the snow. Her progress was very slow, so it hardly mattered when Sally stopped to scoop up a snowball in her hand and to throw it playfully at her mother.

'Here, you cheeky monkey!' Vi laughed, 'And here's one for you.' And she picked up a handful of snow and threw one back.

Elsie bent down to make her own snowball but then had to stand up quickly as she felt very unsteady on the slippery surface. She let the snow slip through her fingers before she had time to roll it into an effective weapon. Feeling a spasm grip her, she put a protective hand across her back.

'Be careful how you go, Elsie. Are you all right, love?' Sally came and slid her arm round her. Elsie clasped hold of the other girl's hand gratefully.

'Thanks, chuck,' she said. 'I feel like an old woman in this state.' And they all laughed.

'Not for much longer,' Vi said.

Sally continued to support her as they set off down the street, eagerly chattering about their neighbours who lived in each of the houses they passed.

'It's a pity our Jimmy didn't make it on leave,' Vi sighed. 'I was so looking forward to seeing him again.'

Elsie made no comment, for she wasn't sure how much Vi knew. 'I see George made it home on leave though,' she said as they passed number 13. 'I saw him going in there this morning.'

Vi and Sally both stopped. They looked at each other. 'Are you sure?' Vi said. 'Because, as I understand it, May has taken the baby and they've gone away.'

'I'm positive,' Elsie said, truth suddenly dawning.

'Madge didn't go,' Sally said. 'You know, May's sister. I'd heard she stayed behind.'

'Aye, I believe she did,' Vi said thoughtfully. They looked at the house but it was in complete darkness with no telltale lights to give anything away. Elsie could only think of the strange noises she had heard throughout the day and all four women exchanged knowing glances.

The cold weather got worse and the snow fell again several more times as the new year of 1940 began. Not a very happy new year, now that it was clear that the war had not ended at Christmas. People had started calling it a phoney war though it was reported that there had been ships lost in the North Sea and the Western approaches. Elsie wondered if that was where Arnold was and fretted about the regular income she might lose if he was lost at sea. She felt a pang of guilt then, not for Arnold but for his mother who would be losing a son. Amy Tanner had been good to her and would be able to see right through any 'saintly wife' picture Elsie tried to paint.

No, this was a year when the immediate prospects were not looking very bright on any front. It was the coldest it had been for years, people said, and Elsie was glad she didn't have to go far from the house. She lit a fire most mornings and wrapped up with all the clothes she could find, including Arnold's oversized dressing gown. She only went out to Elsie Foyle's shop when she ran out of food, for she was finding it uncomfortable to walk any distance. She was pleased when Vi or Sally popped in, for they were the friendliest faces she saw most days. She caught only a brief glimpse of her neighbours on the other side when she saw Madge and George go by, for there was no sign of May or the screaming baby.

No one had asked her what she intended to do about the birth of her baby and she had to admit she hadn't given it much thought. She'd got so used to her mother dropping one each time with people around to help, that she felt confident she would too. She assumed Vi, or Sally, or someone would be on hand to help her when the time came. Ida Barlow had told her how she had been home alone counting the buttons on her new gas stove when she'd gone into labour and that Ena Sharples had delivered her son, called Kenneth. It didn't occur to Elsie that she too might be alone when the time came and wondered who would be on hand to help her. She didn't have any of her younger siblings to act as messengers. So it was only when she was taken by surprise by the first twinges of real discomfort and her cry of pain echoed in the empty house that it hit her she was all alone.

Knowing how much she could hear of her neighbours' goings on through the thin walls on either side, she tried shouting and knocking on the wall. But as the pain grew worse her voice grew weaker and she began to panic that no one was home.

She heaved herself out of the chair, the fire having long since gone out. She wrapped Arnold's old dressing gown round her as best she could and staggered to the door. Someone must be about who could help her. But there was no one on the street.

The pains were becoming really severe and as far as she could tell they were following each other very fast.

She tried to take deep breaths as the midwife had always told her mam to do, but it didn't seem to make much difference to the pain and she didn't know what else to try. She was more frightened than she had ever been in her life. And more alone. She needed help, and she didn't care how she had to beg or where it came from. She stepped into her boots, not bothering with her stockings as she couldn't roll them on. Then she waddled out as fast as she could into the freezing morning, remembering at the last moment to grab her keys. The pavement had mucky, well-trodden trails of footprints that had been covered by a sprinkling of fresh snow. While on the road there was sight of some of the cobbles through the well-impacted tyre tracks and it looked as if they would be dangerous to walk on. But she couldn't worry about that right now. She had to keep going. She wasn't sure where she was heading in her desperation but the next thing she knew she was standing in front of the Rovers Return.

She yanked open the door with all her remaining strength and almost fell into the public bar. The smell of beer fumes made her want to be sick but she could hear the buzz of conversation so there must be people in there who could do something for her.

'Help!' she cried as loudly as she could. 'Someone help me, please.' Her voice was warbling as she slipped down on to the floor. She was aware of a moment of shocked silence then everyone must have started talking at once. The next thing she knew, strong hands were lifting her and half dragging, half helping her to walk through a curtain and behind two heavy doors to a place she'd never seen before. She thought she heard someone screaming and Mrs Walker's voice trilling, 'She can't come in here!'

But then the voice she dreaded most of all shouted, 'Let me through. I'm the only bloody midwife round here. And if you think she can't come in then tell me what other bloody place she can go.'

'Upstairs,' Annie Walker said. But Mrs Sharples only laughed. 'Not right now she can't.'

Elsie knew she was right for she felt the sudden wetness between her legs.

'Her bloody waters have broke, haven't they,' Mrs Sharples said.

Elsie heard Annie Walker moan, 'Oh no, my lovely new carpet. What am I to do now?'

'Someone get a mop or something to clear up this mess from the floor,' roared Ena Sharples. 'And while you're at it, get a blanket for that there couch and let's be getting on with it.'

In between contractions Elsie looked around and tried to make sense of what was going on. She saw Annie Walker quickly removing the well-plumped cushions from the couch, shuffling the other people in the bar out of the way and then watched in horror as her arch enemy Mrs Sharples took her coat off and rolled her sleeves up.

'Not her!' Elsie screeched. 'I'll not be having the likes

of her near me.' And she pointed to the woman she called the Wicked Witch.

'You'll have to put up with me, I'm afraid,' Mrs Sharples said, 'so shut your gob and let the experts do what they need to do.' Then with a half-smile she made as if she intended to walk away. 'Unless you want to deliver it yourself?'

At that moment Elsie was hit by another wave of pain. 'No!' she screamed. 'Don't leave me.' She began to sob. Then she grasped hold of the bib-front of Mrs Sharples' dress. 'I'm so afraid,' she whispered.

'Nowt to be scared of,' Ena Sharples said firmly, taking over. 'Now let's be having you. I need to see what we have here.' Elsie had no choice but to obey.

It was some time later when Sally's friendly face appeared in front of her. She was smiling and laughing in her usual bubbly way.

'Congratulations!' she said as she thrust a glass into Elsie's hand. It was filled with what looked like water, but Sally gave her a wink. 'Mrs Walker said I was to give the new mother a double gin.'

Elsie took the glass, though her hand was shaking. Sipping the gin seemed to steady her nerves, and a moment later Ena Sharples appeared holding what looked like a rolled-up blanket.

'Here,' she said, 'I believe she's yours,' and she thrust the bundle into Elsie's arms.

'Linda,' Elsie cooed. 'My own little Linda, at last.'

And she stared down at the tiny head and its surprising mop of black hair.

'This is to wet the baby's head,' Sally said, and she and Elsie clinked their glasses together.

Annie Walker wrote in her diary almost every night before she went to bed as she listened to one of her Vivaldi records on the gramophone her darling Jack had bought her. And she wrote a daily letter to Jack too, even though she could never be sure that any of them reached him. In those letters, she poured her heart out to him, saying all the things she never could bring herself to tell him to his face. Like how much she loved him and missed him, and all the things they would do together on his return.

But for once she was lost for words to describe the events of the day, how that dreadful slut Elsie Tanner had almost given birth on her best carpet and how Ena Sharples had saved the day. Thankfully, none of her Stuart crystal in the display cabinet had been damaged in all the kerfuffle. The couch was probably redeemable, once given a good clean. Only the carpet would have to be replaced.

She decided not to tell him that their one-year-old son Billy had witnessed everything from his playpen in the hallway. It was to be hoped that his memory of the dreadful things would be lost on a mind so young and be well and truly wiped out once his daddy came home.

But she couldn't help but feel a certain pride and

satisfaction that it was to her hostelry that the desperate woman had come in her hour of need. Not that any of this would matter once Jack came home from the war. As soon as he returned, they would abandon the Rovers Return and move to a proper, refined public house in the leafy environs of Cheshire, leaving Weatherfield – and the memory of Elsie Tanner's brat – behind them.

Chapter 34

Elsie wondered if she ought to try and contact Arnold. Would he be interested to know about his daughter's birth? She had not heard from him and thankfully had never received a telegram or any of those dreadful official letters. But now she wondered if perhaps she should try to connect with him once more. She never was good at writing letters and as he hadn't written to her, she really didn't know where he was. She didn't even know if he was on a ship or in a submarine, whether he was out in the Atlantic or the Pacific. Geography never had been her strong point. For all she knew, he could still be stuck in Portsmouth docks. She could probably get the information from somewhere if she tried hard enough, but she wasn't that bothered. He would find out soon enough, if he ever came home.

The one person she did want to contact was Fay. And in the days that followed, after spending time at home recovering from the birth, Elsie managed to get word to her about Linda. She wasn't sure – and she didn't really care – how her mother would feel about becoming a grandmother, but she knew her sister would be thrilled to know she was an aunt.

Once the snow had begun to clear she also took a small bunch of flowers to Mrs Sharples at the Mission.

'What's that for?' Ena Sharples looked at them suspiciously.

'For helping me and for doing what you did.' Elsie smiled. She genuinely felt grateful and she hoped Mrs Sharples would be able to see that.

'Don't think you can get away with anything with a few flowers. I'll still be charging my regular fee.' Clearly the older woman was back to her usual surly self.

'I'm not trying to get away with anything. This is just a little extra, that's all.' Elsie had never given anyone a present like this before and she was surprised how nice it felt to be giving someone something. It was almost as much fun as it was to receive.

'Can we not bury the hatchet for once and be like proper neighbours?' she said, wondering if it was having a baby that had made her soft in the head.

'I'll say thank you, then. And where, may I ask, are you planning on having the christening?' Ena Sharples said as she took the flowers and stuck them in a jar that was standing on top of the harmonium. 'Happen you could do worse than to have her christened here at the Mission.'

Elsie was surprised. Obviously she'd have Linda christened though she wasn't really religious, but she'd hardly put much thought into it yet and wasn't sure she wanted Ena Sharples lording it over her and Linda. 'I don't know how to go about it, I'm not the church-going type.'

'Maybe you should be for once. What with this war an' all.'

Elsie felt the older woman's glare. 'Maybe you're right. I'll think about it,' was all she would concede and then she wandered back home, mulling it over.

Later that day Elsie was among the many residents of Coronation Street who listened to the BBC news on the wireless at the Rovers Return. The new Secretary of State for War, Anthony Eden, told the country solemnly that what people had been calling 'the phoney war' was over and that a serious offensive was more than likely on its way. He asked for what he called Local Defence Volunteers to come forward and offer their services to their country. It was to be a new home army to help defend British shores from possible attack. Then he warned of more stringent rationing in the months to come and the difficult times ahead.

A heavy atmosphere descended on the drinkers as people took his words to heart. There was no more singing and conversation was subdued. Everyone left the pub that night looking more forlorn than ever. Little did they know it wouldn't be long until the bombing started in earnest.

It was the day Elsie had chosen for the ceremony that the first air raid hit Weatherfield. Linda Tanner ended up being christened in the basement shelter underneath the Mission of Glad Tidings. The short service had no sooner begun in the chapel upstairs when the air raid siren began to wail. The loud drone of the planes and the distant boom of bombs dropping told the congregants this was no false alarm. Elsie and the others had never heard anything like it and the residents had come streaming out of their houses withshocked white faces, hurriedly pulling on coats and huddling infants into siren suits.

Elsie clung to her new baby as if there was a bomber immediately overhead. Everyone had put their gas mask on and Mrs Sharples was trying to encourage Elsie to wear hers and to put one on the baby.

'Kenneth Barlow and Billy Walker have put their Mickey Mouse masks on,' Mrs Sharples said.

Elsie had been given a huge infant mask that she was supposed to pump air into but she couldn't imagine trying to get her wriggly baby inside of it in an emergency, so she covered her daughter's head with a blanket and clutched her close to her breast instead. The lay preacher was in the middle of his final blessing when the boom sounded as if it were overhead. The large room was plunged into sudden darkness. Then there was a collective audible gasp followed by individual panic-stricken shrieks as the whole building was shaken to its foundations. Unidentifiable objects fell from the walls and ceiling, people protesting loudly as they were hit. The air was filled with gritty dust that made everyone gasp and cough.

'I can't see,' someone called.

'Not surprising as there's no bloody light,' someone else retorted.

'No, I mean I can't open my eyes.'

Ena Sharples lit up her torch and it soon became plain that it was plaster dust and the powder of fallen masonry that was causing the problem. There was another boom, followed by another, but it was obvious that the planes were now moving away and were dropping their lethal packages elsewhere.

Finally the all clear sounded and everyone emerged from underground, blinking into the daylight and trying to protect their ears from the whine of the siren and the fire engine and ambulance bells that filled the air. People were shaken and dishevelled, hair greyed by the cloud of dust that hung over the entire street. There was a strong smell of burning and the sparks and flashes from adjacent streets confirmed that fires were still raging in buildings that had taken a direct hit.

Elsie hurried home and was surprised to find Fay waiting for her on her doorstep, a small battered suitcase in her hand.

'Thank God you're all right, I didn't know what to do.' Fay rushed up to Elsie and hugged her. 'And how is this little one?' She peered inside the folds of blanket that filled Elsie's arms.

'She's safe, thank goodness,' Elsie said. 'No thanks to them.' She shook her fist at the sky. 'But what are you doing, hanging about here at this hour?'

'I've come to see my niece,' Fay said, almost too lightly. 'Thought I could give you a hand. Though of course I didn't know about any of this.'

'Well, help is always welcome,' Elsie said. 'But let's go inside. I could murder a cup of tea and I'm sure you could too, so come in and tell me all about . . . ' Elsie stopped speaking as she opened the front door and ran down the passage, Fay following behind.

'Oh my God, Else,' Fay said as the two women stood amid a pile of debris.

It was obvious the building behind the house had been hit, for there was no longer a wall at the back separating her from the neighbouring street. The force of the blast had blown in all the windows. Shattered glass covered the floor of the back room, kitchen and scullery and the unhinged back door was swinging on a single nail. Even the privy had had its roof blown off.

Elsie wanted to cry. But as she stepped outside she was too shocked to show any emotion, for sticking out from underneath the pile of bricks of what had once been the wall between her house and number 13 were two stocking-clad legs.

Elsie was pleased Fay decided to stay with her because she didn't know how she would have managed on her own, clearing up the rubble and fixing as much of the damage as was possible. The whole street was without water or electricity for several days which made things all the harder. And when the body of Madge from next door was finally recovered it made a grim sight and Elsie tried to push the memory of it out of her mind. Somehow with a baby to look after and with Fay alongside her, she just about managed it.

'So tell me, what's going on in Back Gas Street?' Elsie said one night when they had settled down and put the baby to bed.

'You're well away from it all, that's all I can say.'

'How is everybody?' Elsie said hesitantly.

'Mam's the same as ever, I suppose, though she's not pregnant of course. She never seems to do anything much and then I get cross with her because she says she's too busy to be bothered going down to the shelter when the siren goes off. And she doesn't force the kids to go either.'

'And how's Jack?' Elsie asked.

'Still missing you, if that's what you're asking,' Fay laughed. 'Maybe I'll bring him here to see you.'

'And his new cousin,' Elsie said, her voice choked.

'But the best news is that Dad's been roped in to be an ARP warden – can you believe it? Complete with a tin hat!'

'Bloody hell. So is he any different?' Elsie wanted to know.

'You wouldn't believe it, but he is. He's got so many other people to boss around, he leaves us lot alone. And he doesn't have time to get drunk every night.'

'So the war is good for something,' Elsie said.

'But that's not all. I think he must have some kind of fancy woman, because he leaves mam alone completely. She's not complained about him getting on to her for ages.'

'And you think he's getting his leg over somewhere?'

'You bet he is.'

'I ask you, who would want anything to do with him?'

'You never know, do you? But then, you fancied Arnold Tanner!' Fay spluttered with laughter and Elsie stared at her.

'No offence,' Fay said quickly, 'but he's not to everyone's taste.'

'Good grief, Fay. Since you've been working in that office you don't half talk posh.'

'No I don't,' Fay protested, but her cheeks did redden. 'Anyway, there's nothing wrong with trying to better yourself. I was trying not to hurt your feelings too much, that's all.'

Elsie shook her head in disbelief wondering that anyone could ever say anything about Arnold that would bother her now and changed the subject. 'How's the job going? Is it working out?'

'Yes, thanks, it is. The boss is very odd. I think it's because he's old. But with Terry there to keep me sane, I'm managing OK.'

'Is Terry your boyfriend now? You know what I mean?'

'Yes, I know. But you could hardly call him that. He's very cautious and very gentlemanly. He says he doesn't want to pressure me or put me in an awkward position.'

'Does that mean he hasn't kissed you?'

'Only on the cheek.' Fay looked coy.

'How long is it you've known him?' Elsie tried not to let her thoughts show on her face and suppressed a grin.

'That's not the point. He doesn't want to rush things. And right now that suits me too.'

'He doesn't sound like he's going to set the world on fire?' Elsie ventured.

'I don't want anyone who's going to set the world on fire! We can't all be like you, chasing trouble. Anyway, not after all that business with Harry. It's not as if I'm going to marry him.'

'I thought you wanted to get out of Back Gas Street.'

'I do, and that's why I'm here.'

'You can stay here as long as you want, you know that. But surely, with all your fancy ideas, you want better than this?'

'Aren't you happy here?'

Elsie thought about it. 'Happy as I can be, I suppose.

343

I've finally started to have a bit of fun, if you know what I mean. But I don't know how it will be once Arnold's back . . . '

Chapter 35

Life somehow carried on for everyone in the street for the next few months but they were anxious days for those whose loved ones were fighting in France, like Annie Walker and Vi Todd. Vi drove the rest of her family mad fretting about her son Jim, while Annie tried not to think about what might be happening to her husband, keeping herself busy pulling pints. The Allies were retreating, their retreat to Dunkirk had trapped thousands of men on the French coast. An armada of all shapes and sizes of boats and ships was sent to rescue the British and French soldiers stranded on the beaches. Fortunately, rain had prevented the Luftwaffe from flying, so despite huge casualties many thousands were evacuated safely and people began to believe Winston Churchill, who was now Prime

Minister, when he declared that 'Britain shall never surrender'.

Then one night two scruffy-looking soldiers appeared in the bar. Annie looked at their filthy uniforms and mud-streaked faces with distaste and wished she could have ordered them out. She hadn't recognized Jack, her own husband. But then she suddenly let out a shriek as she rushed out from behind the counter and without thinking threw her arms around him right there in the public bar. She quickly excused her uncharacteristic behaviour and ushered Jack through the curtain and into their private quarters.

It was Elsie who first realized the other soldier was Jim Todd, the puny youth from number 9. She welcomed him warmly, glad to see he was safe, then shooed him off home where she knew his mother was anxiously awaiting news.

There was a third soldier who came home with the others that night but Elsie didn't find out till later that it was George Hardman from number 13. He had gone straight home where he thought his lover was waiting, only to find Ena Sharples, who had taken it upon herself to deliver the news about Madge's tragic death. He would see no one after that and all Elsie heard through the wall was the sound of sobbing long into the night.

None of the three men stayed long in Coronation Street for their embarkation papers arrived within a few days. When she knew he would soon be off to war again, Elsie opened her arms to Jim Todd once more even though she had sworn she wouldn't entertain him again. Annie Walker had thoughts of hiding Jack's papers when she saw them come through the door, but realized it wasn't worth the penalty she would have to pay. Only George was glad to be going back into the fray to fight.

Elsie became anxious to go back to work, and encouraged by Winston Churchill's rousing speech for everyone to do their duty, she signed up for work at the local engineering factory, where Sally and her sister Dot worked, which was now making spare parts for rifles and munitions. Many local factories had gone over to war production and most women were now in work. Ida Barlow offered to take care of Linda along with her little Kenneth, and that suited Elsie very well. She hoped that with two babies to occupy her, Ida would stop fretting so much about her husband Frank.

The pay was not as good as her last job, but with three breaks on a nine-hour shift Elsie felt it was as good as she could hope for. There was a cheerful atmosphere on the factory floor and, unlike the mill workers, they were allowed to chat as much as they wanted. When she found out she would be working on a bench next to Sally and Dot, Elsie couldn't wait for her first day in the new job. It was only when she got there she found herself sitting opposite Ena Sharples and her cronies all day as well. But then she discovered the clatter of the machinery made it almost impossible to hear what anyone said, so there was no real chat apart from mouthing and lip-reading. Private conversations had to be saved until later.

Linda was not a good sleeper but Elsie and Fay managed to settle into a routine. When Elsie was too tired to respond to her daughter in the middle of the night, Fay was happy to attend to the baby's needs. Fay also didn't mind babysitting while Elsie went out of an evening. She liked to go to places further afield than the Rovers and would go dancing whenever she got the chance, even if it meant travelling into town. She seemed to come alive in men's company and sought out those who were offering more than a drink in a pub. Several times she brought a man home with her for a few hours of fun, though she made sure he was gone by morning. She was especially taken with those who could supply her with items like matches and soap that were no longer freely available from the corner shop.

Rationing was really biting and Elsie's thoughts took her back to her childhood and her days of foraging for food and clothes. Sugar rations were cut and more and more food items were in short supply. Rows broke out every day in Elsie Foyle's shop when people accused her of favouring some customers above others. Some accused her of running a black market racket in fruit and other items she was always running out of, even though it wasn't true. They would constantly argue with poor Mrs Foyle that such things should have been kept by for regular customers with sufficient coupons.

Air-raid sirens sounded more frequently now, though they were still mostly false alarms and Elsie refused to be dragged down to the Mission every time they went off. When they sounded during the night, either she or Fay would grab the baby and they would scramble together under the kitchen table. But the news was getting worse as France fell and the threat of German invasion into Britain increased, and the mood in Coronation Street became heavier and more wretched, like the rest of the country.

Shortly after the collapse of French opposition, the Germans began to drop incendiary bombs all over Britain and there seemed to be a constant chain of firefighters in almost every city trying to stop the flames and the ensuing panic spreading. Elsie saw the dreadful pictures for herself whenever she ventured to the cinema, though she no longer enjoyed going as often as she once had for it was impossible to avoid the newsreels. Watching London and smaller cities such as Coventry and Southampton being bombed spoilt her appetite for whatever light-hearted film was the main attraction. The mood in the cinema was very sombre these days. Audiences were stunned into silence by the images of communities being devastated and scores of innocent victims losing their homes. It seemed that many people had disappeared following the bombings, leaving their families in limbo, not knowing whether they were alive or dead. It was as though everyone was wondering when the Germans would turn their attention northwards to industrial cities like Manchester and consequently Weatherfield.

As the year went on and the weather got colder, no one seemed to notice that Christmas was approaching. It was hard to feel like celebrating anything and few houses in the street had put up any decorations. Even Annie Walker seemed to be letting her standards slip, for the bar no longer looked bright or cheerful.

The Sunday before Christmas began as any other day. Elsie was enjoying a lie-in and recalling the annual display in the newsagent's window near Back Gas Street. Would it be there again this year? Damnit, that's what we need, she thought: decorations. Linda's too young but Fay and I will enjoy them.

So she decided to spend the morning making up some paper chains and hanging them in the back room and kitchen. Fay had gone to Back Gas Street, as she did every Sunday, to check that everything was all right. It would be a lovely surprise for her when she got back. We could all do with something to cheer us up, Elsie thought.

For the next couple of hours, she forgot all about the war as she busied herself with paper, glue and scissors.

Early in the afternoon she wrapped Linda up warmly and went out for a walk in the local park. She was surprised to find how bare and neglected it looked. All the railings had been removed, no doubt to be melted down to make guns or planes, and the bandstand too had suffered a similar fate. But she gathered some twigs and leaves, deciding she could make her own little Christmas tree. Some holly leaves had fallen on to the grass and she even found a sprig of mistletoe. She put it on her head and that made Linda gurgle with laughter. 'Let's hope it won't have to go to waste,' she said, chucking her daughter under the chin.

Once the small bits of foliage had been carefully arranged in the corner of the room in an old plant pot Elsie thought they really did look like a tree – if you squinted. Elsie wrapped some tiny boxes in the remaining bits of coloured paper and arranged them around the branches on the floor. Knowing the boxes were empty suddenly made her wonder if the boxes in the newsagent's window had been empty too. The thought of how longingly she'd looked at those make-believe gifts made her smile.

She was pleased with her handiwork and was sure Fay would like it as well. When she had finished, she left Linda asleep and, with a word to Vi to keep an ear out for her daughter, popped out to the Rovers for an hour. She was glad to see Annie Walker had also decided at the last minute to bring some Christmas cheer to her customers, for the bar was now bedecked with paper chains and decorations, even if they did look as if they had been dragged up from the cellar.

''Appen the place tooks a bit more cheery, Mrs Walker,' commented Elsie as Annie bustled about behind the bar.

'Mr Churchill has told us all to do our bit, and if that means giving Hitler one in the eye by showing him his bombs won't stop us celebrating Christmas, then that's what the Rovers will do.'

'Hear, hear!' said Elsie, sentiments that were echoed by the other regulars. There were bombs falling all over England and there were times when it felt as if the world was coming to an end. But tonight, here in the Rovers, Elsie thought she was part of something . . . something that Hitler and his bloody Luftwaffe could never destroy.

Despite the grim news, the rationing and the biting cold, Elsie could sense a change in the atmosphere tonight. There was a sense of purpose; of pulling together. They might be down, but they weren't out.

It had been quiet in the public bar when Elsie first arrived but as time wore on there was a growing buzz of conversation. People were beginning to smile and she felt cheered when Elsie Foyle whispered that tomorrow she would have a few oranges hidden under the counter that she would sell to her regular customers.

'Bugger the coupons,' she said with a wink. 'I may as well do what I'm always being accused of.'

The customers sang cheery versions of 'There'll Always be an England' and 'Wish me Luck as You Wave me Goodbye', Mrs Foyle doing her best Gracie Fields impression which Elsie though wasn't half bad. When the whole pub joined in to sing Vera Lynn's 'We'll Meet Again' Elsie was surprised to feel a few tears trickling down her cheeks. Looking across at the snug even Ena Sharples seemed to be moved by the sentiments of the song. *I'm going soft,* thought Elsie, *either that or it's the gin.*

It wasn't until they started singing carols that Elsie felt it was time to go home. Ena Sharples seemed determined everyone should join in.

'Not for me,' Elsie said. 'My daughter might have been baptized but that doesn't make me a God-botherer. I like the tunes but that's as far as it goes, I'm afraid.'

'Well,' Mrs Sharples said, 'I know our good Lord died to save us, but with you I'm not sure there's owt that could be saved.'

'Charming, so much for goodwill to all men – and women!' But Elsie wasn't really offended this time.

On the way home, she popped in to see Ida Barlow to give her a tiny present she'd wrapped up. 'It's to say thank you for all you've done for Linda,' Elsie explained.

Ida was delighted. 'You didn't need to bother. It's been my pleasure. And she's been company for my Kenneth too.' Ida smiled but then she slipped into her own thoughts. She was always worrying about her husband Frank in France, tormenting herself that he'd been killed.

Elsie had bought a bit of minced meat for their supper. She always liked to make something for Fay's return. She looked at it and wondered what unfortunate animal had been trapped and minced up like that. Better that she didn't know. She seasoned it and prepared it in her special saucepan and hung it over the fire so that it would be ready when Fay got back. She also prepared her sister's present, looking at it one more time before she wrapped it up. It was a cotton handkerchief she'd bought specially and Vi had embroidered a lace border. She thought she would give it to Fay before Christmas, probably tonight.

Chapter 36

Night had descended and it was pitch-black by the time the first siren whined its warning into the street. For some reason, Elsie thought it sounded more urgent than usual. Fay wasn't back yet so she ignored the kitchen table, and gathering Linda ran directly to the shelter at the Mission. It was as though everyone felt the same way, for the street was packed with people making their way to the Mission basement. She could already hear the steady drone of the distant bombers and knew she had done the right thing. She hoped Fay would insist the family in Back Gas Street ran for shelter and that she was safely with them too.

'Where's Annie Walker?' Ena Sharples demanded. She was wearing her warden's hat with a large W painted on the front and was checking names off a list.

'She wouldn't leave the Rovers while her Jack's away,' Sally Todd answered. 'She's taken Billy with her and gone down to the Rovers' cellar.'

'Right then. Everyone I expect to be here is accounted for,' Mrs Sharples said with satisfaction.

There were several wardens from the surrounding neighbourhood all directing people to the Mission and it seemed like they were just in time. For the drone of engines that filled the air was getting nearer, and people were rushing to get down the stairs.

Elsie was trying to decide whether it was safe to go into the shelter as more people than ever seemed to be packing in the doors. She stood for a moment, hypnotized by the sky that was ablaze with searchlights and the leaping flames from fires ignited by distant bombs. But then she realized as the throbbing engines grew louder that the bombing was getting closer too and she stood uncertainly, hanging on to Linda, trapped by the milling crowd that was mobbing the entrance.

When she heard someone scream for Mrs Sharples' help, she turned and watched in horror as Marjorie Barlow, who'd been desperately pleading with her sister-in-law Ida to leave her house for the safety of the shelter came into view, holding what looked like a parcel, with Ida right behind her. Both women were keeping close to the wall and moving as fast as they could in the direction of the Mission. Ida seemed to be shouting something, but her words were drowned out as the planes were almost overhead now. Realizing she had no time to get down the stairs to the basement, Elsie clutched Linda to her as tightly as she could and lay down on the floor, trying to protect her head while shielding the baby's body with her own.

Suddenly the street shook, there was blinding flash of light followed by a roar and a deafening noise echoed all around. Then there was the thunderous sound of bricks crashing to the ground and bouncing on the cobbles. In the momentary silence that followed, Elsie lifted her head gingerly but regretted it immediately as there was another crash and a boom and the whole of the factory wall disappeared, along with those trying to reach the safety of the Mission. She couldn't believe what she had seen in that brief moment. It was as if the street itself had been lifted, shaken about and then fallen back in different order.

Those who had witnessed the dreadful scene gave up all attempts to enter the shelter, risking their lives to run to where the wall had collapsed. As word spread, the shelter emptied and others joined them, scrabbling at the bricks with their bare hands to free whoever had been caught underneath. A combination of sirens, bells and shouting filled the streets, mingling with the screams of those who had been injured. Thankfully, the noise of the bombs was getting ever more distant.

To Elsie's relief, Linda seemed unharmed. Apart from having torn her coat when she flattened herself to the floor, Elsie too was untouched. Not knowing what else to do, she ran to the main road and despite the risk of being knocked down in the darkness, she attempted to flag down an ambulance on its way into town.

'We need your help here. Please,' she begged when the ambulance pulled up a few feet away from her. 'People have been badly hurt in the air raid on Coronation Street. I think they may need emergency treatment.' To her huge relief, the crew turned their ambulance round and joined in the hunt for Ida and whoever else had been with her. It was several hours later that they found her, injured but alive. Kenneth too was safe, thanks to the quick thinking of his Aunt Marjorie, who had been with them. But she had not been so lucky. Marjorie Barlow had protected him at the cost of her own life.

Fires burned in Weatherfield well into the early hours and continued to burn in the city too. Many of the city's firefighters had been sent to help out in Liverpool earlier, and had not yet returned. Those who remained fought valiantly, putting out fires even while bombs were still falling during a bombardment that lasted more than twelve hours.

In the morning, the residents surveyed the damage. Not everything was intact but Coronation Street had survived. The corner shop had been hit and most of the stock ruined by the shattering glass if not by the blast of the bomb itself. The main gas pipe to the street had been cut off, the water pipe had been fractured by the force of the explosion and they were informed that electricity would have to be rationed. When Annie Walker emerged from the cellar, she found the shelves had been looted by rescuers who must have been desperate for refreshment.

Amazingly the only fatality on the street was poor Marjorie. Ida was released from hospital after a night's stay to make room for more urgent cases that were coming in from all over the city. The city centre was in ruins and there had been many severe casualties during the night. When she went down to the hospital, Elsie found Ida looking so bewildered that she offered her a bed at number 11, and later that morning she took Ida home to look after her. It helped to keep her mind off her sister.

Fay hadn't come home the previous night and when she hadn't appeared by morning Elsie didn't know what to think or do. She wanted to go out looking for her but she didn't know where to go. News had travelled fast about the devastation of the city centre, but so many people were killed or missing and there was no news yet about a single young girl lost somewhere between Coronation Street and Back Gas Street.

The next night the raids began again at about the same time and went on throughout the night as the Germans tried to dislocate networks and transport links and to terrorize the people. But this time there were no planes directly over Weatherfield. When the alarm sounded, Elsie was content for them to hide under the table once more where they felt safe enough listening to the bombs blasting in the distance.

If the Germans hoped to destroy the morale of Manchester, they had miscalculated. The blanket bombing had had the opposite effect. For while many buildings had been destroyed in the city centre, the heart of the people and their spirit of cooperation had not been touched. Everyone, young and old, pulled together, helping to drag the injured from the burning and flattened buildings. The Women's Voluntary Service arrived with their trucks on street corners distributing spare clothing and much-needed strong tea. If Hitler thought the people of Manchester — or anywhere else in the country — were going to crumble, then he clearly had another thing coming.

On Christmas Day Weatherfield enjoyed a rest from all the air raids and it seemed like the blitz on Manchester was over, for the time being at least. No one was in a mood to celebrate, but a small crowd gathered at the Rovers, and people tried to pool their meagre resources to help them get through what should have been a festive day.

When Elsie heard a knock at the front door, she ran to open it, thinking it was Fay at last. Instead, a wild-looking man she didn't recognize stood on her doorstep. He was wearing a dishevelled uniform and had several days' growth of beard.

'Elsie?' a local-sounding voice said. 'I hear my Ida's with you.'

Elsie gasped. 'Frank Barlow? Is it really you? You're a sight for sore eyes!' And she pulled back the door to let him through.

Ida, despite her bad leg, came rushing out as quickly as she could. 'Frank! I thought you were dead. And I was convinced I was a goner too.' Ida sobbed and told him about his sister Marjorie and how she had saved Kenneth's life.

Elsie left them together while she went up to the Rovers, hoping she might hear some news of Fay. But she was greeted with the kind of information she didn't want to hear.

'Don't you come from Back Gas Street way?' someone asked her as soon as she set foot inside the door.

'What of it?' She was used to defending her home from the snooty types who liked to look down on anyone who came from the slums.

'Rumour has it they didn't fare so well the other night.' Ena Sharples always liked to be in first. 'I was going to nip over and tell you, if you hadn't come in.'

Elsie gave a shiver and a sudden hush fell in the room.

'How do you mean, "not fared well"?' Elsie tried to keep her voice steady.

Someone pushed a chair towards her. 'Here, you best sit down.'

Vi put a glass of gin in her hand, but Elsie ignored it. She was looking straight at Mrs Sharples, who as usual didn't mince her words: 'They bore the brunt of one of the explosions. A shelter took a direct hit. Incendiary bombs started fires all over the place. They spread quickly because those flimsy houses in the terraces were all so close together. And then they couldn't get to the pumps.'

She looked as though she would go on, but Elsie had heard enough. As if suddenly realizing what Vi had put in her hand, she downed the gin in one gulp and ran out of the pub.

She went the way she always went, past the news-agent's, which was still standing though with empty, glassless windows. But when she got to the Field she had to stop. Suddenly she didn't recognize anything and lost all sense of where she was. Where there had once been streets and houses, all she could see were piles of rubble and the shattered remains of what had once been people's homes. Several fires were still burning, she could feel the heat. Even now there was frenzied movement and activity as emergency workers and volunteers continued to pick through the debris, looking for the injured and the dead. Here and there she saw a chair leg, a kitchen drawer with a melted tangle of knives and forks. She nearly stumbled over a window frame, and skirted round a mattress that was still smouldering. Everything was covered in a film of masonry dust as fine as powder.

'Here, come and look at this,' a fireman called to his mate. Elsie went over to where he was standing so she could see too. There were dozens of tins of what had once been spam. Most of them had exploded, but a pile of jars of fish paste had somehow remained intact.

'Bloody hoarders,' the second man said, and went back to his digging.

As she went on, Elsie saw a papered wall still standing, complete with mantelpiece and photo frame. A door was attached to the wall and was swinging on its hinges, though the rest of the house had disappeared. The fireman yelled, 'Be careful, it's not safe!' and she gave it a wide berth. Small children, unaware of the hidden heartbreak and dangers, were scurrying around looking for souvenirs.

'You don't want to be hanging about here,' the fireman called to her, 'it's far too dangerous. You never know what might be lurking.'

'How else will I find my family?' Elsie shouted back.

The fireman came up to her, his face lined and weary. 'This your house then?' he asked.

'I don't know. I can't rightly tell. I can't see owt familiar, at any rate.'

He took his helmet off and scratched his head. 'I'm sorry. I don't think anyone could have survived this lot. And the same goes for that shelter there, an' all.'

Elsie nodded. She was so numb her mouth couldn't form words to answer him. As tears trickled silently down her cheeks, she continued to make her way through the debris, hoping to find something or someone she recognized. Her hopes rose when she spotted Mrs James, their old neighbour, picking up bricks and putting them down again.

'Oh, Elsie love. Whatever have you come home to?' And she clasped Elsie tightly, tears pouring from her eyes.

Elsie clung to her for some time. 'What's happened to them all? Where is everyone?' she sobbed.

'I can't say for sure,' Mrs James said. 'The whole street was hit right bad. They never had a chance. Strange thing was, they never usually went to the shelter, you know. Your mam, bless her, wasn't always wanting to go. But they did that night, 'cos we was warned things were looking bad.'

'Were you in the shelter with them? I thought—'

'Oh no. I don't think anyone survived from there. I ran down to my daughter's, in the next the street. Thank God, there were no direct hits there. But from what I've heard, your house was just . . . blown away. And the shelter too. I'm so sorry, love. I don't know what to say.'

Elsie didn't know either. Eventually she took a deep breath and said, 'And Fay? Where is she?' She could hardly recognize her own voice it croaked so badly.

'Fay? Wasn't she with you?'

There was a sudden shout and Elsie looked to where several firemen were gathering together, peering into a small crater, their faces grey and drawn. Something fluttered in her chest and she tried to steady her breathing. Then she picked her way carefully over the hot bricks and fractured concrete, trying to avoid the shards of glass. Some of the volunteers working on the site followed her too.

'Stand back, please,' the firemen's leader warned the gathering crowd as people began to surge forward. 'Here, love,' the original fireman called to Elsie. 'Looks like there were several people in this hole here. Happen it's who you're looking for.'

Elsie thought she was going to be sick. But she forced herself to peer down where the fireman was pointing. Her eyes began to swim and she could barely see. But she did manage to see the torn brown felt of a teddy bear's foot.

Chapter 37

Elsie couldn't believe she had lost her entire family in one night. At first she felt completely numb. When she got back to number 11 and found the Barlows had gone home, she was glad to be alone. She was grateful they had taken Linda with them and she wasn't in a hurry to fetch her back.

'My mam and dad may not have been up to much, but they were my family,' she cried out loud, 'and all those innocent little ones – it's not fair, what did they ever do to hurt anyone?' She squeezed her eyes tight shut as an image suddenly came to her and there was a stabbing feeling in her chest. 'My beautiful little Jack,' she cried, 'my lovely boy.' Her only brother. She was overwhelmed by a vision of the blond-haired child clinging to her skirts. She could actually feel the warmth of his embrace. She could see him trailing his battered brown teddy along wherever he went, and it was then that she sat down at the table and sobbed her heart out.

She didn't know when thoughts of Phyllis crept in, the sister who had gone from them such a long time ago. The angry child who Arnold had discovered hiding underneath the arches at Exchange Station. Elsie felt a sudden ray of hope that at least one member of her family might have survived and, without thinking about where she was going, set off into town to try to find her.

The scene in town was not any better than in Weatherfield, for the entire city centre had been damaged or destroyed. All major routes into the city were blocked and the only way to approach it was on foot. A network of hoses criss-crossed the once busy streets while a smoke cloud hovered over the debris. Buildings that hadn't taken a direct hit had been destroyed by fire from incendiary bombs and water was still spurting in all directions over the smouldering remains.

Emergency workers were out in force and had been joined in their grim search efforts by soldiers. Displaced residents wandered in despair, calling out the names of their missing loved ones. Such was the scene of carnage laid out before her eyes, Elsie couldn't begin to take it all in.

A soldier in a metal helmet shouted to her: 'Get back! It's not safe, love. You shouldn't be here.'

Elsie stared at him blankly, as though not understanding his words, then carried on wandering among the wreckage of the damaged buildings. 'Watch out for hidden craters,' he warned, 'and there still might be unexploded bombs in there.' But Elsie merely nodded and moved on. Everywhere she looked, huge piles of bricks, fallen masonry and shattered glass were all that remained of the magnificent Victorian structures that had once been the pride of Manchester.

Whole sections of the centre had been cordoned off, but Elsie managed to find her way through to the twin stations of Victoria and Exchange, only to find the station buildings and platforms had been completely destroyed. The arches where Phyllis had last been seen were still standing though, and she could see people were moving about. She made her way down and, remembering what Arnold had said about Phyllis having changed her name to Mattie, asked everyone she saw if they had seen her. But no one had, until Elsie mentioned her sister's flame-red hair. 'Like mine?' she said eagerly when two young boys, who looked like brothers, thought they might have known her.

'Yes,' the younger looking one agreed, 'she used to live with us down here, but I haven't seen her in a bit.'

Elsie looked round anxiously. 'When did you last see her? Please try to remember. It's important. Was it the night of the air raid?'

The older boy shrugged. His eyes were unfocused and had a haunted look. 'There's been loads of bombs,' he said vaguely.

But the younger one was more specific. 'I remember when we last saw her and the rest of the girls. It was bloody freezing that night, right brass monkeys, and we all went up to the waiting room on the platform to try to get some sleep. But there wasn't enough room for everyone, so we let the girls stay and us lads came back down here.'

Elsie's heart began to pound with hope. Was it possible that Phyllis had survived? But when she went to look at where the boy had pointed she felt crushed and all hope died. There was no station there now. No platform. No big waiting room. The station roof had been reduced to a bare skeleton of tangled girders. A mangled advertising hoarding for Bryant and May matches lay abandoned on the twisted track. The station where they had been sheltering had taken a direct hit. No one could possibly have lived through that. Her last hope had gone.

She turned away disconsolately and peered over the bridge. Down by the fresh fish and cheese markets, the Falstaff Hotel was nothing but an empty shell, yet by some miracle the centuries-old Shambles pub, with its original Tudor timbers, had survived the blast. Such is the way of life, Elsie thought miserably.

By the time she reached home, Elsie was inconsolable. When there was a knock at the door, she didn't answer it. But whoever it was persisted, so she went into the front room and peeked through the curtains. Seeing Ena Sharples standing on the step only strengthened her determination not to open the door, but Ena, eagle-eyed as ever, had spotted the twitching of the curtain and began rapping on the window.

Elsie had no choice but to open the front door.

Before she could say that she wanted to be left alone, Ena had her foot over the doorstep, wedging open the door.

'I'm really sorry to hear what's happened to your family,' the older woman said. 'It's a terrible day for the Grimshaws, that's for sure. But I need you to come down to the Mission – right now if you will.'

'What the bloody hell for?' Elsie snapped. 'I'm not suddenly going to get religion after this.'

'I don't doubt it. As I've told you before, you're beyond saving. But don't let that stop you coming with me now. Here, put this on and let's be having you.' She picked up Elsie's coat from the chair and handed it to her. Elsie put it on, still in a daze. Grumbling all the while, she went with Ena down to the Mission.

Ena didn't go into the Mission Hall or the basement but entered through the side door to the vestry, where she lived, with Elsie following grudgingly in her footsteps. As she entered the room, Elsie gasped at the sight before her and had to grab at a chair for support. A curtain hid the bed, but there lying on the couch, covered by a grey blanket, was her favourite little sister.

'Fay?' Elsie moved to touch her, for she couldn't believe what she was seeing. 'How did you get . . . I thought you were . . . Weren't you with the others when the bomb . . . ?'

Elsie sank to her knees beside the couch as Fay sat up, then she buried her face in Fay's shoulder as the two embraced. Neither spoke for several minutes.

'I was on my way back. I was running for cover, hoping to get into someone's Anderson shelter in their garden. But before I made it to safety I caught some shrapnel in my leg.'

Elsie gasped, squeezing Fay's hand as she continued: 'They managed to drag me into the shelter, and then after the all clear they took me to the hospital. That's where I've been ever since. I'm so sorry, but I didn't know how to get word to you.'

'I don't care about that now. I'm just glad you're all right.' Elsie sobbed and kissed her again through her tears.

'Mrs Sharples told me what happened to the rest of the family.' Fay's eyes began to stream and her voice was choked with tears.

Elsie hugged her and they clung together. 'I can't bear it, Fay, let's not talk about it now. Let's just go home. Can you walk?' Elsie asked.

'A little. But I'll need help.'

'No rush,' said Elsie. 'We can take it slowly.'

Fay threw off the blanket and Elsie helped her to her feet. She noticed the heavy strapping on her leg.

'Here, lean on me,' Elsie said.

'Are you sure you can manage?' Ena asked. 'You

know you can stop here as long as you need,' she added gruffly.

Fay had made it to the door. 'I'll be all right, thanks, with Elsie's help. And thanks for rescuing me,' Fay called over her shoulder. 'Mrs Sharples found me hobbling along the road,' she explained to Elsie. 'And then, when you weren't home and no one knew where you were, she took me in. I was so worried.'

'*You* were worried!' Elsie gave a laugh.

'Yes. Where were you?'

Elsie frowned, knowing she wouldn't be able to tell Fay everything, but she said, 'I'll tell you all about it when we get home.'

As they left, Elsie turned to Ena. Ena Sharples, the closest thing she had to a sworn enemy but who always seemed to be there when comfort and a steady hand were required. Elsie couldn't find the words that she needed at that moment, perhaps there weren't any. Instead she reached out a hand to Ena and touched her arm. Ena covered Elsie's hand with her own. She didn't speak, but nodded, and briefly the two women were united, drawn together by the tragic events that had unfolded around them.

Chapter 38

Ida looked after Linda for the next couple of days while Elsie and Fay shared their memories and their grief. But by then Elsie couldn't wait to have her daughter back.

'Enough,' she said, lifting Linda high into the air. 'That's quite enough misery for one lifetime. Now we all need to be thinking about the future, don't you agree?'

To her delight, Linda gurgled in response.

'At least we've got each other,' Fay said, hugging her sister and her niece at the same time. 'We can't bring the others back, but we can live our lives for those that have had theirs snatched away. And we're going to beat that bloody Hitler, you mark my words.'

Everyone in Coronation Street seemed to feel the same way. News of the tragedy that had struck the

Grimshaws had spread, and Elsie was overwhelmed by people's reactions. She'd lost count of how many stopped to speak to her offering their sympathy and any help they could give. It had been a desperate time for many of the residents. Most families had suffered in some way as a result of what they referred to as the 'Manchester Blitz'. Though it was a sad event that had brought them together, people were rallying to help less fortunate neighbours, taking time to pop in for a chat or to check if they needed anything.

Frank Barlow was home for the foreseeable future as the wound in his leg was not responding to treatment, but Ida was happy to continue looking after Linda. This left Elsie free to work. As soon as the gas, water and electricity services were restored, the factory reopened. Their war work – assembling parts for rifles – was now more important than ever.

Fay's shrapnel wound was healing well and she began to wonder what she should do about going back to work. Talbot and Jones' offices had been hit and whole sections of the building had collapsed. What little remained had been badly scarred by incendiary bombs and had been deemed unsafe.

So it was that Fay was sitting in the seldom-used front parlour one morning after Elsie had gone to work, considering her options. Suddenly, she thought she saw someone she recognized passing the window; moments later there was a knock at the door. She went as quickly as she could to open it.

'I imagine you're surprised to see me,' the visitor said.

'Oh Terry!' It was such a surprise to see him, his serious face was in some way so welcome that Fay could not stop herself throwing her arms around him and giving him a hug. Awkwardly at first, but then more tenderly, Terry returned it. Fay felt a brief sense of safety and security in his arms, before they both pulled away. Terry had a flush on his cheek and Fay tugged at her hair self-conciously.

'Would you like to come in?' said Fay, and she stood aside to allow him to enter.

He took off his hat as she showed him into the back room where they could sit in front of the fire while she explained about her bandaged leg.

'I'm very sorry about your family,' Terry said balancing his hat across his lap, 'that really is terrible. Please accept my sincere condolences.'

'Thank you,' Fay said, 'but I'm sure that wasn't the reason you came.'

'No, I came to see if you'd heard from Mr Talbot that he's winding up the business,' Terry said.

'No, I haven't, what's happening?'

'Mr Talbot has decided to close the office entirely and offer everyone references. I asked him for your address so I could come and tell you myself,'

'Thank you, Terry. But I'm not sure what I'll do now. Have you decided yet?'

'You're very well qualified – you shouldn't have any difficulty finding a new position,' Terry said.

'But not in the centre of Manchester at this moment.'

'No. Quite. I'm thinking of returning to Saddleworth to work.'

'Oh.' Fay felt her cheeks reddening and looked away.

'I've been offered a good position not far from where my mother lives, so it makes sense for me to move back home permanently.'

'Oh?' Fay said again, surprised at the tight feeling in her stomach at this news.

'The thing is . . . ' Terry fingered his hat nervously now. 'I wondered if you might consider coming to Saddleworth to work alongside me, much as we did at Talbot and Jones.'

'Work beside you?' Fay, her thoughts and feelings in turmoil, wasn't sure what he meant.

'Yes, well, I had hoped we might over time be able to get to know each other better. Perhaps consider courting. But this damned war puts things in a different light.'

Fay nodded. Her heart had begun to beat faster. She didn't know what to make of his little speech. But he hadn't finished.

'So what I really wanted to ask you was . . . would you consider coming to live in Saddleworth . . . as my wife?'

Fay sat silently for a moment, breathing hard as the meaning of his words sank in. There had been a time when she wouldn't have even considered him; Terry had always been so cautious and methodical in his approach. But after the tragedy of recent events she looked at him with different eyes. They may not share the kind of love like in the films. But she could see in his face what he was proposing was a future filled with kindness and affection. He was offering her a new life, and that certainly seemed very attractive right now.

'I don't know what to say,' Fay began. 'I'm flabbergasted, I mean . . . '

'I apologize,' he said quickly, misunderstanding her hesitation. 'I've been too forward and I'm sorry.' He stood up, hat in hand.

'Not at all,' Fay hurried to assure him. 'I was going to say . . . well, I'd be honoured to accept.'

He sat down again abruptly, a smile spreading across his face.

'And once my leg is better, I can come to see you in Saddleworth so that I can meet your mother and we can begin to . . . make arrangements.'

Terry stood up again and Fay did too, hesitantly moving towards each other. Terry twiddled his hat in his fingers. 'You've made me so happy, Fay.'

Fay smiled, 'You've made me happy too, Terry.' And she took his hand in her own.

As Christmas and New Year had slipped by without much celebration, 1941 began without anyone in Coronation Street seeming to notice. So when word went round at the factory that there was to be a bit of a knees-up at the Rovers one night in early January, Elsie looked forward to joining in.

'We mustn't go too early, mind,' Sally Todd said. 'Why don't I knock on for you about eight?'

When they arrived, Elsie was surprised to be greeted by Annie Walker, who invited them into the select. She could see almost immediately that it was festooned with baubles, tinsel and all manner of glittering decorations and as she stepped inside she realized it was also full of familiar faces. As she entered, everyone stood up and raised their glasses, and Sally thrust a large glass of gin into Elsie's hand. Then there was a loud chorus of 'Merry Christmas and a Happy New Year, Elsie!' and Elsie noticed a long table groaning with plates of food in spite of the austere rationing.

Elsie looked around her, bewildered. She had no idea what was going on until Ena Sharples stepped forward and began to speak.

'Thanks to the bloody Luftwaffe, Christmas and New Year were as good as cancelled. We all suffered, but you, Elsie Tanner,' she turned to face her, 'you fared worse than most and we all wanted to acknowledge that fact.' She raised her glass to everyone in the room. 'We wanted you to know we're right behind you. So we all chipped in and we're taking the opportunity to celebrate Christmas and New Year today. You may have lost your old family, but the people of Coronation Street have always thought of themselves as one big family. Even with all our squabbles and disagreements, we all do what's right by each other. You're part of Coronation Street now and that means you're one of us, so let's remember absent friends and welcome the new ones.'

There were murmurs of approval and shouts of 'Hear, hear!' and glasses were raised again. Elsie was too overwhelmed to respond. She stood with the gin in her hand and looked around the room at the eager faces all wishing her well. When Elsie had arrived at Coronation Street just over a year ago, she never could have guessed at the events that lay ahead or the people that she would meet. Ena was right, they might fight like a bunch of kids sometimes but Coronation Street was a place like no other.

'This is quite some celebration. I've never had a Christmas present like this before,' she said, finding her voice at last. 'I thank you all from the bottom of my heart.'

'And that's not all,' Ena added. 'We've kept some food back for a kiddies' special, a party tomorrow at the Mission. All are invited. We can celebrate Linda Tanner's first birthday in January and there's young Billy Walker and Kenneth Barlow to think about – they're our future now. It's time to show them how we celebrate, Coronation Street-style. To let them know that we'll never be beaten.'

Elsie was busy lighting a cigarette to stop herself bursting into tears. She'd never had much of a child-hood and had certainly never had any presents as a child but Linda was having a different start in life. One surrounded by people who cared. She was overwhelmed by the generous spirit in the room.

But the night had one more surprise in store. Through the busy crowds of the pub, Elsie saw a young woman pushing through the throng, heading in her direction and calling her name.

'Elsie, Elsie, is that you? It's me, I'm all right!'

For a moment, Elsie couldn't place the young woman. She was dressed smartly in a new brown woollen coat with a touch of fur at the collar and a neat hat cocked sideways on her head, as was the current fashion.

'Elsie don't you recognise me?'

Elsie stared open-mouthed at the woman standing in front of her, who had now been joined by an equally smart older man, his arm drapped protectively around the girl. Elsie felt a sensation creep up her spine as the realisation dawned. 'It can't be, I thought you were . . . the bombs down by the arches . . . Phyllis, is that really you – you look all grown-up?'

The young woman beamed. 'I'm glad you barely recognise me, I've got a new life now, this is Roy Bailey and he got me off the streets. I live with him in Oldham and I was with Roy when the bombs fell. We're going to get married when I'm old enough, aren't we, Roy?'

Elsie stood stock still for a moment unable to believe the sight before her, though a small thought niggled away about what the relationship might be between Phyllis and Roy. She wondered at her sister's new-found affluence – but Phyllis had always been good at getting what she wanted. Well, good for her, thought Elsie. This was no time for speculation so she exclaimed in excitement, 'Look at me stood here gawping, come here you!' and she enveloped her sister in a fierce hug. 'Phyllis, I hate to spoil the moment, I'm right happy to see you but, there's been bad news . . .'

Phyllis stopped her. 'I've heard all about it . . . I know . . . One of the lads down at the arches heard what had happened to Back Gas Street and came and told Roy. That's why I'm here now, I wanted you to know I'm safe.'

Elsie and Phyllis regarded each other silently for an instant, joined in the memory of their lost family. But nothing was going to spoil Elsie's happiness and joy – she had her sister back and that was all that mattered right now.

'Come on, we've got to celebrate and first thing tomorrow we're going to tell our Fay that you're alive!'

For a moment, Elsie remembered Stan Walsh and the thrill of her first-ever present, but she knew that tonight she had been given the biggest and best present she would ever receive. Life was definitely looking up.

'I want to raise another toast,' she shouted above the din. 'Here's to Coronation Street, long may she reign!'

Elsie downed her gin in one gulp, and as Mrs Foyle took up the piano, the noisy cheers drifted out of the Rovers Return, across the cobbles, and into the night.

THE END

Coronation Street – Still the Nation's Favourite

Coronation Street was the creation of Tony Warren, a scriptwriter at Granada Television in Manchester. The story goes that Tony was frustrated with the scripts he was being asked to write and jumped onto a filing cabinet in the office of the Head of Drama, Harry Elton. Tony refused to come down until Harry allowed him to write about something he knew. Looking out of the office window towards the brick terraces of Salford, Tony said he could write about an ordinary street and the people who lived in it . . . and so *Coronation Street* was born.

It was initially rejected by the studio, who didn't believe that audiences would take to a drama about the ordinary lives of working-class Northern characters. It was Harry's idea to screen the pilot episodes to Granada staff, many of whom were 'ordinary' Northerners themselves. After proving the programme could connect with the target audience, twelve episodes of *Coronation Street* (it was originally called *Florizel Street* before being renamed) were scheduled and the first episode aired on ITV on the 9th of December 1960.

The critics did not immediately warm to *Coronation Street* but audiences didn't agree. It was the first time that genuine Northern accents were consistently used on television and viewers were hooked by the series' storylines, the portrayal of 'ordinary' characters and the brilliant acting on display.

Early storylines embedded strong female characters such as Ena Sharples (Violet Carson), Elsie Tanner (Pat Phoenix) and Annie Walker (Doris Speed) in the nation's consciousness; the squabbles and the skirmishes kept viewers glued to their screens along with storylines that featured a young and idealistic Ken Barlow, played by William Roache, who is now the world's longest running soap character to have been played by the same person.

Within a year, the programme was top of the ratings and stayed there throughout the decade, regularly pulling in audiences of 20 million viewers. As the programme headed into the 1970s, many of the older characters were leaving the series, allowing a new generation to sip their drinks at the Rovers Return. Bet Lynch (Julie Goodyear), Rita Fairclough (Barbara Knox), Deirdre Hunt (Anne Kirkbride) and Mavis Riley (Thelma Barlow) all started to carve out their own legendary statuses and the women who played them cemented their acting credentials with storylines showcasing their admirable talents.

Coronation Street, along with all ITV programmes,

was forced off the air for eleven weeks in 1979 as the whole country was caught up in industrial action. But this did nothing to dent the series' popularity and with barely any competition from the other channels, it reigned supreme until the 1980s when both the BBC and Channel 4 introduced hard-hitting new soaps *EastEnders* and *Brookside*. *Coronation Street* writers met the challenge head-on and some of the programme's most dramatic storylines were played out during the eighties. Who could forget the love affair of the decade between Deirdre Barlow and Mike Baldwin? The ensuing feud between Mike and Ken would last for years. Rita Fairclough's mental abuse at the hands of Alan Bradley and the dramatic conclusion which saw him fatally struck by a Blackpool tram has gone down as one of the defining plotlines in any soap. Hilda Ogden's poignant breakdown in the aftermath of the death of her husband, Stan, has come to be viewed as one of the most outstanding performances in the programme's history.

As the millennium approached, Bet and Alec Gilroy (Roy Barraclough) were manning the pumps at the Rovers but it was a time of upheaval for the show. The series had increased to three episodes a week. The show had relocated to a brand new set with new houses and shops and fresh characters had replaced some of the old guard and were taking root in the nation's heart. The touching but ultimately doomed romance between Raquel Wolstenhulme and Curly Watts (Kevin Kennedy) broke millions of hearts nationwide and made Sarah Lancashire a household name.

While the trademark humour of the series was much

in evidence, the show's plotlines reflected shifts in society and tackled modern issues such as drug abuse and transsexuality with the introduction of the character of Hayley Patterson. On the 8th of December 2000 the show celebrated its 40th year on air and the Prince of Wales made a cameo appearance. As the show entered a new century, new families such as the Battersbys and the McDonalds dominated the street. A new feud emerged between Karen McDonald, played by Suranne Jones, and Tracy Barlow, who had been played by a number of actresses over the years, though it was Kate Ford who embodied Tracy's most turbulent storylines.

In 2010, *Coronation Street* celebrated its 50th birthday, not long after it had officially become the world's longest running soap in the *Guinness Book of Records*. The show marked the occasion with one of its most dramatic storylines when The Joinery bar exploded, destroying the viaduct and sending a Metrolink tram hurtling down on to the street. There were seven episodes screened that week with a special live one-hour episode, which sent the programme's ratings soaring into the stratosphere.

In 2011, the character of Dennis Tanner returned to the street after an absence of forty-three years. As Elsie Tanner's son, Dennis' reintroduction into street life provided a tangible link to those early days, when Elsie, Annie and Ena held sway over Weatherfield life. The nation's favourite street has now dominated the airwaves for almost sixty years and seems destined for many, many more. The trials and tribulations of the people of Weatherfield continue to delight audiences the world over. Life is never simple for them but the good humour and witty one-liners have seen them through many a crisis. As Ena Sharples wisely observed, 'I don't expect life to be easy. I'd think very little of it if it was.'

1961: *Left to right*: Elsie Tanner (Pat Phoenix) Ena Sharples (Violet Carson) with Annie Walker (Doris Speed) behind the Rovers Return bar.

Pat Phoenix – The Woman Who Made Elsie Tanner

While Elsie Tanner and the other strong female characters of *Coronation Street* might have been the creation of Tony Warren and the scriptwriters at Corrie, it was the actress, Pat Phoenix, who made Elsie the woman we all know and love.

Patricia Manfield was born in Manchester on the 26th November 1923, to parents Thomas and Anna Maria Manfield. Like the character she played in *Coronation Street*, Pat was born into a working-class family and grew up to become a tough and strong-minded young woman.

From an early age, Pat had yearned for a career on the stage and, despite a lack of encouragement at home, submitted a monologue to the BBC which they liked enough to give her employment on *Children's Hour*. This experience whetted her appetite for acting and she spent much of her free time enthralled as she watched stage greats such as Laurence Olivier and Ralph Richardson treading the boards at the Palace Theatre. Her school report stated that, 'Patricia is not exactly a model pupil, but on stage she is marvellous.'

On leaving school, Pat got a job working for the Manchester Corporation's gas department while still pursuing amateur dramatics in the evenings. She joined the Manchester Arts Repertory Company, and her big break came in 1948 when she won the part of comedian Sandy Powell's wife in *Cup-tie Honeymoon*. The film also featured a young Bernard Youens, who would later play Stan Ogden in *Coronation Street*.

But her career struggled to get off the ground as she was only cast in small roles in small films. She received acclaim for her part in the play *A Girl Called Sadie*, which had a racy plot about a vicar and a tart. During that production, Pat had a fling with her co-star Anthony Booth, but it was an illicit one as he was married with two daughters (the elder, Cherie, would go on to marry Tony Blair, the future Prime Minister). Pat felt despair at her lack of success and later spoke of near-starvation and of a failed suicide attempt which was thwarted because she didn't have any money for the gas meter.

The wheel of fortune turned for Pat when she won the role of Elsie Tanner in *Coronation Street*. She was up against a huge amount of competition from other actors for the role and Pat recounted arguing with the Granada team on the day as she was so highly strung. Whatever she did that day won her the part and Elsie Tanner was a hit with audiences from the very beginning. The Prime Minister, Jim Callaghan, once described Elsie as 'the sexiest thing on television', and Pat clearly revelled in her role as the street's fiery redhead. 'I was one of the first anti-heroines – not particularly good-looking and no better than I should be,' said Pat. She was the perfect embodiment of 'the tart with a heart' and her ongoing storylines, featuring her tortured love life and clashes with Ena Sharples (Violet Carson), were highly addictive for audiences.

Pat Phoenix loved her fans and was often charm personified, but she built up a reputation for being difficult on set. She regularly clashed with the equally headstrong Carson and often fell out with her co-stars. Pat embraced the glamour and the fame that came with the role of Elsie and poured much of herself into the role. Like Elsie, Pat's love life was bountiful fodder for the tabloids and her turbulent relationships often made the headlines.

Her first marriage to Peter Marsh ended in divorce after just a year. She went on to marry her *Coronation Street* co-star, Alan Browning, who played her on-screen husband, Alan Howard. The marriage was as turbulent in reality as it was on screen. The two had already separated by 1979, when Browning died of alcohol-related liver failure.

Pat had become disillusioned with *Coronation Street* and had left the programme to pursue her stage career. However, alternative roles with the high-profile that Pat desired never quite materialised. By 1976, Pat had returned to the street, although she still clashed with the producers who wanted to tone down the character and have her behave in a more age-appropriate fashion. Pat was having none of it and was insistent that Elsie should not grow old gracefully. In 1983, Elsie Tanner packed her bags for the last time and headed off to Portugal for a new life with an old flame, Bill Gregory.

Another old flame had made a reappearance in reality too. Tony Booth had walked back into Pat's life; he had found fame as Alf Garnet's socialist son in the TV series *Till Death Us Do Part*, but Booth had suffered terrible burns after setting himself on fire in a drunken accident. Pat nursed him back to health and Booth credited Pat with saving his life. She went on to have a good relationship with his children and campaigned for Tony Blair in the 1983 General Election, helping him to win his first seat.

A lifelong heavy smoker, Pat died of terminal lung cancer in 1986. She had hidden the disease from family and friends, including Booth, and the two only married a few days before her death. Tributes flooded in and Tony Warren, the creator of the show, said, 'She was fiercely loyal, frequently impossible and I wouldn't have missed knowing her for anything.'

Without Pat Phoenix, Elsie Tanner as everyone knew her would never have existed. Pat said of herself, 'I don't know what the word "star" means. I am a working actress.' But she was one of the biggest stars of the show's history and her light still shines on those famous cobbles today, almost sixty years on.